ARKHAM HORROR

It is the height of the Roaring Twenties – a fresh enthusiasm for the arts, science, and exploration of the past have opened doors to a wider world, and beyond...

And yet, a dark shadow grows over the town of Arkham. Alien entities known as Ancient Ones lurk in the emptiness beyond space and time, writhing at the thresholds between worlds.

Occult rituals must be stopped and alien creatures destroyed before the Ancient Ones make our world their ruined dominion.

Only a handful of brave souls with inquisitive minds and the will to act stand against the horrors threatening to tear this world apart.

Will they prevail?

ARKHAM HORROR™

The TWILIGHT MAGUS

TIM PRATT

ACONYTE

First published by Aconyte Books in 2025

ISBN 978 1 83908 314 3

Ebook ISBN 978 1 83908 315 0

Printed in the United States of America and elsewhere.

9 8 7 6 5 4 3 2 1

ACONYTE BOOKS

An imprint of Asmodee North America

Mercury House, North Gate,

Nottingham NG7 7FN, UK

aconytebooks.com

For Maria,
mil gracias

Carl Sanford sat on a bench in one of the small plazas lined by theaters and open-air markets, situated just off Las Ramblas, the bustling pedestrian concourse near the heart of Barcelona, Spain. Once upon a time, that series of streets had been a streambed that regularly transformed into a river of sewage and filth when the seasonal rains flowed down from the hilly Collserola mountain range. Watching the locals and expatriates bustle in their pointless multitudes this dry morning, Carl couldn't help but sneer. The flowing sewage was still here, after all; now it just had arms and legs, hopes and dreams, thoughts and opinions.

The exiled magus, once of the Silver Twilight Lodge, fanned himself with a newspaper, acknowledging the heat made him irritable. Though it wasn't yet noon, the specter of another scorching Mediterranean afternoon loomed. The newspaper was in English and nearly two weeks old. There were international editions of some prominent American papers available in Barcelona, but the *New York Times* didn't tend to cover the fortunes of small cities in Massachusetts, and, frankly, the *Boston Globe* was only a little better. Importing copies of his hometown paper, the *Arkham Advertiser*, was an irritatingly roundabout process that involved far too many steps, especially since he didn't want anyone back home to know he was in Spain… or, indeed, that he was anywhere at all. Better for them to continue thinking he was dead, at least for now. The time for his glorious resurrection was coming, but the groundwork was not yet in place.

The sorcerer Randall Tillinghast had stolen everything from him: his wealth, his home, and most of all, his control of the Order of the Silver Twilight. But Carl Sanford would be revenged. Tillinghast hadn't worked alone to complete his machinations; he'd co-opted Sanford's bodyguard Altman, his employee Ruby Standish, and even Sarah Van Shaw, the longtime Warden of the Order's Lodge. That last betrayal stung. But those betrayers were just weapons. Tillinghast was the one who wielded them, and Sanford would see the man destroyed for it. After that, he could focus on rebuilding his *own* empire.

Or… perhaps ruling a new one. He'd lost the Silver Twilight Lodge to Tillinghast, but he was done with silver, anyway. These days, he rather fancied red.

Whatever power he acquired in Europe would be used to fuel his return to America. He would not become one of those expatriates who fled the New World for the Continent forevermore. He *would* go home again. Though it wouldn't be the home he'd left behind. Sanford's flow of news from the States was irregular and sporadic, but he knew that in the year since he'd fled, his beloved Arkham had suffered an apocalyptic flood that destroyed large sections of the city, helped along by frustratingly unspecified "social unrest" and "mass hysteria." Arkham was apparently something of a shambles these days. That was devastating… but it also gave him a glimmer of dark satisfaction.

See? I leave, and everything promptly falls apart.

It was a shame he couldn't take advantage of the situation to buy up great swaths of distressed property at disaster-area prices. It was too dangerous to arrange that kind of transaction at a distance, even through intermediaries, and his supply of funds was rather diminished these days, anyway. Carl Sanford would never be *poor*, but there were strata of wealth, and he'd tumbled a long way down from the upper crust.

But he had a plan to get back on his feet, hence his presence on this uncomfortable bench. A shirtless young boy in tattered pants lingered near him for a moment too long. Sanford raised an eyebrow, sending the youth scuttling. The pickpockets had tried their luck with him a week ago when he first started coming here in the mornings and he'd allowed them to succeed. They hadn't much liked what they filched, though, and word had spread among the petty thieves that he was a foreigner best avoided. Sometimes he caught the phrase *bruixot malvat* – the Catalan equivalent of the Spanish *brujo malvado*. Evil warlock.

Close enough. At least the locals seemed to understand that magic wasn't inherently evil or good – it was a tool that could be used for anything.

Carl Sanford used it to help himself.

A man sat down on the bench beside him, as pale and insubstantial as a wraith, dressed in a loose white shirt and pants of the thinnest linen. His hair was not so much white as colorless, and the same was true of his eyes and thin lips. He looked like a monochromatic figure from a photograph somehow escaped into real life.

"I see you haven't eaten today, Fantasma." Sanford kept fanning himself with the paper. Fantasma looked insubstantial enough that even a slight breeze might send him tumbling from the bench, but looks were deceptive.

The man – at least, he looked like a man, though he wasn't precisely human – curled his lips into a smile. The first time Sanford met Fantasma, the creature had recently fed, making his lips full, his cheeks ruddy, his hair dark and lustrous. He'd still been a wisp of a figure, though. Fantasma didn't take up much space in the world. Unlike Fantasma's brother, Akh, who was invisible but so immense that he would have broken the bench if he'd sat on it. Sanford had met people like them before – the Whateley brothers in Dunwich came to mind, the offspring of mingled human and inhuman parentage, exhibiting… unusual qualities passed down by their Outsider parents. Such people had their uses, and Sanford had a knack for finding them.

"I told you not to come here." Fantasma's voice was a whisper on the wind. "You scare away my clients. You distress my employees. You are becoming a problem, Mr Phillips." He spoke English well, with a hint of Catalan softness in the vowels.

The necessity of a pseudonym rankled Sanford. He'd gone to great lengths to build up his own name over the decades, making it a synonym for power, danger and strength. If this creature knew who he really was… well, it wouldn't make much difference. Sanford had lost much of his stature when Tillinghast drove him from Arkham. Fantasma would be delighted to sell him out to an enemy who wanted to make sure Sanford *stayed* dead. Better for this creature to believe he was Mr Phillips, an American magician of no great renown and undetermined power.

The square was clearing out. Fantasma's thieves moved swiftly into the adjoining alleyways while the tourists and locals simply felt a frisson of discomfort they couldn't identify, a feeling strong enough to make them depart without being so overwhelming they were alarmed by the urge to leave.

Sanford felt the edge of that discomfort himself, and unlike the mundane people around him, recognized the feeling for what it was: Fantasma's brother Akh had entered the square. Unlike his brother, Akh had inherited more from his inhuman parent than his mortal one, and even though Akh was invisible, there was a sense of wrongness emanating from his presence. Being close to him made your hair stand on end and the back of your mind scream, "Run." Get much closer and you would fall down, gibbering and clawing at your own eyes. Most people would, anyway.

Sanford yawned and kept fanning himself. He observed a disturbance in the air, like a heat shimmer, near the center of the square. "You're going to try to kill me, Fantasma? It would be so much simpler to acquiesce to my request. I am a much better friend than I am an enemy."

"I think I would prefer you as neither. Corpses do not make alliances or hold grudges." Fantasma waved his hand in a gesture of lazy beckoning. The shimmer moved toward them. That urge to run got stronger. Sanford caught a whiff of the charnel house, though he doubted Akh actually smelled like anything. His brain was simply trying to translate that sense of wrongness in a way that his organic body could understand.

Sanford reached into his suit's inner pocket and withdrew a small leather pouch, then shook a handful of the gray dust inside into his palm.

"What is that?" Fantasma asked, not yet alarmed. "Some American drug? You wish to dull your pain before the end comes?"

The dust came from an apothecary case Sanford had

brought with him on the Transatlantic crossing, a satchel packed full of useful items painstakingly collected over the years. He'd lost most of his treasures when Tillinghast ousted him, but he'd always hidden stashes and caches for the possibility of such a fall. "This is the powder of Ibn Ghazi," he said. "Mingled with a paralytic one of my agents brought back from the Amazon, made from toad venom, I believe. Watch." He blew the dust across his palm at the approaching shimmer.

The powder struck him, rendering Fantasma's brother visible. Akh was smaller than Yog Whateley – *that* entity probably had more rarefied parentage – merely the size of a carriage instead of a barn, but the Abomination of Barcelona had similarities to the Horror of Dunwich. His oblate spheroid body was studded with a profusion of eyes of varied sizes, sported uncountable writhing appendages like the trunks of elephants, and possessed scores of slack and drooling mouths. Balanced atop the whole, like a small hat on a large head, was the upper half of a human face, the only trace of humanity in the monster. The face was clearly kin to Fantasma, pink-eyed and pale.

Akh was floating above the ground when the powder struck, but the paralytic agent interfered with his flight, making him stutter before toppling sideways, crashing on the stones of the plaza, drooling now-visible ichors onto the ground.

Sanford rose and drew the sword concealed inside his walking stick and took a few steps toward the mewling monster. He glanced back at Fantasma, saying, "'Akh.' The word means 'brother' in Arabic, does it not? And something like 'spirit' in the language of the ancient Egyptians. Odd choice for a name. I took you for a Spaniard but after some hefty research, I tracked down that your mother perhaps hailed from North Africa, so I suppose that accounts for it."

Fantasma stared at his fallen sibling, frozen in shock.

Sanford sighed. No one appreciated the work he put into his endeavors. "Shall I put your brother out of his misery?" He set the point of the blade just below the largest of Akh's eyes. When he glanced over, he was amused to see Fantasma's face transform into protective fury. "Or have you never seen your brother before? Just touched him, I suppose, and made guesses about his appearance, like that old Indian parable about the blind men trying to work out the nature of an elephant by feeling its various body parts."

Sanford prodded Akh with his toe, the monster's flesh gelatinous like an aspic. The powder's effects also reduced the aura of discomfort the creature emitted. "He does make you look handsome by comparison, doesn't he, Fantasma? Don't worry, he'll vanish from sight again in a moment. The effects of the powder only last for a dozen heartbeats or so but my heart is beating slowly, because, unlike you, I am very calm."

The monster shimmered back into invisibility, but Sanford's sword didn't waver.

"The paralytic agent, however, should work for an hour or more, even on something your brother's size. That gives me plenty of time to carve him into steaks and chops. This blade has tasted fouler blood, believe me. These stones will be awash with his blood – or whatever flows in his noxious veins. No one will be able to see the mess, of course, so that's all right."

"Stop!" Fantasma said, finally rising. "You are more formidable than I realized, Mr Phillips. And better informed. How did you know about my brother?"

"I make it a point to be the most informed party in any negotiation," Sanford said. That was certainly true these days. He'd let himself slip before last year – had become too complacent, too sure of himself. As a result, he'd been bested by a rival and lost almost everything. He hardly needed to bring this degree of preparation to deal with a lowly figure like Fantasma, but the nice thing about overkill was the people you used it on tended to stay dead. "Now. Do you think you might be able to assist me after all? I'm not asking for so very much. Simply an introduction."

Fantasma licked his lips. "I… yes, of course. I'll make inquiries. Meet me here tomorrow–"

"No, I think not," Sanford mused. "You may call on me at the Hotel España. You know the place? It's not far."

"Si. The people you wish to meet… I can reach them, send your message, but I cannot compel them, you understand?" He stared at the place where his invisible brother lay. "I can only *ask*, Mr Phillips."

"Tell them what I did to compel you to ask, then. Perhaps that will pique their interest." He sheathed his sword in the walking stick and sauntered away.

There was a flower market nearby he thought he might visit. Perhaps he'd acquire a red blossom to wear in his lapel, to mark this first step on his long road to ascendance. The only jokes he had these days were private ones. He suddenly missed Ruby Standish. They'd never been friends, but they'd had an easy rapport, and she could give as good as she got when it came to verbal sparring.

As he strolled down Las Ramblas, between the plane trees, he allowed himself to be distracted by the sights, his mood uplifted considerably. Barcelona! The city was too hot this time of year, but otherwise not such a terrible place. He appreciated the signs of great age all around him: the ancient churches, the fountains, the sculptures, and the twisted cobbled lanes, some nearly two thousand years old. In the New World, all the cities Sanford had explored were… well, relatively new. There was vigor in that newness, but there was something to be said for the strength of long centuries.

Spain's neutrality in the Great War had spared it from the devastation that struck other nations on the Continent, many of which Sanford had visited since leaving the shores of Massachusetts. Of course, the country had hardly come out unscathed. The war had brought economic devastation and social unrest. The Spaniards had ample internal quarrels, anyway, from their interminable skirmishes with the Berbers in Morocco to unrest among the Catalan separatists. There'd been a coup, a military dictatorship, and martial law had only just been lifted. The country had abandoned its hereditary monarchy in favor of leadership by strength of arms. As a strong man of no great lineage himself, Sanford approved of that political shift in principle if not in terms of the specifics.

From what Sanford could see now, the Spaniards were doing well. The country had become a beacon for artists and thinkers, both homegrown and from abroad, especially to the west in Madrid. As a whole, the people of the country seemed eager to enjoy the rest of the Twenties, to celebrate the end of the war and their new prosperity along with many others in the world – apart from the Germans, of course, who'd be licking their wounds for a bit, but perhaps they'd learn some valuable lessons from the drubbing they'd taken and proceed with more care in the future.

As Sanford walked, sweat trickled down his back, and he mused on the common image of the "lazy Spaniard" so prevalent in the American imagination: the broad hat pulled down low, the cigarette drooping from the corner of a slack mouth. Now that Sanford had experienced a few weeks of Iberian summer, he understood the truth: in the heat of the late afternoon, it was impossible to do much of anything except wait for the cool evening. The Spaniards were as industrious as anyone else, during those hours when the temperature permitted it. Sanford didn't take naps during the daily siesta when the whole city shut down, but he was not averse to finding a shady spot and allowing his deep thoughts to turn over more slowly than usual.

His stomach grumbled. It was nearly lunchtime by his old standards, but of course these Europeans didn't sit down for that meal until mid-afternoon, and as for the evening repast? They didn't eat until ten or eleven at night, when most good citizens of Arkham would have been tucked up in bed – Sanford always kept later hours, being in business with so many creatures of the night.

To distract himself from his hunger and the general disorientations of life abroad, he walked first toward the waters of the Mediterranean Sea, pausing to admire the Monumento a Colón, an ornate pedestal and column topped with a statue of the explorer Christopher Columbus, surrounded by immense lions and winged figures of victory. Sanford admired Columbus in certain limited ways; his entrepreneurial spirit and willingness to explore, at least. Sanford had discovered strange countries himself, after all, in the Dreamlands, others sometimes by accident, and always in search of riches and power. Though he'd approached and treated the denizens of his discovered countries better than Columbus had; to read the accounts of how the great explorer had treated the native peoples he encountered, you'd think the man must have been half ghoul.

From there he turned north, walking on to the Barri Gòtic, the Gothic Quarter, the heart of the oldest part of the city and his favorite place here. History was on display everywhere, including remnants of the old Roman wall and monuments dating back to the Medieval era. Even the newer constructions fit into the spirit of the place, notably the restored Gothic façade of the Barcelona Cathedral, and the recently renovated Centre Excursionista de Catalunya. The renowned architect Lluís Domènech i Montaner had taken a humdrum structure of no particular distinction and transformed it into a spectacle with Gothic windows and soaring battlements.

The neighborhood was quiet, even somber, suiting Sanford's general mood. The streets were labyrinthian, twisting and doubling back on themselves, often dead-ending in tiny squares and plazas. Sanford liked to wander there. The warren of streets reminded him of the deep basements beneath the Silver Twilight Lodge, designed to make sure any intruders became irredeemably lost. Sometimes, he sensed magic in the Gothic Quarter and suspected folds in space, hidden pockets of geography, or secret portals to other realms existed here, but he hadn't tried to penetrate any of those yet. He didn't want to tread into secret places uninvited and upset more of the local *bruixots malvats*. At least, not unless he had a good reason.

The hour finally grew late enough to plausibly dine, so he returned to the Hotel España and their lavish dining room, La Pecera, "The Fishbowl." The walls were decorated with sgraffito art by Ramón Casas, depicting frolicking mermaids amid more mundane sea creatures. Sanford had encountered a few of the Deep Ones, the closest thing to the mermaids of folklore, and far less alluring than the *sirenas* depicted on the walls.

The staff led him to a table in the corner, where he could

sit with his back to the wall and see the main doors. They'd learned his preferences quickly enough. Despite the hotel's origins as a humble boarding house, this establishment was as comfortable and luxurious as the Excelsior back home in Arkham, if a long step up from the frayed opulence of the Independence Hotel. Sanford wondered if those venerable establishments had survived the floods. It was terrible to imagine dark waters flowing through the Excelsior's ornate lobby. He shook off the dark musings and ordered a plate of fish. He'd permanently lost his taste for fish after an ordeal in the charmless seaside town of Innsmouth, but when in Rome and all that. He also accepted the inevitable heavy pour of red wine, rougher than the French varietals he favored, but not wholly unpalatable, in a common way.

Sanford never felt lonelier than he did at mealtimes. Back home, he'd often been too busy for a proper meal, choosing to eat at his desk in his study with dishes prepared by the staff at the Silver Twilight Lodge. Other meals were opportunities to use his power: allowing his favored devotees to dine with him, or forcing them to sit and watch while he took his repast and they were served nothing. He thought again of Ruby Standish, and the good-natured way they'd so often traded barbs over lunch or drinks in her favorite booth at The Songbird's Perch. Ruby had stolen from him, then saved his life, then worked for him, then betrayed him for Tillinghast, but he was willing to admit she turned on him only under duress. Yet in these diminished times, he ate alone, and no one clamored for his attention. There were days where he had nothing to decide at all beyond what to order at mealtimes. Such idleness, when he had once effectively ruled the city of Arkham, Massachusetts (or at least the parts that mattered), had wielded influence over much of the East Coast, and even held secret sway in national politics!

"Oh, how the mighty have fallen," he murmured before patting his lips with a napkin and pushing his plate away. He rose and strode out through the airy Modernist lobby, planning to return to his room to wait out the heat, when the desk clerk waved to him. "Señor Phillips! There is a letter for you."

Sanford frowned. Could Fantasma have made arrangements that quickly? Unlikely. Which meant this was something else. Perhaps something welcome, and perhaps not.

He went to the desk and accepted the heavy cream-colored envelope liberally covered with stamps. He expected to see his alias, Ward Phillips, but there was a sigil drawn in reddish brown, and the shape writhed on the paper. Sanford glanced at the clerk, who exhibited no confusion or discomfort, and when he looked back at the envelope, he instead saw neat letters, albeit in the same off-putting hue: Ward Phillips, c/o the Hotel España, Barcelona, Spain.

"Thank you," Sanford murmured, turning away. Someone had used magic to locate him. That sigil was drawn in a drop or two of his blood mixed with ink. He'd always been careful about keeping his bodily fluids to himself, and even routinely incinerated his fingernail and hair clippings lest a rival use them against him in a ritual. But there at the end, when everything in Arkham fell apart, when the deep basements collapsed on him and the Lodge began to burn… he knew he'd left quite a bit of his blood splashed and smeared. Everyone thought he was dead, with his corpse lost forever in another world, beyond the gates of a closed portal, so why would anyone bother to look for him? Clearly, someone had found a reason.

He wasn't surprised. The only question was why they'd bothered to send a letter instead of showing up with knives drawn.

Back in the safety of his room with invisible wards drawn on the doors, walls, and windows, he sat down at the small writing desk and considered the envelope. He didn't open it right away, of course. If he wanted to kill someone from a distance, he could do it easily with the right symbols carefully inscribed on a piece of paper. There were arrangements of lines and curves that could steal breath, stop hearts, and flense away sanity, and he wasn't the only person who knew how to write them.

He twisted a monocle into his eye and looked over the missive. The lens revealed many forms of spellwork, and there was nothing magical about this letter, apart from the sigil of seeking inscribed on its front. Even so, he proceeded with caution, slitting the envelope with a letter opener and carefully tipping out thin folded sheets to rest upon the desk.

He used the letter opener to unfold the pages without touching the paper – you could soak paper in poisonous substances, not magical, but no less deadly for that – and

peered at the first lines, written in flowing ink. Sanford teased apart the sheets until he revealed the last page and looked at the signature, which confirmed his suspicions.

This letter was from Ruby Standish.

Just a letter, nothing magical at all, but that didn't mean it wasn't dangerous. Sanford began to read.

Ruby's voice was strong and somehow inarguably *her* from the first word, and he felt another pang of homesickness. He'd endured that longing often in the months since he fled the shores of America, of course, but they'd usually been pangs for the things he'd lost: his possessions and his power. He hadn't longed for a person before today, and mere moments after thinking of her, he'd arrived to find a letter. Not all the magic in life came from sorcery. Sometimes it was just serendipity.

As he read the letter, Sanford imagined he was sitting across from Ruby in their booth at the back of The Songbird's Perch, listening to the tone of her voice, which could be as changeable as New England weather.

"Old friend, old foe, old fellow." He imagined Ruby swirling her martini, making the olive bob in the glass like a bit of flotsam. Sanford pictured her glamorous, not in any of her various dressed-down disguises, but wearing a shimmering knee-length dress, with a black feather fascinator in her hair, dark makeup around her eyes, and berry-red stain on her lips.

"Traitor," Sanford murmured, but fondly.

Ruby sighed and went on. "First of all, since I know how your mind works, let me set it somewhat at ease. Tillinghast is gone. He left Arkham a disaster, but he *did* leave Arkham. Your precious city is no longer occupied by your enemy. I won't go into all the ins and outs of his machinations – it's not as if I understand them all myself. I know what Tillinghast did, at least a large part of it, but I still can't fathom why he wanted to bring about such destruction. Maybe the destruction was only a side effect. Suffice to say, he gathered magical artifacts, and he attempted a ritual."

"I know." Sanford had a glass of good Canadian whiskey in this fantasy, and he took a sip. Europe didn't suffer under the rigors of Prohibition the way Sanford's homeland did, but most of the local alcohol didn't appeal to him: those rough red wines and sickly-sweet ports and sherries. Sometimes a bottle of Scotch managed to drift this far south intact, but not often enough.

Sanford had still been present in Arkham when Tillinghast's relic hunters came to call – at least the first few. After the man stole some of Sanford's artifacts – including the Ruby of R'lyeh – Tillinghast let the magical community at large know he was in the market for more relics associated with R'lyeh, the fabled cyclopean city in the sea. What anyone would want with that barnacle-encrusted graveyard from antiquity was beyond Sanford's understanding. A few objects purportedly from R'lyeh had passed through his hands over the years, mostly bits of statuary and the like, and they were unpleasant things, chilling and squamous. The lovely Ruby was a rare exception, and he'd personally doubted its provenance was really related to the sunken city.

Sanford even managed to intercept some of Tillinghast's

treasure hunters, lurking on the outskirts of the city, offering them money for information and artifacts, back when he'd believed revenge was a dish he might enjoy served hot. But after two meetings – one that went well enough and one that went badly, for the treasure hunter, anyway – he realized he was playing with fire. Sanford didn't learn anything of consequence about Tillinghast's plans after those meetings, just that that man was avaricious and power-hungry, which was hardly news. Sanford feared that if he continued to meddle, word would get back to Tillinghast that he'd survived their prior confrontation, and the old man would use his vastly superior resources to hunt Sanford down and make sure he was *really* dead. So Sanford had reluctantly packed his bags and taken passage to Europe, to recover his strength and plot his *cold* revenge.

But now, it seemed, Tillinghast had departed Arkham, anyway. Could I go home again? he thought, hope fountaining in his chest. But he gestured for Ruby to go on, and she did.

"I don't know if the ritual did whatever Tillinghast intended," she said. "The only obvious result was a terrible flood, and a wave of terror throughout the city. You wouldn't even recognize Arkham now, Sanford. You don't have much of a heart, I know, but what you do have would break if you saw what this place has become."

"Then I need to come home and fix it," he said.

"You probably want to come home." Her gaze was steady and sad. "I wouldn't advise it. I'm not the only one who knows you're alive. I found out because I know you're the master of the contingency plan. I couldn't believe you'd allowed yourself to be crushed by rocks and trapped in a broken-off clot of unreality. I poked around, found some of your blood, consulted the relevant texts, and did a minor divination to confirm you were still out there, drawing breath. That made me happy, by the way. I never *wanted* to turn on you and work for Tillinghast. When bribing me didn't work, Tillinghast threatened me, and at the end, he was much more dangerous than you were. I had no choice but to betray you."

"The first and foremost concern of Miss Ruby Standish," Sanford said, "is and always will be the wellbeing of Miss Ruby Standish." He could hardly fault her for that. He was much the same when it came to the wellbeing of Mr Carl Sanford.

Ruby sipped, swirled, and went on. "I wish I hadn't sided with him now, though. I didn't agree with everything you did, Sanford, but you cared about this city. I don't know what Tillinghast cares about, other than power. He wrecked everything and then disappeared, leaving us stumbling around in the ruins. If you want revenge on him, you won't find it in Arkham. You won't find *anything* of value here. The Silver Twilight Lodge… it's gone. I don't just mean the house, though that burned and collapsed into a sinkhole. I mean the whole Order. It's shattered."

Sanford sighed. His former bodyguard and driver, Altman, had conspired with Tillinghast to kill Sanford, and Altman had been promised leadership of the Order of the Silver Twilight as his reward. It was gratifying, in a way, to know that Sanford's secret society had not survived without his leadership, but what a waste! The Order possessed real power, and its membership had included luminaries from up and down the East Coast in the higher echelons, and an ample supply of zealous cannon fodder among the rank-and-file.

"Altman tried to seize control of the Order," Ruby said, "but he's not the politician you are. Or the blackmailer, or the manipulator, or the briber, which might be redundant, since I already said 'politician.' High-ranking members of the organization immediately turned on Altman and tried to seize control themselves, all claiming to be your true heirs. Some of them even came up with documents proving that you'd chosen them to be your successors. Everyone accused everyone else of forging their proof."

Sanford smiled. They weren't forgeries. He'd promised to make various powerful people his heirs over the years to inspire their loyalty and had drawn up all sorts of beribboned and calligraphed proclamations to that effect. He'd expected to outlive all those useful idiots, so he'd never worried about his deceptions coming to light, but it was amusing to know how his old plots had muddied Altman's waters.

"At this point, there are at least five different organizations claiming to be the true Order," Ruby said. "There's one called the First Order of the Silver Twilight, and another called the Eternal Order of the Silver Twilight, and the Argent Brotherhood, and the Fraternity of Dusk, and the Clan Crepuscular – I think that last one only has two members, and they hate each other's guts. These offshoots and sects are all more or less at war with one another, squabbling in the muddy flooded streets. You might think you could come back and impose order on the various Orders, but they've all had a taste of power now, and they *all* resent you for ruling them. Every one of them suffered various indignities and humiliations at your hands, and now that they're out from under your thumb, they're never going back. I think the only thing that could make those factions join forces is if they found out you were still alive. Then they'd forge an alliance long enough to kill you."

Sanford tut-tutted. "Ungrateful. Foolish. Typical."

Ruby smirked. "On the bright side, the only person the assorted Orders hate as much as you is Altman, who tried to take over the whole shebang even though he doesn't even know the real secret handshakes. They laughed him out of every room. He even got roughed up a couple of times. Altman thought he could buy his way into power, but Tillinghast took most of your money when he left town, even though he'd promised it to Altman. The poor sap is just squatting in some townhouse these days, occasionally scraping through the ashes of the Lodge to look for anything that survived the fire and sinkhole. The Warden is with him."

Sanford gritted his teeth. Sarah Van Shaw, the Warden of the Silver Twilight Lodge, had allied with Tillinghast to betray him, too. Ruby was an adventuress, loyal only to herself. Altman was a hired thug who'd developed pretensions above his station. But the Warden… she'd been as devoted to the Order as Sanford was. More, perhaps, since she was bound by powerful oaths to protect the Order at all costs and endowed with supernatural powers to help her do so. Tillinghast had convinced the Warden that fulfilling that oath meant getting rid of Sanford, that the Order would be better off without him. Ha. How had *that* turned out? "She must be suffering." He sighed.

"The Warden is not well," Ruby said. "Her oath to protect the Order is killing her, now that the 'true' Order has been reduced to her, Altman, a house burned to the foundations, and a handful of singed grimoires they mostly don't know how to read."

Sanford had managed to smuggle out many of his treasures, the relics he'd gathered assiduously over the years, before the

Lodge house fell, but he'd been forced to leave behind most of his impressive magical library. He hated the idea of Altman having even scraps of that much power.

Ruby took a deep drink, then set her glass down carefully on the table. "The Warden and Altman are desperate, Sanford, and you should know… they're coming for you."

Sanford sat up straight and smiled. They were, were they?

"I didn't tell them you were alive. Altman has gotten paranoid, convinced you were lurking in the shadows, orchestrating his downfall, like he couldn't fail comprehensively all on his own. He scraped up some of your beard hairs and did the same sort of divination I did, and now they know you're in Europe. The Warden thinks you can release her from her oath since you're the one who administered it."

"Oh, does she? How nice for her."

"Altman wants revenge, though when I asked, 'Revenge for what?' he just said, 'For not dying like he was supposed to.' He also has this idea that he can force you to declare him the one true heir and rightful ruler of the Order. I don't understand him anymore. He's gotten strange, Sanford. I think he… did something with your books, some rite that was meant to give him power, to help him vanquish his enemies. I don't dabble in that kind of magic, and I didn't want to know the details, but he's a lot more dangerous than he used to be."

"It's amazing he survived, if he performed such a ritual without supervision," Sanford said. "Oh dear, he didn't use *that* book, did he? It's the only one of any value he could have possibly recovered, so he must have. Hmm. How much time do I have before they arrive?"

"They're making preparations to leave now. Altman managed to borrow or steal enough funds for a voyage, and they expect to take passage on a ship in the next few days. They asked me to come along, thinking I'm still part of their merry little band, or that I have some ill feelings toward you, but all I have is ambivalence. After what I've been through these past months, the things Tillinghast demanded of me, I can't face getting on another ship. This letter is all the help I can give you, and the closest I can come to making an apology. I'll send this tonight, so it will reach you before Altman and the Warden do, by a few days, at least. You might want to hide. Or set a trap, knowing you." She pushed the glass away and stood up from the table. "Goodbye, Sanford. I can't say it was nice knowing you, exactly, but it sure was interesting. And after all the time I've spent working for Tillinghast, I can say with certainty: you aren't so bad after all, old man." She disappeared into the gloom that surrounded their booth.

The salutation was a simple "Ruby."

Sanford let the fantasy withdraw and looked around his hotel room with a sigh. He folded up the pages and started to slip them back into the envelope, then thought better of it and rose to burn them in the washbasin instead, along with the envelope. He wasn't going to leave a sigil that could reveal his present location lying around.

So, Altman and the Warden were coming. Most of his security lately had come from obscurity: no one came looking for the dead, so he'd been effectively hidden. But the letter had found him, and that meant his old employees could, too. The Warden was formidable, but if she was weak and dying, he was confident he could best her. Without Tillinghast's backing, Altman was just a professional killer and liar. Sanford had tangled with many of those. Even in his reduced circumstances, he was equal to the challenge.

Unless Altman had found something truly powerful in those books… and he might have. It was possible.

Overconfidence had led to Sanford's downfall at the hands of Tillinghast last year, and he resolved not to let himself fall prey to such hubris again. Even so, forewarned was forearmed; he was cautiously confident that he could cope with this development in a satisfactory way. It was all happening faster than he'd intended, true, but he was nothing if not versatile. His plans would go on.

Ruby's warning had altered the details of those plans, but not the essential substance. His goal was to acquire power here in Europe and to create a network that would rival the Order of the Silver Twilight. Once he was more formidable with the proper allies, he'd planned to return to Arkham and destroy Tillinghast. Now that Tillinghast was in the wind, he'd need to add an extra step: tracking down the old man and *then* destroying him. But that would be easier with a new organization under Sanford's command, anyway, so none of his immediate plans needed to change.

Of course, it would take years to build such an organization from the ground up, and Sanford wasn't that patient. He could serve his revenge cold, but not frozen. Fortunately, there was a shortcut: he simply needed to join an existing mystical organization, take it over, and twist its goals to his own purposes. Sanford had done that before, after all. Even the Order of the Silver Twilight had begun life as someone else's little cult before Sanford came along to seize control and improve it.

That loathsome Fantasma was going to introduce him to a leading figure in one such organization, and from there, Sanford would work his way in and up, all the way to the top.

He checked his pocket watch. Barcelona was still slumbering, which made this a good time to handle certain necessary arrangements. Sanford spent time in the bathroom pulling strands of hair from his head and gathering copious drops of his own blood. He cut the back of his hand, of course, to acquire the latter. Neophytes often sliced across their palms while doing blood magic, a sure sign of an amateur. The palm was much more sensitive, and there were numerous nerves there, and every time you curled your fingers, you'd reopen the wounds.

He had a few empty vials among his personal effects, and for good measure he rinsed out a few marmalade jars he'd collected from his breakfasts. He dripped his blood and nestled his hairs inside the small vessels, sealing the tops with candle wax and inscribing the appropriate sigils on the seals with the end of a needle. With a bit of effort, he pulled up a floorboard and hid one of the jars underneath, restoring the board and covering it with a rug.

Then he set out into the city with a satchel over his shoulder, roaming far and wide, walking for hours with no particular plan, and hiding the jars of blood and hair inside drains, gutter spouts, behind loose bricks, and even throwing one into the shallows of the sea.

The blood, hair, and a bit of sympathetic magic made each and every one of those jars the mystical equivalent of Sanford himself, a series of doubles. Anyone attempting to divine his location would now see a dozen results scattered across Barcelona. All that remained was making sure they couldn't locate the *real* him.

He returned to the hotel and went to the front desk. The young man working behind the counter was vaguely familiar, but Sanford had never gotten the knack of learning the names of nobodies. "May I help you, señor?" the man asked in adequate English.

Sanford extended his right hand across the counter. "I just wish to say, I have stayed in many of the finest establishments in the United States of America, and none of them can rival the luxury and attentiveness I have experienced in your exemplary hotel. I wish to congratulate you and shake your hand."

The clerk looked a bit dazed, doubtless more accustomed to complaints than compliments, then smiled and extended his hand. Sanford took his hand and *squeezed*. The clerk looked at first puzzled and then slightly pained. Sanford withdrew his hand, tipped his hat, said, "Keep up the good work," and then went toward the stairs that led to his room.

He glanced down at his hand as he walked. He wore a ring on his right hand, a hollow one with a tiny needle protruding from the bottom, like the poison rings favored by the Borgias, but this one had a different purpose: it drained blood, just a drop, but that was enough for a skilled magician. And Sanford was no mere magician, he was a magus.

A hotel clerk's blood wasn't much use to anyone in the normal course of things, but it would serve perfectly well for Sanford's purposes. He paused on the landing of the stairs, made sure no one was ascending or descending, then put the drop of mundane blood in a tiny vial sealed with wax and inscribed with a different sigil. He hung the vial around his neck from a thin silver chain.

There. Now his magical personhood was muddled with that of the clerk's. Any divination meant to find Sanford would slide right off the obfuscation. The effect wouldn't last forever, or stand up to sufficiently strong scrutiny, but he wasn't too worried. It was only Altman and the Warden coming for him, after all. The Warden didn't do spellwork; she *was* magical, her powers inherent and granted through a ritual long ago. And Altman was a dilettante at best.

Sanford tut-tutted at himself as he continued up the stairs. That overconfidence again! No, it was best to treat the two of them like a real threat. An abundance of caution would do no harm and could conceivably do some good. He should leave the hotel soon and take different lodgings. A shame – he'd finally gotten the rooms arranged to his liking – but moving on was a basic precaution. He couldn't leave quite yet, though. He had to wait for Fantasma to send him a message first. With luck, he wouldn't have to wait long.

Sanford opened the door to this room and stepped inside.

Fantasma sat in the same chair where Sanford had read Ruby's letter, one leg crossed casually over the other, a pistol pointed straight at Sanford's heart.

"Do come in," the pale man said, baring his teeth.

CHAPTER THREE
Altman at Sea

Altman tossed and turned in his bunk on the ocean liner *Ebon Lion*, his mind filled with visions of black fire. The Warden sat in a small chair in the corner, watching him as he moaned, writhed, and sweated. He hated being weak in front of her, but she insisted on keeping watch. She was significantly diminished from her peak, but she was still powerful by human standards and did not need to sleep. The small black dog curled up at her feet was the only creature truly resting in this berth tonight.

The *Lion* was a faded glory, its once-opulent rugs now threadbare, its wallpaper scratched in places, rust showing through the paintwork even on the upper decks. They'd chosen this vessel because it was the first passenger ship departing from Boston for Portugal after they'd discovered Sanford was alive and tracked him to Spain. Altman had… acquired… enough funds to purchase a cabin in first class; they could hardly bunk in a room with ten other people in steerage, even if that was more appropriate for their financial situation. They required privacy to make their preparations and for Altman to come to terms with his new condition.

He turned over on the bunk, facing the metal wall, unable

to bear the Warden's steady gaze any longer. He knew she was watching to see if he was going to be trouble. She had a pistol in the purse on her lap and a knife hidden in her boot. She knew what he wrestled with, and if the thing he fought with won, she was prepared to take the necessary steps. She could cut his throat and easily use her vestiges of power to hide from sight while she threw his body overboard to feed the fish and Deep Ones below the waves.

But he wouldn't lose this battle. He would win. He would master the thing inside him–

Altman blinked.

He was no longer in the bunk, no longer in their cabin at all, but back in Arkham, standing amid the ruins of the burned Lodge on French Hill. The once great mansion had been entirely lost, the foundation cracked, the basement rooms partially collapsed and infested with ghouls, but he'd returned anyway, with a shotgun and a flashlight, to see if anything could be salvaged. He'd moved aside fallen timbers and entered the remains of the basement, finding his way to a room that contained a few mystic tomes, stained by soot and smoke but largely unharmed. Most of the Order's impressive collection of magical books was lost. The more common items upstairs burned when the house went up in flames, along with the truly valuable ones lost forever in the deep basements, an extradimensional space that had been cut off from the mundane world, impossible to access ever again.

But there were a few volumes that survived, recent acquisitions picked up by the Order's roaming scouts, brought to this room for Initiates and Seekers gifted in languages to sort, inventory, and translate. A scant dozen titles of unknown value, but they were the only assets left to the Order of the Silver

Twilight, and thus to Altman as the new head of the Order. So, he gathered those books up, put them in a satchel, and trudged through the crunching coals back up into the light.

See? A voice seethed in Altman's head. *You* chose *this. No one* made *you do this.*

Altman whimpered and slapped himself in the face, trying to return to consciousness, to come back to the ship making its weeks' long trip across the Atlantic. However, he remained steadfastly trapped in this memory – if it was a memory, and not some sort of mental projection, sending his present mind into his past body. That sort of thing was possible. Sanford had imprisoned a mental time traveler like that in the deep basements, a woman with the mind of an inhuman creature from the far future lurking behind her eyes. She'd escaped in the chaos, though. Another of the Order's once-great resources, lost.

If Altman's mind *was* being projected into the past, then he could change things, couldn't he? He could make different decisions. He didn't have to take these books with him, didn't have to blackmail that linguist at Miskatonic University into translating them for him, didn't have to perform the Rite of Invitation–

Why would you want to change any of that? the thing sharing his brain whispered. Altman recoiled, but how could you recoil from something inside you? He tried to hurl the satchel of books to the ground, but then the world

twitched

and he was suddenly sitting in the back room of the shack he and the Warden had rented by the river, a shack that was gone now, utterly obliterated by the floodwaters, but he didn't want to think about that either.

Tillinghast had promised him money, no, *wealth* in the form of access to all of Carl Sanford's and the Order's accounts, but there were legal delays, logistical problems, and somehow the funds never materialized. For a time, Altman and the Warden had stayed in the home of Tillinghast's departed assistant Gloria Dyer, but then a man from the bank came and told them the house had been foreclosed, and they'd been forced to move on. Around that time, Tillinghast stopped communicating with them entirely, more interested in whatever grand ritual he was performing.

Altman had eventually been forced to sell the Rolls Royce that Tillinghast had given him just to afford food and housing. And what meager housing it was! That car remained the only real asset he'd ever gotten, and it was poor payment for Altman's role in assassinating Carl Sanford. Who wasn't even dead, although Altman hadn't realized that until later.

He'd only found out the magus was alive because he discovered one of Sanford's rings in the ashes of the Lodge where the old man's study had been. Altman sat at the table in that horrible shack, holding the ring up to the lamplight, and asked the Warden if she knew anything about it.

Altman didn't will himself to speak, it simply happened: he was trapped in this vision. He tried to rise from the table, to fling the ring aside, to break the chain of causality that led from the past to the present, but nothing happened. It seemed he was merely a passenger in the past now, observing the memory but unable to change it.

The Warden was seated in a chair against the wall, her head tipped back and a cold wet cloth draped across her eyes. She'd been getting terrible headaches lately. Her wellbeing was tied to that of the Order of the Silver Twilight, and as the Order suffered, so did she. "I know about everything," Van Shaw said querulously. "The ring has a bodiless servitor bound to it. A sort of spirit, but a brute of a thing, invisible but tangible, only really useful for carrying heavy things, or frightening fools, I suppose."

"I need any resource I can get," Altman said. Feeling his mouth move without his volition repulsed him. He twisted the ring onto his little finger, the only one it would fit. "How do I summon the thing?"

"Simply command it to appear." The Warden always spoke to him like he was a child who hadn't yet learned to tie his own shoes.

Altman cleared his throat and said, "I command you to appear, servitor!"

The ring trembled on his finger, like the vibration of a tuning fork, and a faint shimmer appeared in the air before him. "I do not serve you," a groaning voice said. "I am bound to another."

"What other?" Had Tillinghast somehow stolen this, too? "I wear the ring, so I possess you."

"No. Carl Sanford is my master," the shimmer said.

"Sanford? He's dead, creature, and death breaks all bindings."

"Not all bindings," the thing said. "But that is of no consequence, for my master is not dead."

Altman froze. "What do you mean?"

"My master is not dead," the servitor said again. "I await his summons, not yours." The shimmer vanished, and the ring began to grow hot, so hot that Altman tore it from his finger and flung it away, cursing. He stared at the Warden, hiding his confusion with fury, as was his custom. "Did you hear that? That thing says the old bastard is still alive!"

"Yes." The Warden removed the cloth and looked at him slowly. "I suspected Sanford had survived."

"You might have said something!" Altman roared.

The Warden winced, not from fear – she didn't fear him at all, which was part of the problem – but doubtless because of her aching head.

"I knew nothing for certain." Her voice was low and hoarse, not the commanding tones she'd once used for nearly every utterance. "But Carl Sanford is not easily killed, and we did not see his body."

"The ceiling fell on him," Altman said. "He was buried in rubble. And then the place where he was buried in rubble was torn away from this reality. So what if he's alive? He's surely lost, floating in a pocket-sized world in an endless void full of monsters, beyond the back of the stars, slowly starving to death."

The Warden barely shrugged, lifting one shoulder and then letting it drop. "Perhaps. But he is Carl Sanford. Such a situation would be an inconvenience at most for such a magus. Don't forget that Tillinghast exiled Sanford to the Dreamlands, and he made his way back home. Even Tillinghast seemed impressed by that."

"If Sanford is alive and at liberty, why hasn't he come back here?" Altman looked over his shoulder, as if afraid Sanford might be lurking beyond one of the shoddily glassed windows.

"Tillinghast is ascendant here," the Warden said. "Arkham belongs to him. If he believes Sanford is dead, that allows the magus time to regroup, marshal his powers, gather resources and allies, and return with a plan. Sanford underestimated Tillinghast once. He won't do so again. When he returns, it will be in strength."

Altman licked his lips. "We should tell Tillinghast that Sanford still lives."

Van Shaw scoffed. "Run along to daddy, then, and ask for his help? Remind me, has Tillinghast been returning your calls? Do you even know where his shop is now?" Tillinghast Exotics and Esoterica had a disconcerting tendency to move around, and its last known location was an abandoned dusty storefront now. "We barely ever met with him directly anyway. He always sent his assistant, or apprentice Gloria, and *she's* disappeared, too."

"He still works closely with Ruby," Altman said. "If we can reach out to her–"

The Warden shook her head, slow and ponderous. "She is gone. Tillinghast has sent her on some mission. I do not know where. She told me she was going on an expedition with a group of people Tillinghast put together. They are out working on the next step to achieving his Great Work, whatever that might be. We are *alone*, Altman. Tillinghast used us and cast us aside. We were only ever a method to remove Carl Sanford, the one person who might have been a threat to Tillinghast's machinations."

Altman rose from the table and looked out the window at the squalid night. The mental passenger – the delirious, fever-dreamed Altman of the future, locked inside this memory – stared, too. The moon was high and bright, which made the churned mud of the street and the bowed roofs of the sagging warehouses dreadfully visible.

Then a wall of churning water burst from between two warehouses, tearing the structures down as it came rushing straight for their shack. The inner Altman gasped, but the body at the window seemed to take no notice, even though they were going to be washed away, obliterated–

He lurched upright in the ship bunk, looking around wildly, but there was no threat, only a dimmed lamp and the Warden sitting upright against the wall.

That inundation… that hadn't happened. When the flood – the Great Flood – came, he and the Warden had been up on French Hill, sifting through the ruins of the Lodge again in search of valuables. From their high vantage, they'd seen the wall of water wash in from the sea and watched it smash apart the poorest parts of the city. They'd also seen… *things*… moving in the water, and then–

But that whole time was a jumble in his mind. Altman had spent dark months in Afghanistan working as a mercenary, and he had clear memories of every atrocity he'd witnessed there. But for some reason, the day of the flood, and the hectic, desperate, drowning time that followed, was all smoke and fog fragments. His mind refused to order or collate those experiences, and something fundamental to his psyche recoiled every time he tried. He was left with a vague impression of something immense and rotting, dragging itself forward…

"Warden," he croaked. "What were those things we saw in the water? When the flood came?"

"I don't know," she said from her chair. "Sanford would have known. But I think Tillinghast called them up. Summoned them. The flood was a result of his Great Work."

Altman swept sweat from his brow. He was feeling lucid, at last. The past released its grip on him. Why was he so feverish? He'd never suffered much on sea voyages before. Had he eaten tainted fish, or caught something from another passenger? He'd survived the Spanish Flu, and even that hadn't addled him like this. He remembered something, candles and blood and chanting, but his mind recoiled from that, too. He tried to focus. "Why would Tillinghast want to wipe Arkham from the map?"

"I don't know if he did," she said. "If that was his goal, he didn't quite succeed. Arkham is battered, but it still stands. For all we know, the flood might have been a side effect, or an unintended consequence, or perhaps his ritual simply went wrong. All we know is that his plans were grand and complex, and when grand and complex rituals fail, the consequences can be disastrous."

"When… when the Order is mine, properly mine, we can help rebuild." A great weight seemed to settle on Altman's shoulders, and he sank into the mattress. "Once Sanford… gives me what he stole, the treasures… once he's really dead… once he names me his heir… then I'll be… I'll have… what Tillinghast promised."

"Tillinghast's promises are moonbeams and fairy dust," the Warden said. "You should know that by now. He promised me freedom. But I'm still bound and dying. All because you…"

Her voice faded away, everything

twitched

and darkness rushed in. When that darkness receded, Altman knelt on the warped boards of the place they'd squatted in after the flood, a townhouse devastated by mold and mildew. The rightful inhabitants were among the missing, presumed dead, no doubt pulled by currents out to sea – or worse, judging by the body parts that sometimes washed up on the banks of the Miskatonic River. Some of them were covered in bite marks. The theory was that the flood waters brought in sharks. Altman found that more comforting than the various alternatives that occurred to him.

Now Altman was surrounded by candles, waiting for the paint on the floor to dry. He'd painstakingly copied the sigils from the book, the single book of true power he'd successfully recovered from the basement in the Lodge. The title of this grimoire was partly obscured, scratched off the leather cover and eradicated from the interior as well; the only part that was still legible read "serpentum nocturnorum," with words on either side that were impossible to make out. Something – Serpent of the Night – Something. The missing words were somehow even more evocative, as mysteries were often more compelling than facts.

Altman only knew this book had value because the Warden told him so. She had an affinity for magic – she was, in fact, more than half magic herself, her life sustained by her connection to the Order. Altman had found a linguist willing to translate the relevant portions for him, and he was finally ready to perform the ritual.

Don't, his feverish mind willed his past self, but it was too late. Immutable.

A brass bowl sat in the center of the sigil, filled with samples of his blood, hair, spit, and fingernail clippings, even one of his teeth wrenched from the back where it wouldn't be much missed. His jaw still ached. The roots had come out bloody. There were other things in the bowl, too: herbs procured from a witch in the woods of New Hampshire, and ground-up mushrooms, and a rare cactus small enough to fit in his palm.

He poured brandy into the bowl and lit the whole mess on fire with a long match. The smoke that rose was vile. He sat down in the circle and chanted, slow and even, having practiced the words over and over. He barely understood what they meant, memorizing them phonetically, but after weeks of practice, the Warden had grudgingly said his pronunciation was adequate. If he said the words wrong, he didn't know what would happen, but as the Warden said – or would say? – incorrectly performing a ritual could lead to disaster.

Correctly performing a ritual could lead to that, too, though.

Altman chanted, and the smoke took on a shape – were those arms, legs, and a head on a long and writhing neck? He breathed in a deep lungful of the smoke, and his vision blurred. He fell back, twitching. In the center of the symbol on the floor, the smoke figure hovered over him, looking down at him, and then he was somehow looking down at himself, at his weak human flesh, and then he was rushing down into the mouth, through the nostrils in through the eyes and ears and every other opening, into *everything*–

The world

twitched

again, and his surroundings writhed into a blur before settling into a new configuration.

"I just need power," Altman told the Warden, back in their little shack, after discovering that Sanford had survived but before the flood changed their world for the worse, before the ritual broke his mind. "Strength enough to show those fools that I'm the rightful ruler of the Order."

"You *are* the Order." The Warden's voice was dull. "An Order of one. Two, if you count me, but I'm more... part of the infrastructure. I must free myself of this binding, or I will die with you."

"If I'm stronger, will it make you stronger?"

She shrugged. "Perhaps. I don't expect that situation to

arise. Now that the servitor has confirmed Sanford is alive, I have other options. If I find the magus, he can free me from my oath. He laid these bindings upon me, tied my life to the Order, and he can sever those ties. I'm sure of it."

She didn't sound even remotely sure of it.

"If I can find him, I can make him give me back the treasures he stole. Make him name me his heir. I can bring his head back here and show it to the traitors and upstarts, and make them realize *I* am the only rightful Grand Magus."

"You? Make Carl Sanford do anything? Pah."

"Maybe I couldn't now," Altman admitted. "But we found that grimoire. There's a spell there, and it promises great power. The power to destroy one's enemies."

"You speak of things you do not understand."

"Look at us." He spread his hands. "We live in squalor. If we go on like this, neither of us will survive. Or worse, we will, and we'll have to go on living like this forever. Or else I can give up my dream of ruling the Order… resign, renounce my claim… and then what would happen to you? When the Order of the Silver Twilight is truly gone?"

"I do not know." The Warden shuddered. "Agony at worst. Death at best."

"Then isn't it worth a try?" Altman said. The plan appeared in his mind. Like some sort of divine, or infernal, inspiration. "I'll perform this ritual and gain great power. Then, we'll track down Sanford, force him to free you, and give me all that I was promised. Are you with me?"

"I have no choice," Van Shaw said and turned her face away. Smoke began to pour in through the windows, black and acrid. It smelled like the pyres they'd made in Afghanistan, the stink filling the room–

Altman screamed and sat up in bed again, kicking the blankets off. Light streamed in through the tiny porthole window. The Warden stood by the door.

"Where are we?" he asked, panicked. How long had he been dreaming?

"Lisbon," she said quietly and turned away again.

CHAPTER FOUR
I Bind and Adjure Thee

"You invite me to enter my own room?" Sanford sighed. "What a gracious host you are. The hospitality of the Spanish was truly not overstated." He shut the door behind him and stood, hands clasped loosely before him. This wasn't surprising, but it *was* mildly disappointing. You always hoped people would learn. Ah, well.

Sanford spoke a few words, a combination of Latin, Attic Greek, and the incantatory langue of Aklo, murmuring them swiftly under his breath.

"Are you praying?" Fantasma said. "I do not think your gods will answer you. Not before my gun can speak." He shifted on the chair, ostentatiously making himself more comfortable. "I would have preferred to feed you to my brother – he is so very hungry, you know, always. Failing that, I would have loved to sup on your blood myself." He sniffed, then frowned. "Though you smell different, somehow." He shrugged. "No matter. Perhaps it is the smell of fear. But I think this is better. The American businessman who came to Europe desperate to make deals, only to fail and face poverty. Who could blame him for choosing to turn his pistol on himself rather than return home in disgrace?"

"If you think you can convince me to shoot myself, you are much mistaken," Sanford said.

Fantasma waved the gun idly. "It hardly matters. We have some influence with the *policia,* and once the scene is properly staged no one will ask too many questions. I am so glad you told me where you were staying, Mr Phillips. You spared me the trouble of trying to track you down. Do you have any parting words?"

"I do," Sanford said. "How kind of you to offer." He cleared his throat. "I bind thee and adjure thee to put the gun down."

Fantasma's eyes widened as his hand moved, seemingly of its own volition, to place the gun on the table.

"Now rise and face the wall," Sanford said. "I grow rather weary of your smug features. I've never seen anyone so pale sneer so condescendingly, and I've spent time in Cambridge." He paused. "I mean the one near Boston, but the one in Britain fits too, I suppose."

Fantasma jerked to his feet and then spun to look at the wall. He trembled, his shoulders twitching as he fought the binding.

"Would you like to see something beautiful?" Sanford said. "Behold." He gestured, and sinuous shapes began to glow golden yellow and blood-red over every space surrounding Fantasma. The previously invisible sigils ranged in size from inches across to yards.

"Aren't they lovely?" Sanford said. "This entire room is a circle of binding. I don't know the details of your inhuman heritage, but I made some educated guesses and inscribed my room with an array of sigils and signs to cover all plausible possibilities." He smiled, thinking of Ruby's sobriquet: the master of the contingency plan. Well, indeed. His plans hadn't kept Tillinghast from destroying his Order and driving him away, but they *had* kept him alive, which was the important thing. Everything began with survival.

"I– you can't– this is–" Fantasma sputtered.

Sanford said, "Hmm," as if the man had made a good point. "If you're wondering, the *Aklo Sabaoth* proved to be the relevant rite."

He gestured to one particular large sigil in front of Fantasma's face that seemed to pulse in time with a fast heartbeat, which must have been Fantasma's, since Sanford's was quite steady. "It's exceedingly difficult to bind and control a human, unless you can obtain blood or tissue, and even then, the results are generally quite crude, more puppeteering than elegant compulsion. But you aren't entirely human, and so you are subject to a different set of laws. All that bodily resistance is unsightly, but that's just your human side coming through. A pity for you it's not strong enough to cause me any trouble."

Sanford sat down in the chair, picked up the pistol, and opened the chamber. He shook out the rounds, dropping them in one jacket pocket, and then put the pistol in the other. He didn't usually bother with guns, but they had their uses from time to time.

He shifted his chair around until he was angled properly to see Fantasma's profile, enjoying the sight of the creature's jaw clenching. "I didn't ask you to do so very much, Fantasma. You would even have been compensated for your assistance. I only asked you to make an introduction. I would kill you for this rudeness but, fortunately for you, I find myself short on time and don't wish to cultivate another contact. You are the only thread I have that connects me to the people I need to meet. I haven't pulled that thread very hard yet. Would you like me to pull it harder?"

"You will not get away with this–" His voice shook.

"I could tell you to pluck out your own eyes and eat them, and you would rush to comply," Sanford said. "I would find such a thing unsightly – ha, forgive me – but if needs must…"

"Enough!" Fantasma said. "Who *are* you? How do you have such power, such resources?"

"Mr Phillips is a good enough name for now. I don't need you to know any more than that. How does the saying go? I wish to speak to the organ-grinder, not the monkey? I'll introduce myself properly to your masters."

"They are not my masters. I only work for them intermittently at best. They are the ones who sent me!" Fantasma clenched his hands into fists. Sanford was impressed. He had a strong will. Just not as strong as his own. "I passed on your message, as requested, and attempted to arrange a meeting. But Thorne told me to come and kill you, instead."

"That seems rude," Sanford said. "I'd heard the One in the Red Cravat was less… volatile than some other members of his group." Thorne wasn't the leader of the so-called Red Coterie – the structure of their organization was a bit unclear, to Sanford's annoyance, though the enigmatic Red-Gloved Man seemed the most likely to be its head – but Thorne was said to be rational and efficient. All Sanford had *ever* needed was someone willing to listen to him. Once people started negotiating with Sanford, he'd already won.

"It was a test!" Fantasma blurted. "Thorne said if… if you could be killed by someone like *me*, then you weren't worthy of their time."

Sanford chuckled. "I like them already. They are quite right. What if you proved unable to kill me?"

Fantasma gritted his teeth. "Then I am supposed to tell

     Arkham Horror

you… that you can meet Thorne… in a certain plaza in the Gothic Quarter tonight."

"Then why don't you give me the rest of the details of this rendezvous now, and you can go on your way?"

The creature dully recited a series of directions which Sanford absorbed without needing to take notes. Long decades of memorizing complex rituals had made such matters trivial for him. He didn't doubt the creature's words or fret about being led into a trap, or at least, not a trap Fantasma had set; honesty was a condition of the bindings Sanford had laid upon him.

Once the creature finished, Sanford released Fantasma unharmed from his paralysis – he was, after all, an errand boy, or an errand entity, technically – but declined to return his pistol to him. "Stay for a drink?" Sanford said. "You made everything unnecessarily difficult, but I have half a bottle of single malt Bowmore I'd be willing to share to toast the conclusion of our business relationship."

"Scotch?" Fantasma said. "*Islay* Scotch? Those taste like someone set a muddy rubber boot on fire."

"Ah, yes, you Spaniards prefer your sangrias. You have the palates of children sucking on boiled sweets. We have one last bit of business before you can run along."

Fantasma cast him a murderous glare, but Sanford merely smiled before forcing the creature to swear a binding oath to do no harm to the magus now or in the future, or cause others to do him harm. After that, Fantasma was a toothless dog and safely ignored. Sanford could have killed the creature, or even bound him to become his personal servant forever, but he hadn't. You'd think the fellow would be a bit more grateful.

Once the pale man had departed, full of ill humor and

grating promises to do as he was told, Sanford checked to make sure none of his signs and bindings had been damaged during the encounter, then settled down to wait. He'd been instructed to meet Thorne at midnight, so he had hours to kill and plenty of time for Fantasma to report back to Thorne that Sanford had passed his "test." All this hoop-jumping was rather tedious, but Sanford was the one seeking an audience, so he would go along.

For now.

Sanford went to the dining room around 10 PM. The mealtimes here were abhorrent, and while the food was adequate, it wasn't truly to his taste. He imagined a rare steak in the Excelsior's dining room, and then grimly returned to his sole. Fish again.

Finally, the hour grew late enough to set out for his rendezvous. He took his walking stick, with its concealed blade, and had several magical items hidden about his person. He had no reason to think this meeting would turn hostile, but… contingencies.

Barcelona was very different from Arkham. Back home, this close to midnight, everything would be silent and buttoned-up, all the good citizens home in bed. But the Iberian summer nights were cooler than the brutal days, and he passed many crowds of locals and visitors strolling through the streets, making merry. He tipped his hat and returned greetings when he was greeted first, and that was different, too. Back home, anyone he passed would be head down, intent on their own affairs, and with the strictures of the Volstead Act, few of them would have been so obviously intoxicated.

Massachusetts had been founded by Puritans, though, and

          Arkham Horror

here, Catholics abounded. Perhaps that accounted for some of the differences in cultural character. Catholics were so much more *dramatic*.

It was only a ten minute walk or so from his hotel to the Gothic Quarter, which was darker and more sedate than Las Ramblas. He'd memorized Fantasma's instructions, which were simple enough: enter from a particular intersection, take two lefts and a right, follow the winding path to a square, and if there was a fountain with a statue of an octopus in the middle, he was in the right place.

After that final right turn, however, the winding path did not take him to a plaza, with a fountain or otherwise. Instead, it meandered before finally splitting into three paths. The walls on both sides had gradually closed in until they were almost close enough to brush his shoulders. He craned back his neck and saw only blank stone walls on either side of him, without windows or lights. The narrow strip of sky overhead was black, without even a hint of moonlight. Sanford cursed and reached into his pocket for his monocle, then peered through it.

Magic shimmered all around him, so bright that he could discern nothing else through the lens. "Another test?" he demanded aloud, but nothing answered him. He put the monocle away and considered the three paths before him. Straight ahead, he could see a streetlamp and a group of three people walking beneath it, chatting and laughing. That, he suspected, was the way out, back to mundane reality – and a tacit admittance of defeat. The path on the right was cobblestoned, and he heard the faint strains of flamenco music and caught a whiff of what might have been hashish.

The leftward path was puddled with black water and so dark

he could see only a few yards along its length. Well, Sanford was never afraid to walk in the dark. He chose that path, stepping over the puddles, squinting until his eyes adjusted to the gloom. He could see well enough to avoid bumping into walls, but not much more.

A soft scraping sound behind him made him freeze, and he spun, peering into the darkness. A titter up ahead made him whip his head around to face the front again. A low growl rumbled behind him, and an answering chuckle came from another direction. Were they true threats or mere trickery from Thorne? Sanford reached into his pocket for a gold-plated lighter, murmuring, "Ignis" when he flicked it on.

A head-sized ball of fire burst into life in the air, six feet in front of Sanford at roughly eye level. It dispelled the shadows and revealed… nothing at all. No muggers lying in wait, no strange monsters hiding in the shadows, no pits or pendulums.

Sanford let the light fade, pocketing the lighter and frowning. The unnatural shadows didn't push in again, perhaps dispelled forever, perhaps merely gathering strength to enshroud him anew. Thorne was taunting him.

"Enough," he said.

He pulled on a pair of kidskin gloves he'd had specially enchanted after Ruby gave him a demonstration of her cat burglar skills one night back in Arkham. She'd scaled a nearly sheer wall – in skirts – and then stood on the edge of the roof and curtsied to him. Sanford was not as young or limber as Ruby, but he was in good shape, and when he tried to follow her example, he failed completely, unable to climb even a couple of feet up the façade, his fingertips slipping from the grooves in brickwork, unable to find purchase.

That failure was an outrage, of course. Anything *anyone*

could do, he could do better. He resolved to become better than Ruby, and indeed to exceed even the skills of Harry F. Young, one of several building climbers also nicknamed the so-called "human fly," who'd scaled the side of the Martinique Hotel in New York freehand a few years ago before an audience of thousands. Of course, Young had fallen to his death after making it ten stories, but Sanford did not intend to emulate him *exactly*.

The gloves and the tasseled loafers he wore were thus laid with enchantments that increased Sanford's agility and tactile sensitivity, as well as made slight alterations to local gravity, sufficient to let him outdo Ruby *and* the unfortunate Mr Young.

Sanford turned to the four-story high wall on his right and began to scale it, his fingertips and toes unerringly finding tiny imperfections in the stones sufficient to support his weight. The going was awkward with his walking stick shoved through his belt, but he made it to the roof and gazed at his surroundings.

The lights of the city glowed around him. He glimpsed the unfinished spires of the Sagrada Família, by far the tallest thing in sight. He looked down, tracing the paths below, and realized he'd doubled back somehow and returned nearly to his starting point. All the illusory paths had conspired to guide him nearly out of the Gothic Quarter entirely.

Was all that growling meant to make him panic and run, and to feel relieved when he emerged into the light again? What an insulting illusion.

Sanford walked along the rooftops, untroubled by further specters and glamors. Apparently, the baffling magics didn't extend this far above the ground. He followed the directions

Fantasma had given him, but from above, and soon found the proper square, with its small betentacled fountain.

And there, seated at a small table with a candle burning in the middle, was a tall, slim, pale-haired figure with a red cravat. A gray scarf covered the lower half of their face.

Sanford scaled down the wall and then jumped the last bit, using one of the minor enchantments in his pockets to drift down elegantly and spare him any embarrassment. He sauntered to the table. "Thorne, I assume?"

The One with the Red Cravat surprised him by saying, "Of course. And you are Carl Sanford."

Rattled but refusing to show it, Sanford took the chair across from Thorne and sat, propping his walking stick against the fountain. "I see my reputation precedes me."

Thorne's shoulders lifted in a barely perceptible shrug. "People said you died, but when Fantasma described you – and especially when Fantasma reported back and described how you bound him – I considered the possibilities. Carl Sanford was the most likely candidate. Congratulations on your continued existence. Condolences on the destruction of your Order of the Silver Twilight. I understand Randall Tillinghast is a formidable foe."

Sanford hated to admit that, but did so. "He is," he said simply. "But I will make him pay for his trespasses against me in time."

"Is that why you wanted to meet?" Thorne said. "To enlist our help in some revenge plot? I don't think any members of the Red Coterie have dealt directly with Tillinghast, but we are … aware of him. There are clearly areas where our interests overlap, and may, perhaps, even come into conflict someday. But we aren't looking for a fight with him at the moment, I'm afraid."

"I don't need others to fight my battles for me," Sanford said. "No, you quite misunderstand. I haven't come to enlist your services. I'm here to offer my services to *you*." He leaned forward. "After much thought and consideration, I have decided I would be willing to join the Red Coterie."

"Ah," Thorne said. "I see." They leaned back, looking Sanford up and down before gazing around the square. "This used to be a Roman village. We're not far from what remains of the old Roman wall, in fact. Remind me, what happened to the Roman Empire?"

"It fell," Sanford said. "There were barbarians at the gate. They forced their way inside, and they pillaged." He sighed. "I suppose you're drawing a parallel between what happened to their empire and what happened to my own?"

"Extraordinary," Thorne murmured. "You compare your little Order to the might of the Holy Roman Empire?"

Sanford shrugged. "My organization was less holy, I suppose, but superior in other respects."

Thorne didn't seem amused. "The fall of Rome was more of a labor dispute, in some ways. Those barbarians didn't attack Rome at random. They were hired as mercenaries to fight Rome's myriad battles abroad, but the politicians declined to pay what they were owed in a timely fashion, and the so-called barbarians grew tired of waiting. So they came back and took what they were owed. And a bit extra, which is only fair."

"You sound like a socialist," Sanford said.

"Should I claim capitalist, that they took acquired interest? Or perhaps I'm just a pragmatist. Do you still see parallels? Wasn't your empire toppled when your own undervalued employees turned on you?"

Sanford scowled. This person knew more about his business

than he would have preferred. "Those employees were valued appropriately for their worth. Overvalued, even. I gave them everything, and how was I repaid? They were seduced away by a treacherous sorcerer. A man who turned them against their best interests and poisoned them against mine. And look what happened in my absence! Arkham is a flooded ruin. That would have never happened if I'd been there."

"But you weren't," Thorne pointed out. "The point I am trying to make is this: you were bested. You were driven away. You *failed*. The name Carl Sanford used to have a certain renown attached to it, even on the Continent, but the bloom is off the rose. Why should we let you join the Red Coterie when you've proven incapable of managing your own affairs?"

"I have much to offer," Sanford protested. "Tillinghast took me by surprise, yes, but he didn't kill me. I escaped, and with my treasures indeed, some of which would surely interest your group–"

"Your fabled vault, yes." Thorne yawned. "I'm not sure how much you know about the nature of the Coterie."

"Each member holds a Key," Sanford said. "A para-dimensional artifact of great power. You wield them, protect them, to keep them from falling into the wrong hands."

"That is one facet of our work, yes."

"It will not surprise you to know that I possess numerous relics of power–"

"You had one thing that might have interested us." Thorne held up a single long finger. "Just one. The Ruby of R'lyeh."

Sanford frowned. He hadn't expected that; he'd had a different relic entirely in mind to secure his membership. "Really? I never even found out what that thing was *for*."

"Magical artifacts aren't tea kettles or egg timers," Thorne said. "They aren't necessarily 'for' any purpose at all, and their effects can vary based on time, location, and the individual who is using them. But, broadly speaking, the Ruby affords a certain protection to travelers through other realms, or through regions distorted by magic. I understand you spent some time wandering the Dreamlands?"

"I… how do you know all this?" Sanford hadn't told anyone about his journeys through that place, mostly because it would have required admitting that Tillinghast had banished him there in the first place.

Thorne shrugged. "We have eyes everywhere, even in other worlds. Didn't you ever wonder how you managed to survive such a journey with your body *and* your mind intact? The Ruby protected you."

"I was nearly killed many times," Sanford objected. "I was nearly devoured by a stone man filled with fire at the end!"

"*Nearly.*" Thorne tapped a finger on the tabletop. "Nearly, nearly, nearly. Without the Ruby, you would have been carried away and eaten by a nightgaunt in the first five minutes."

Sanford didn't like being in the presence of someone who knew so much more than he did. "So you say. I think I would have survived anyway. I suppose we'll never know."

"Believe what you like. If you still had the Ruby, you might be of some interest to the Coterie. You might even be a viable contender to take over the Venice territory, which has recently opened up. But since you don't… you aren't." Thorne made a gesture like flicking drops of water from their fingertips. "We weren't sure if Tillinghast took the Ruby from you or not, but now it is clear that he did. That is good to know, anyway. We do try to keep track of such things."

"How do you know I don't have the Ruby?" Sanford patted

the breast of his jacket, as if the jewel might be hidden away in a pocket. In reality, Ruby Standish had stolen the relic from him in the basements beneath the Lodge and given it to her new employer.

Thorne sighed heavily. "If you had possessed the jewel, the illusory maze I laid for you would have given you no trouble at all. You would have passed through the false paths without even noticing them. Safe passage is what the jewel offers – or safer, anyway. Tillinghast has the jewel, now. That is all I wished to ascertain during the course of this meeting. I bid you good evening and good luck." Thorne began to rise.

"I have other relics," Stanford said. A whole steamer trunk full, encrusted with protective sigils and locks, his painstakingly gathered collection, smuggled out of the Lodge last year when he began to doubt the place's security and subsequently carried with him across the sea and rails to Barcelona. He didn't expect any of them to truly tempt the Coterie, but it was worth a try.

Thorne nodded. "You possess some interesting items, but nothing we need to lay our hands on right away. We can wait until you die and acquire them from your estate. I do hope you enjoy them in the meantime."

"I do not intend to die anytime soon," Sanford snapped. "I will live a *very* long life."

"By the standards of ordinary men, I'm sure you will," Thorne said. "But the Coterie does not operate on such timescales. We are an *ancient* order, Sanford, not like your feeble cult. Our roots date back to the eleventh century. Some of our members do, too. We are very good at being patient."

Sanford waved that aside. "Fine, yes, you're all very impressive, of course you are. I wouldn't be interested in joining your group if you weren't venerable and important. Listen. What if I told you I had plans to acquire an object of power you and your colleagues would find most impressive? Something imbued with energies from beyond this plane, capable of great feats of defensive *and* offensive magic?"

Thorne gave another minute shrug. "Then we might kill you and take it from you, if you would not part with it willingly."

Sanford reared back, stung. "Why do you seek conflict with me when you could simply welcome me into your order?"

Thorne put both hands flat on the table and spoke in a clear, resounding voice. "Let me be clear: there is no place for you in the Coterie, Mr Sanford. You do not possess an object of power worthy of being called a Key. Even if you did, you have proven incapable of managing your own affairs. The members of the Coterie operate independently, controlling our own territories, and we could not trust you to do so. Indeed, what territory could you even claim? You were driven from Arkham, and that was your stronghold. You are Keyless. You are stateless. You are powerless."

Sanford struggled to remain calm. "I have suffered setbacks, yes, but anyone who knows me at all understands I thrive in conditions of adversity. I *will* rise again."

Thorne surprised him by saying, "I don't doubt that. You are a man of considerable talent and determination, your current circumstances notwithstanding. I said you were not in a position to join the Coterie, and that is true. However..."

Thorne sat back down, and Sanford thought, ah *ha*. Thorne dismissing him and rising to leave had been a negotiating tactic, to put Sanford on his back foot and make him grateful for whatever scrap he was about to be offered.

The One with the Red Cravat said, "Had you come to

me as the head of your Order, this conversation would have gone differently. We could certainly have collaborated. If you possessed the Ruby, we might even have invited you to join the Coterie, with a territory encompassing the Northeastern United States. The situation, alas, has changed, and your circumstances are much reduced, but you still have things to offer, I think. The fact that you survived when someone like Tillinghast was so eager to see you dead speaks of a certain resilience, too. I might have work for you, if you're interested. The Coterie has agents everywhere, as I believe I mentioned, and if you intend to settle in Europe, I could find a use for you–"

"I am no one's agent or errand boy," Sanford said. "But you're right. I *am* very capable, and my circumstances are only temporarily reduced. You'd much rather have me as a friend than a rival, Thorne."

"Oh, my. Are you actually threatening me?" Thorne did not sound threatened, only amused.

"I am merely pointing out an immutable law of the universe. It is better to be with Carl Sanford than it is to be against him." Sanford spread his hands. "Listen. I understand that I have suffered failures recently. I have even exhibited certain small lapses in judgement. But I have learned from those mistakes and will not make their like again. You doubt me. You need me to prove myself. I understand that. So set me a task. Not an *errand*. Something that will prove me worthy of joining your Coterie when I succeed."

Thorne shook his head. "You would still need a Key, Mr Sanford."

He leaned forward. "I will acquire one. You needn't worry about that. A plan is already in motion to do so. Just assume

I will have a Key. What can I do for you in the meantime to prove that I'm worthy of wielding that Key as part of the Coterie?"

"You wish to offer your services for free, then?" Thorne stroked the red cravat thoughtfully.

"Not for free," Sanford said. "Consider it a down payment on my membership dues."

Thorne chuckled. "Really, Sanford. You come to me like a knight in search of a quest. You wish to be set an impossible task to prove your worth? Shall I send you to fetch the Golden Fleece? To kill the Nemean lion?"

"Your mythological metaphors are getting jumbled there, Thorne, but, yes, if you like. No task is too Herculean for me. Or Argonautic, either. What do you have to lose? If I fail, I'll trouble you no further. And if I succeed, you get something you want. And so do I. And the Coterie benefits."

Thorne's face was hidden by that scarf, but their eyes were smiling. "Well. There might be one little problem you could help us with. Have you ever heard of a magician called the Blood Moon?"

Estrella hurried through the bustling streets of Madrid on her way to the Residencia de Estudiantes on a mission for the Moon.

The sprawling complex was home to many university students, but more importantly, it was the place where great artists, musicians and writers congregated, discussing heady things and sharing their visions of the future.

They were all wrong, of course, about what that future would look like, but it wasn't their fault. Estrella simply had more information than they did.

She was seventeen, dressed modestly in a white blouse and long skirt, hair pulled back into a no-nonsense ponytail, and clutching a book to her chest. She could move among the residents and their visitors without particularly standing out, and anyone who took notice of her would think she was a newer student, nervous about this new stage in her life. She *was* nervous, but mostly because of the needles hidden away in the pockets she'd carefully sewn into her skirt.

"Estrella" was not the name she'd been born with, but it was the name her savior had given her, and so much more meaningful because of that. She was an orphan, raised in an overcrowded home for such children – her mind skittered away from her still-sharp memories of that place. The Blood Moon found her when she was only five years old, and they were someone who believed in her, loved her, and placed her in a good home with a good family, instead. The Moon had whispered to her, through one of their many mouths, and said, "You will be called Estrella. A shining star, fit to share the sky with the light of the Moon."

The Gullettes were wonderful parents, but most of the time, Estrella didn't really talk to her mother or father. She talked to the Blood Moon, who spoke *through* her mother and father, using their voices. Her closest relationship in the world was with the Moon, who was father and mother, sponsor and mentor, and more. For most of her life, the Moon guided her studies, especially her gift for languages, by sending her a parade of tutors, even teaching her magic, too. In the past few years, she'd been permitted to put that learning to use, and now she went about the city of Madrid doing the Moon's good work.

It was an exciting time in Spain and in the world, Estrella thought – the Great War was over, the influenza epidemic had passed. New ideas blossomed everywhere, and there was a feeling of hope and renewal in the air, like it was springtime the whole year 'round. That feeling of hope was justified, though no one realized why. The Blood Moon had plans for the future, and that future would be bright.

True, the country was ruled by the military now, with a general for a dictator, and it troubled Estrella to know that men who thrived on war were in charge of her country, but the Blood Moon said the dictatorship brought stability, and the Moon would make sure the general and his associates didn't do anything bad. Or, if they did bad things, they were doing them in the service of a greater future.

"No birth is painless," the Moon told her, "and we are bringing a whole new world to life."

Her musings about that future were interrupted by a voice. "Are you ready for this?" A pretty blonde stepped onto the sidewalk beside Estrella, her hair pulled back in a shining ponytail, her checkered dress swaying with her neat steps, books held before her in both hands. She was like another version of Estrella, taller and glossier. Estrella felt dowdy and plain beside her, small and brown, like a sparrow in the presence of a phoenix. But she was also fascinated, the way she often was in the presence of confident, beautiful young women. She couldn't decide if she wanted to be them, or... no, stop, she had a purpose, she had to *focus*.

"What did you say?" Estrella asked. She could talk to boys just fine without a bit of nervousness, perhaps because they didn't interest her, as a rule. But around girls like this, a little older and a lot more sophisticated, her tongue became tangled and dull.

"It's me, Estrellita," the girl said. Estrella's face heated in a blush. This wasn't a young student making conversation: it was the Blood Moon, inhabiting one of the many members of their extended family.

It wasn't Estrella's fault she hadn't realized right away. Their family was vast and growing larger all the time.

"Let's sit and talk for a moment." The girl – currently the Moon's vessel, and thus made holy – sat on a stone bench by a pathway leading to the Residencia, neatly tucking her skirt beneath her in a smooth motion. The Blood Moon was so effortlessly comfortable in so many different sorts of bodies when Estrella wasn't even comfortable in her own, the one she lived in every single day! But then, the Moon was much older, "as old as my namesake," they'd said once.

Estrella sat beside the vessel, tucking her knees together, trying to imitate the host's perfect posture. The girl smiled, her face open and beaming, her eyes lively; the Blood Moon's eyes were always lively, regardless of what face they looked out of, dancing and filled with humor. "I haven't sent you on a mission like this before," the Moon said. "I wanted to make sure you weren't feeling overwhelmed or worried."

"Oh, you don't need to be concerned, Moon. I can do it. I won't fail you–"

"Estrella!" The girl's eyes widened. "You couldn't possibly fail me. I might fail *you*, by sending you out before you're ready, by asking for too much, by pushing you too hard. That is what I hope to avoid. You are my protégé – you are my *heir* – and it is my duty to prepare you to take over the golden world we're creating once I'm gone."

Tears welled at the corners of Estrella's eyes. "Don't talk like that, Moon. You're so powerful. You can live forever."

"Even I grow old, my star. I could go on beyond the death of my body, it's true, but only by taking over the body of someone else, forever, not just a temporary borrowing like this. And that would be wrong." The voice was mildly chiding.

"You could take over the body of a bad person," Estrella said. "Someone who doesn't deserve to live. You could use their body for something better. That would make the world a better place." They'd had this discussion many times before, and Estrella thought she was winning the Moon over to her point of view.

"You do make a compelling argument," the Moon said. "I will continue to ponder the issue. But we can put that aside for now. I am hardly on death's doorstep."

Estrella wondered, for the millionth time, what the Moon really looked like in their actual body. Were they a man or a woman? Did they look as old as they must surely be, or did they appear young, or middle-aged, like the Gullettes? Were they strong or spindly, curvy or stout, dark or pale? Estrella had asked, but only once. The Moon had said, "There are secrets I cannot share with you, little star. The nature and location of my true form are the most important ones, for my safety. If you don't know where I am or what I look like, no one can force you to tell them." There were so many people who wanted to kill the Moon, because the Moon was going to make the world a better place, and the bad people preferred the world to be worse: there was more profit that way.

The Moon didn't let anyone know the location of their lair, not even their heir. Except Estrella did know where the Blood Moon lived. She'd always known. She resisted turning her head and looking in the right direction, instead keeping her head bowed, demure and meek. The Moon didn't know that she knew. That was her one secret, the one thing she kept close, because… well, because she didn't want the Moon to be upset, mainly. And because it felt good to have something that was just hers, a kernel of forbidden knowledge. But she would never tell anyone that secret – all the Blood Moon's secrets were safe with her.

The woman-vessel put her hand over Estrella's, and she reminded herself it was a parental sort of touch and not any other kind. Whoever this girl was at other times, right now she was synonymous with the Moon. "This is a big day for you," the vessel said. "An important assignment. I want to make sure you're ready."

"I've practiced it a million times, Moon. I can do it. But if you don't mind me asking… why do you want to bring these people into the family? They aren't politicians, wealthy, or even powerful."

"Do I only invite the powerful to join our cause?" the Moon asked, amused.

"No, but the poor, the criminals, the people of the street, I can see their use. They move freely throughout the shadows of the city, overlooked and unremarked upon, and that gives you eyes in the low places. But these people… they do not move in the halls of the mighty or the illicit. They read, write, and paint, but mostly they just talk and talk and talk. What good can they do for the cause?"

"Ah, Estrella. The artists are *so* important. They shape the minds and hearts of nations, do you see? My family is growing, yes, more and more every day, but it will be a long time before everyone in the world is part of us. These writers and painters and musicians, they can reach so many people quickly. True, the people you will meet today are young, but some of them will become great in time. If they can spread the ideals we espouse throughout the world, through the medium of their art, then they will help prepare the world for our ascension. You know I don't want a world of puppets, Estrellita. I want a world where people willingly choose to be part of our family because they realize we are stronger together. A single twig may be broken, but a bundle of them lashed together, is strong. That we can stand united against those undesirables who refuse to take part in our great plan. The artists you induct into our family today will help us shape those minds." The vessel paused. "Also, these students sometimes meet artists who are already great and influential, and by inducting them now, we will gain access to those people, and it will be that much easier to bring them into the fold, too."

"I understand." Estrella looked at the building full of windows, rooms, and searching minds. "I wish I could go to school like they do, Moon. I want to write poems and songs…"

"Ah, my little star, your time will come!" The girl moved her hand and patted Estrella's bare knee. "When you are the empress, you will be able to spend all your time in contemplation of beauty. But for now, I need you out in the world, performing great deeds that songs and poems will be written about!"

Estrella straightened up. Yes. She was important. The work she did mattered. "All right. I am ready."

"You have your needles?" the Moon asked.

"I do." She patted her hip.

"Then go forth and bring me the blood of the future." The vessel rose and walked away. Estrella watched her as she swayed, and sighed a little, and then went to work.

She wandered the grounds of the Residencia until she found a boisterous crowd of two dozen young men and women, variously paint-and-ink-stained. They were sprawled on the grass over a succession of blankets, sharing around a bottle of wine and laughing as they conversed. Estrella sidled up to the edge of the group, smiling and nodding, getting smiles and nods in return; everyone would assume she was someone else's friend, as long as she didn't stay for too long.

"Did you hear what happened with Dalí?" a man with intense dark eyes and curly black hair said, as if beginning a great joke.

"I know he was expelled," a young brunette wearing a daringly cut blouse said. "Did he really insult his professors? During his final exams?"

"He told them they weren't qualified to judge his art!" The young man burst out laughing. "Our Salvador has never suffered overmuch from humility. Though he may have a point. He can paint as well as any of his teachers, but his interests are so far beyond theirs. After they threw him out, he spent some time moping, but I heard he's off to Paris now."

"Oh, Federico, he'll fit right in," the woman said. "In Paris, being terribly rude is a virtue. You know, *you* might be right at home there, too."

The man burst into raucous laughter, and Estrella felt a terrible pang of longing for this kind of easy fellowship as she settled on the grass. She was very busy, always rushing around doing her important work, delivering packages, carrying messages, and she met a great many people, but most of those people were actually the Blood Moon. Or else they were people who soon would be. Oh, it was true, the members of her family all had their own lives – most of their lives were their own to run, in fact. The Moon only popped in to use their bodies when he needed to convey a message or guide them onto a better path or perform a particular decisive action, but most of the time when Estrella met people, the Moon was using them as vessels. Sitting here, listening to these people chat, made her alert to the virtues of a less extraordinary life. To be able to drink wine, talk about art, and gossip about acquaintances would be such a pleasure.

There would be no gossip in the Blood Moon's golden future. There would be no need for gossip, because everyone would share a single mind, united in a radiant purpose. That idea should have made her happy. A world without strife, without abuse, without conflict. Why did the idea, instead, strike her as… a little dull?

"Remember the American artist I told you about?" the woman said, and the man frowned. "Pickman, from Boston?"

"I think so, yes. He paints ghastly stuff, doesn't he? Portraits of demons and all that?"

"One critic said Pickman turned New England into an 'annex of Hell,'" she reported with relish. "I saw a few pieces in a traveling exhibition, and I think he's the closest thing the modern world has produced to Hieronymus Bosch. Except Bosch was driven, ultimately, by his religious faith, and Pickman… I don't know *what* he believes in, apart from monsters."

"There are plenty of monsters worth painting," Federico said, amiably enough. "I saw a few of Pickman's smaller pieces at a gallery once. They were a bit too… pulp magazine cover, for my taste."

"Ha!" the woman said. "I think you underrate him, but either way, you'll wish you'd bought those paintings, because they're only going to increase in value. The man disappeared recently, simply vanished! I've heard the police suspect foul play."

"Really?" Federico toyed with his wine glass. "There are worse things than being expelled, I suppose. I wonder who Pickman insulted?"

Estrella opened her mouth to ask a question, then stopped herself. She wasn't here to make conversation or further her understanding of art. She had a purpose, and she would fulfill it.

The curly-haired man, Federico, yes, he was a good choice. Someone so full of tidbits of knowledge doubtless moved in interesting circles. She made sure the tiny needle was secured on the underside of her special ring and then reached out with her hand, just brushing the side of the young man's hip.

Federico gasped and looked around, and Estrella chose that moment to leap up with a shout. "Something stung me!" she said. "There are wasps in the grass!"

This declaration led to a general uproar and chaos as people leaped to their feet, snatching up blankets, bottles, and books, allowing Estrella to slip away in the chaos. She ducked around the corner of an ivy-covered building, made sure she wasn't observed, and removed the needle from its holder. A shining drop of red was suspended inside its hollow body. Good. That was another family member secured. *Welcome, Federico.* She had a slim leather case in her pocket filled with a neat row of small needles. She slotted Federico's blooded probe into place, then carefully removed a fresh needle and slid it into her ring. Perhaps she'd look for a group of musicians next.

For the next few hours, Estrella roamed the grounds of the Residencia, and then ventured inside, through the conference halls and meeting rooms, hovering on the edges of gatherings both officially sanctioned and informal. She pricked a man in passing at a lecture on Cubism, and drew blood from a woman in the restroom who caught Estrella when she "slipped" on wet tile, and let another fellow back right up onto her needle in a crowded room. Before the day was done, she'd collected a full dozen blood samples, and by the end, she'd become so deft that people didn't even notice they'd been stuck.

With a last longing look at the young people discussing evening plans, she lowered her head and walked on, heading south, back toward the neighborhood she called home. A statuesque brunette, more likely a professor or administrator than a student, fell into step beside her. "You have the samples?" she asked.

"I do." Estrella surreptitiously passed the case over, and the woman nodded and strode away. Estrella smiled. That vessel would take the case to another of the Blood Moon's proxies, and then another, and another, passing hand-to-hand to obscure their route until finally being delivered to the Moon's secret lair by someone whose memories of the journey would be fully erased, along with the rest of their day, just to be safe. The Blood Moon believed in security through secrecy, which was understandable, but it was a bit silly, since Estrella could have taken the samples to the Moon directly. The Moon was *right there*, just half a dozen kilometers to the south. She was even walking in that direction.

Estrella could see the Blood Moon's pillar of power rising out of the city even from here. It appeared to her as a shadow tower shot through with pulsing veins, like branches of scarlet lightning. That swirling wizard's tower was the tallest thing on the horizon. There were smaller flares of power throughout the city, too, spires and minarets, molehills and anthills, where other individuals who used magic – or *were* magic – moved to and fro, but none of their esoteric abilities compared to those of the Moon.

Estrella had never told the Moon she could perceive magical power that way, as a visible column rising up from those who possessed it. When she was young, she'd believed everyone could see those shadowy spires, and only gradually realized that wasn't true. It had taken longer for her to understand what the towers represented, and at that point, it seemed odd to mention it at all. That's what she told herself, anyway, but these days she could admit that she liked having secrets. Maybe because the Moon had so many secrets, and Estrella wanted to be *like* the Moon.

Or maybe because she was afraid of how that secret would be used. She had other unusual abilities, after all, ones the Moon did know about, and that led to… certain demands. When she was halfway back home, a soldier in uniform trotted up beside her and said, "Little star! You did so well today, and I hate to ask for more, but I'm afraid I have another errand for you."

"Oh, really, Moon?" Estrella asked, heart falling. "What's that?"

"As you know, some people cannot be persuaded to do the right thing."

Estrella nodded. There were people out there resistant to the Blood Moon's influence because of their irredeemable wickedness. "If someone has even a scrap of virtue in their heart, I can bring them into the family, but some people… their souls are shriveled and dark. When they stand against me, and against the family, we have no choice but to remove their threat."

Estrella was sometimes tasked with that removal. She'd dispatched two dozen of the wicked over the years. Some of them looked like ordinary people, the rot within them hidden, but for most of them, their wickedness was actually manifest, in the form of inhuman physiognomy or monstrous physiology.

Most of those people had power, too. Almost all of them radiated the darkness that only Estrella, it seemed, could perceive. Power and wickedness went together so often, somehow. She supposed when you had such power, you could use it for great good or for great evil. She was glad the Blood Moon chose to do good. Think of what grim purposes that unmatched spire of magic could be turned to in less virtuous hands!

"Where can I find this threat to our family?" Estrella asked.

CHAPTER SIX
How to Slay a Hydra

"The Blood Moon is a member of the Red Coterie," Thorne explained to Sanford. "As I said, we all operate independently. Our group is more a loose affiliation than the sort of hierarchical system you are more familiar with." They adeptly navigated their scarf to sip their wine.

Sanford thought their group could benefit from a little more hierarchy, particularly one where he was at the top. A bunch of people in possession of artifacts of great power, all pulling in different directions? What a waste. But he could work on that sort of reform once he was accepted into their ranks. "I thought the Red-Gloved Man was your leader?"

Thorne sniffed. "A common misconception. He is… first among equals, perhaps, but we have members who would dispute even that."

"How many members *do* you have?" Sanford asked. "I thought I was familiar with all of them – Amaranth, the Beast, the Watcher – but I confess I've never heard of this Blood Moon before."

Thorne chose not to answer his question, but sidestepped it neatly enough. "The great Carl Sanford, admitting ignorance? I'd tell my friends, but none of them would believe me."

Also, I doubt you have any friends, Sanford thought, but since the same could be said of him, the thought brought little satisfaction.

"I'm not surprised you're unfamiliar with our rogue Moon," Thorne went on. "Some of us in the Coterie operate more… quietly than others. The Blood Moon is more of an enigma even than the Red-Gloved Man. I don't think more than one or two of us have ever met them. Even those who have, only conversed with a shrouded figure hidden in darkness. It might not even have been the Moon, but a proxy sent in their place. The truth is, we don't know the Blood Moon's true name, age, origin, or even if they're a man or a woman or something else. I, personally, have only communicated with the Blood Moon through their proxies and heralds."

"Speaking of enigmatic," Sanford said. "What do you mean by *that*? Proxies and heralds?"

Thorne sighed. "This all grows a bit tedious. If I'd wished to be an educator, I would have pursued a career at university."

"And yet, if you want me to kill the Blood Moon, you have to tell me about them," Sanford pointed out. "Even if you're hoping they'll kill me so I'll stop bothering you, I still need information so I can find my way."

Thorne chuckled and swirled their wineglass. "I thought we were going to leave my unspoken motivation, well, *unspoken*, but you Americans are so very forthright. It doesn't bother you that I'm sending you on a suicide mission?"

Sanford showed his teeth. "I've been on suicide missions before, Thorne. They all turned out to be homicide missions instead. At least one was a regicide, technically."

"Ha. It's a testament to your confidence that even being

thrashed by Tillinghast and driven into exile doesn't weaken your self-regard."

"I have made mistakes," Sanford said. "Perfection is unattainable, and so mistakes are inevitable. The point is to learn from those mistakes. I have."

Thorne nodded. "It's not as if I'd be unhappy if you succeeded in eliminating the Moon. I just don't think it's likely. All right. I'll offer what guidance I can." They leaned forward, putting their elbows on the table, settling in. "The Blood Moon operates out of Madrid... at least, we think so. Their web of influence leads back to that city, and we believe it to be the center of the Moon's network."

"When you say 'we'...?" Sanford asked.

"There are... factions in the Coterie."

"Such fragmentation is always a danger in an organization without a hierarchy," Sanford pointed out. "Such groups can be destroyed from within. Whereas with my Order, it took someone coming from the outside to destroy things."

"And yet many an authoritarian regime has crumbled due to internal divisions as well."

Sanford waved a hand. "They had poor leaders. But no matter. Go on. These factions – you're part of one, and the Blood Moon is part of another?"

"The Blood Moon is a faction of one," Thorne said. "I am part of a small group that has taken an interest in the Moon's actions. Some of those actions have given us pause. One of the longstanding divisions in our organization has to do with the use of violence. Some of us are willing, or even eager, to inflict pain and damage to achieve our goals. Others prefer a softer approach, using stealth and persuasion, and we don't mind that it takes us a bit longer to get results. We are an old group and most situations we encounter aren't that urgent."

"Hawks and doves, war and diplomacy, yes, I'm familiar," Sanford said. "It will please you to know that I eschew violence myself whenever possible." If you killed your enemies, they were merely dead; if you defeated them comprehensively and left them alive, they were *so* much more miserable.

"So I've heard. It's one reason I agreed to meet with you. Some of your moves over the years have demonstrated a certain elegance."

"And yet you want me to assassinate your rival?"

"Elegantly, if you can." Thorne's tone gave no indication that they were joking. "The Blood Moon is less a rival and more of an existential threat to the entire world order. I didn't say we *never* resort to violence. Even the more peaceable among us are realists, and there are times when diplomacy is pointless. It is impossible to negotiate with the Blood Moon. They admit no equals and operate only in bad faith."

"The Blood Moon believes in using violence, then?"

Thorne sighed. "It's not that, or at least, not violence in the way you mean. The Blood Moon doesn't torture or kill, or at least not immoderately. Their approach is so much more insidious than that. They *control.* I don't know the precise nature of the Blood Moon's Key. I've heard it's a crown, and I've heard it's a scepter, or perhaps it's both, two objects working in combination? Whatever the specifics, the Blood Moon's relics allow them to compel the obedience of humans. The precise limit of that power is unclear, but I have it on good authority that the Blood Moon can overwhelm the will of any person in their presence and force their unquestioning obedience, even ignite their fervor."

Sanford nodded appreciatively. "Mind control, eh? A

formidable ability, but one with limited utility if the Blood Moon prefers to hide in the shadows. You can't control people in your presence if no one is permitted into your presence."

Thorne held up a finger. "Ah, but the Key has other uses. It amplifies the power of blood magic in a particular way. If the Blood Moon has a sample of a human's blood, they can see through their victim's eyes and give them psychic orders which must be obeyed, as long as the victim isn't too far away. Even at a greater distance, the Moon can make subtler changes: inflaming passions, planting intrusive thoughts, and influencing behaviors in such a way that the victims don't even realize they're being controlled." Thorne's tone was troubled. "We don't think the Moon can read the minds of their thralls, even those nearby, although anyone dominated that way would happily spill all their secrets if asked. In some cases, the Blood Moon can even take direct control of a victim's body, possessing it on a temporary basis, speaking with its mouth, and using its limbs like a puppeteer manipulating a marionette. The Moon may be able to control multiple bodies at once that way. We're not sure."

"What sort of range does the Blood Moon's power have?" Were they safe in Barcelona, three hundred miles from Madrid?

"The Moon probably can't reach all the way across the Atlantic Ocean," Thorne said, and Sanford sucked in a breath. "Their influence does not yet extend to the New World, as far as we can tell. But they can certainly control people directly, even many hundreds of kilometers away, and they can subtly influence people at ten times that distance. The Moon's powers, to some degree, extend throughout Western Europe. Moreover, those powers are getting stronger. We believe that, as the Blood Moon's army of thralls grows, their range grows, too. As if each thrall is a sort of… node in a network, do you see, acting as an amplifier for their master's power. The more thralls there are in a given place, the higher the concentration of puppets, and the greater the Blood Moon's range becomes. Given enough thralls, who knows? They might be able to directly control people anywhere on the planet. And the Moon has been growing that network for decades."

"It seems like acquiring so many samples of human blood would be rather difficult," Sanford said. "It's not a process that scales well, surely?"

"The Blood Moon infiltrated the hospitals early on," Thorne said. "And sent agents to join the military medical corps of various nations during the Great War. There are ample opportunities to acquire blood in those situations. The Blood Moon's magic is so powerful that even a single drop of blood is sufficient to grant power over a thrall. The Blood Moon is rumored to have a vast library of glass blood slides in their lair, wherever that is, each one representative of someone in the Blood Moon's thrall, perhaps a person wholly unaware that they could be possessed at any moment, and ignorant of any subtler manipulations. The Moon gathers samples in other ways, too. You've heard, I suppose, of the famed pickpockets of Barcelona?"

"Heard, experienced, and taught the appropriate lessons," Sanford said.

Thorne winced, visible around the eyes. "Yes, I'm sure. Many of the street-level criminals of this city and others serve the Blood Moon, knowingly or otherwise. They circulate in crowds with needles, so fine and sharp you might not even notice the prick, or might easily mistake it for the bite of a fly. Then those needles are bundled up and sent back to the Blood Moon to add to their collection. The truth is we have no idea how many people are in the Blood Moon's network now, but surely many thousands are compromised, most of those here in Spain, and most of *those* in Madrid."

"That all speaks of impressive power," Sanford said. "But power is pointless without a purpose. Why is the Moon amassing this army?"

Thorne hesitated. "To answer that, we must move into realms of pure speculation. But we believe the Blood Moon was instrumental in the start of the Great War. It's certainly interesting that the Moon's homeland of Spain stayed neutral throughout the conflict, and Madrid didn't suffer the devastation that other European capitals did."

The Blood Moon was that strong? Perhaps Sanford should have arranged a meeting with them instead of Thorne. "The Moon has thralls in places high enough to instigate a war?" he asked.

"Even if the Moon doesn't have direct control of authority figures in, say, Austria, they can certainly influence thralls at that distance, inflame their emotions, and push them toward rash acts. Small pebbles can start an avalanche, after all."

Sanford raised an eyebrow. "You think the Blood Moon nudged the hand of the Black Hand society and led them to assassinate the archduke in 1914?"

"The Blood Moon certainly wants us to think that," Thorne said, frustration creeping into their voice for the first time. "We believe there was some sort of unnatural meddling in political affairs around that event and others, and we have heard whispers that credit the Blood Moon. But they are adept at spreading misinformation as a one-person rumor mill, capable of sending a message through a city with ease, speaking in a thousand voices! And should we truly give the Blood Moon so much credit for influencing humans when many more powerful people of the Coterie cannot? Bah, the Moon is adept at inflating their own reputation. Maybe the Moon is not as powerful as we fear. But it's equally possible they're more powerful than we dare to imagine."

"All right, let's say they did foment the Great War. Again, why? Is the Moon simply a war profiteer?"

"No, kitten."

Sanford was almost more amused than offended. *Kitten?*

"Money isn't an issue when you can control people's minds and actions," Thorne went on. "The Blood Moon surely owns the minds of many of the wealthiest people in Madrid. No, put simply, we think the Blood Moon wants to rule the world. They may prefer to be the shadowy figure controlling a figurehead, but they might emerge into the light once they achieve total dominance. We think the Moon is… very vain. There are plausible signs that the Blood Moon worked with Napoleon – they're at least that old, yes – and the Moon was definitely involved in the military takeover of Spain. Something like that doesn't happen here without the Blood Moon's approval. They have connections in fascist organizations, and anarchist ones, which may seem contradictory, but–"

"Fascism grows best in the soil of chaos," Sanford said. "The Blood Moon can use the anarchists to create panic, fear, and destabilization, and then people will yearn for a strong leader to restore order, yes?"

Thorne gave a brief nod. Sanford thought he'd earned an iota of respect. "That is our suspicion."

"If the Moon could control some great dictator, someone who could put all of Spain, or the Peninsula, or the Mediterranean, or even all of Europe, under a single boot… they could organize some scheme to collect blood from everyone. In the guise of an inoculation program, perhaps? That would ensure their control of the Continent. Unless you think there's a limit on how many people the Moon can add to their network?"

Thorne's head shook back and forth in negation. "There is probably a limit on how many people the Blood Moon can actively control on a moment to moment basis, but if the Moon has your blood, you are available to them. If their network spreads to encompass even a significant percentage of the population of Europe, and their powers continue to grow at an exponential rate, they will become, for all intents and purposes, a new god."

"So that's my mission, then?" Sanford said. "Go to Madrid and kill a god?"

"A demigod, at this point," Thorne said. "At most."

"Hmm. Their power only works on humans, you say?"

Thorne nodded. "That much we have confirmed. Paradimensional beings are entirely immune to the Blood Moon's power. People with some inhuman lineage in their ancestry, or those who've altered themselves supernaturally are at the very least highly resistant. That's why some Coterie members are less concerned than I am. The Moon can't control them, after all, since they've moved beyond the limits of baseline humanity, or else they were never human in the first place."

"I think I have sufficient information to proceed," Sanford said. "Can I call on you for aid or resources?"

"Absolutely not," Thorne said. "In fact, I'd prefer if you never speak my name to anyone ever again."

"Until I succeed in this mission, and you gratefully induct me into the Coterie, you mean. I assume I'll take over the Blood Moon's territory? To the victor go the spoils, and so forth?"

"A reasonable assumption, certainly. If the territory will accept you. If you resonate with it. As an American with no real ties to Europe that may be difficult."

"A true gentleman is at home wherever he finds himself," Sanford said. These were problems to be dealt with later.

Thorne rose, and after a moment's hesitation, extended a hand. Sanford rose, too, and shook their hand. "I wish you luck," Thorne said. "I really, truly do."

"How will I contact you when I win?"

Thorne laughed. "If you kill the Blood Moon, Mr Sanford, believe me, I will hear about it. I will find *you*." The One with the Red Cravat turned and strode off into the darkness.

They left the wine bottle behind, though, so Sanford sat down and took a long pull directly from the neck. "Well. Hell and damnation," he muttered. He'd joked about being sent to kill the Nemean lion, but the labor of Hercules this mission most closely resembled was slaying the Hydra: a beast with too many heads, and once you cut one head off, two more sprang up in its place.

But in the end, the Hydra *was* slain.

"If a dimwit like Hercules can do it, I certainly can," Sanford said aloud and went to make his preparations.

Thorne and Sanford were not the only ones present for that meeting. A hidden observer watched from the safe distance of a nearby rooftop, listening with keen hearing despite a total absence of ears. Akh, the brother of Fantasma, bore a closer resemblance to their strange father than to their human mother, who'd been the priestess of a minor cult dedicated to a holy purpose she'd lived long enough to regret.

Akh's mind was not like others. In some ways, his was simpler, concerned only with need and sensation. In other ways, it was infinitely more complex, capable of seeing the past, the present, and the branching possibilities of the future; a gift from his father, an entity who stood outside the normal flow of space and time. Fantasma would have used the ability to see those possible futures for personal gain and find the most advantageous path, but Akh was incapable of such conniving slyness. Akh studied the sprawl of possible futures and mostly felt confused. When he was confused, which was often, he deferred to the judgment of Fantasma, the one person who loved him, and protected him, and made sure he got enough to eat.

Fantasma had asked Akh to follow this Sanford from a distance but not to harm him, despite the indignities they had suffered at his hands. That was strange. Fantasma usually liked it when Akh hurt the people who caused them difficulties. But his brother knew best. So Akh floated at a safe distance where Sanford couldn't sense him or blow that terrible powder across his body again. Akh's keen eyes were many, as were all his senses, and he was adept and experienced at floating invisibly and watching people. People were interesting. They had so many branches ahead of them, so many multiplying possibilities but most of the time, they acted like they had no choices at all.

Akh knew Thorne because Fantasma knew Thorne, and

Fantasma's thoughts were as clear to Akh as his own. Clearer, sometimes, because Fantasma was better at focusing. Thorne was someone Fantasma feared, respected and admired, a person of power and influence. Fantasma was at the outer edge of that sphere of influence, but he'd proven useful and willing to do dirty jobs, and so Thorne kept the lines of communication open.

And Thorne, apparently, knew this Mr Phillips. Or Carl Sanford, as he seemed to truly be. By reputation if nothing else.

After the meeting ended – after Akh heard everything there was to hear – he floated across the rooftops, tentacles undulating beneath him, tasting the air. He paused to descend on a drunkard asleep in an alley, drawing the man up into his tentacles and the great maw hidden on his underside, consuming the man whole, clothes and all.

The alcohol Akh absorbed into his system gave him a pleasant warmth as he returned to the small house Fantasma kept. His brother waited in the courtyard, seated in a wooden chair, his feet up on the lip of their cracked, dry fountain. Akh drifted down and Fantasma nodded at him – he could see his brother, though a bit hazily, as if through a flawed pane of glass – and then blew out a cloud of sweet smoke from his cigar.

"What did you learn, my brother?" Fantasma asked.

Akh had trouble speaking. When he opened his smaller mouths, only noises emerged, or the voices of those he'd consumed. But he and Fantasma had other ways to communicate.

Akh extended a long tentacle, thick as a thigh at the base and tapering to the diameter of an eyelash at the end. Akh inserted that end into Fantasma's nostril, deeper, until his brother's eyes rolled back in his head and Fantasma lolled loose-limbed in the chair.

After a moment, Akh withdrew the tentacle. Fantasma sat up, gasping. He'd just seen and heard everything Akh had, the experience compressed into seconds. He did not understand everything that Akh understood, though, and that gap between seeing and understanding was the place where sorrow was born.

"Carl Sanford," he muttered. "Leader of the Order of the Silver Twilight. The Red Coterie. The Blood Moon. Hmm. I will have to ask around, learn what I can, and set people to watch Sanford and his hotel… This man is our enemy, Akh. He hurt us both. We must make him pay."

Akh wriggled a tentacle, making the rudimentary signs they'd developed as a sibling language. *Kill him?*

Fantasma hunched, scowling at the ember on the end of his cigar. "He cast a binding spell on me, brother, to prevent me from harming him or causing him to be harmed. I wanted to tell you to… to… no. I still can't say it! Also, what if you tried to… to… and failed? Phillips, Sanford, he was able to paralyze you once. He might not leave you alive if he does so again. But this spell he cast on me, I think it does have limits. The magic was meant to bind creatures like our father, but we have human heritage, too, meaning the binding is incomplete. I cannot hurt Sanford. I cannot ask you to hurt him – if you took my meaning anyway, and tried to do so, I might even be compelled to fight you. But I think I can do things that I believe will cause Sanford harm indirectly." Fantasma smiled. "Like telling the Blood Moon that an American magician is coming to kill them. Let the Blood Moon take care of Sanford for us. Or, better yet, hollow out Sanford's mind and make him into a puppet. Let's see how *he* likes being bound against his will."

Akh bobbed in the air. The branches that opened into the future when his brother made that declaration did not, by and large, lead to happy outcomes for either of them. But Akh said nothing. There were no words or signs to explain those future possibilities, and he'd never found a way to share the visions he saw with his brother.

And anyway. Fantasma knew best.

CHAPTER SEVEN
Strangers on a Train

Altman woke and looked around, blinking. "Warden? Where are we?"

"On a train. I should think that much would be obvious, even to you." She was reading a newspaper. He squinted. Was it written in … Portuguese? She could read Portuguese? She'd told him once that she could, "Do anything necessary to protect the Order," but what did that really mean?

The two of them were seated across from each other in a small compartment, the quarters so confined that their knees nearly touched. Altman looked out the window, where scenery rolled by, all golden hills and elegantly twisted trees beneath a pale blue sky dotted with fluffy white clouds. The landscape was idyllic, so clearly Mediterranean, not at all like the gloomy topography of Arkham with its muddy hillsides and iron-gray skies. "But … where is the train? Where are we going? What is this place?"

"I grow weary of repeating things to you," Van Shaw said. She seemed much more robust than she had before, alert and stern. Altman had the fleeting impression that she was somehow feeding on him, like a vampire, that his sickness must be connected to her level of strength. He chuckled.

No, wait.

Someone else chuckled. Or… had the laughter been in his mind? Like a thought? But it hadn't been Altman's thought. Was he still feverish?

Then he remembered that he and the Warden were, in fact, connected, but in a symbiotic way. *His* health was *her* health; she thrived when the Order thrived, and he was the head of the Order. Splinter factions and upstart cults crawled over Arkham, all claiming the mantle of the Silver Twilight, but as long as Altman lived, he was the true head of the Order. The Order was him. What had that French king said? "I am the state." Since the Warden looked so much improved, did that mean he was getting better?

If so, it was an odd sort of improvement, given the yawning gaps in his memory.

"We have left Portugal and entered Spain," she said. "We are on our way to Barcelona, but it will be some time before we arrive. I checked the compass again this morning, and Sanford is still in the east."

Compass? What did she mean by that? He decided to pretend he understood her. But… Sanford? Yes. They were hunting Sanford, to punish him, to recruit him, to… eat him? That couldn't be right. Altman rubbed his eyes. "I feel so strange. Is Ruby here?" No, he'd been dreaming about her, hadn't he?

"Ruby Standish? No, Altman. We haven't seen her since before we departed Arkham." She lowered the newspaper, the better to focus her glare upon him. "She stopped by our squalid house. You ranted about how Sanford was tormenting you from the shadows, how you were going to take your revenge. You threw a teacup at a wall by way of punctuation.

After that, she made her farewells rather rapidly." The Warden folded the newspaper neatly in her lap. "How much do you remember about these past several weeks? Since the ritual?"

"The … ritual?"

Yes: the smoke, the chanting, *serpentum nocturnorum*.

"Oh, God. I went through with it, didn't I? I invited something *into* me?" The idea horrified him now, like he'd voluntarily swallowed a parasite.

"You did. You have been in some mental disarray ever since. You experience occasional stretches of lucidity, but then you relapse, and you seem to forget the lucid moments the next time you emerge."

"What is happening to me?" he whispered, more to himself than the Warden.

Van Shaw answered anyway, having no interest in boundaries she didn't set herself. "You invoked dark forces." She shrugged. "As a consequence, dark things are happening to you. But…" She cocked her head. "You are stronger now, even if you don't realize it. As a result, I am stronger. My head doesn't hurt anymore, I only need to sleep an hour or two a night, and I can summon as many as four hounds. I am still far from the peak of my puissance, but I am far from my nadir, much better than I was during the chaos right after the flood. Your lucid periods are growing more frequent, too. I keep hoping the next time you wake up, you will stay awake, or at least maintain continuity of consciousness. In the meantime, I am using what magic I still possess to drag you along without drawing undue attention."

"We undertook an entire sea voyage? I scarcely remember it, just flashes of bedclothes and a cabin." *And you, by the wall, staring at me with your nose wrinkled in disgust.*

She sniffed. "You scarcely left our room. You didn't eat, hardly drank, but you didn't waste away. Whatever spirit you invited into yourself seems to sustain you by magic alone. At least we didn't have to spend much of our meager funds on provisions."

The idea that he'd been so profoundly changed was disconcerting, but he brushed the concern aside. "I have some memory, or, no, it must have been a dream? That we were carried across the sea on the back of a… an immense black cat? That can't be right."

She actually smiled, or at least moved her lips. "Our ocean liner was called the *Ebon Lion*. Your delusions are whimsical."

He groaned. "Please, Warden, Sarah, will you just fill me in?" The rocking of the train should have soothed him, but instead the jolting made him nauseated. "What happened since I opened that accursed book and shattered my memories? Why are we in Spain, of all places?"

"Fine. I'll go over it all again." She rearranged her legs, kicking his shin in the process. "You translated the one useful grimoire we found in the ruins and discovered a ritual that promised power. You gathered the proper components, performed the rites described, and successfully summoned something. You made a bargain with the entity. I am not privy to the details. You hoped to gain power sufficient to bring the squabbling sects back under your control and to revenge yourself on Sanford, but I think that power came in the form of an infestation. There is something living inside you now, sharing your body. It will grant you power, I have no doubt, but at what cost?" She shook her head. "Sometimes your mind is your own. At rarer times, the thing inside you peers out at me with cold, blazing eyes, often terribly amused. Most of the time you've been twitching, drooling, or delirious, though."

"There's always a period of adjustment when one of my kind takes a new host." The words emerged from Altman's mouth without him consciously willing them to do so. It was like being in one of those dreams again, where he was a passenger in his own body, forced to relive something he could not change. He could tell this was no memory: this was happening for the first time *right now*.

"I needed to acclimatize to my new partner, and he had to acclimatize to me. Think of the way water from a strange well can make you sick, or the pollen from foreign trees makes you sneeze. There can be… conflicts… until your body accepts the change."

The Warden bared her teeth. "Hello, beast. It seemed more like Altman's body was fighting off an infection to me. And his mind, too, perhaps his soul. Can you hear me, Altman? You invited an unclean thing to share your body. And for what?"

"For power," Altman's partner said. "Look." He held out his hand, palm up, and a black flame burst into life there, six inches high, giving off darkness and cold the way a normal flame emitted light and heat. He closed his fist and the impossible fire vanished.

"How wonderful. If we become overheated, you can cool us down. That will actually be useful in this dreadful place."

Altman seethed, offended on behalf of his new inhabitant. Was the Warden *ever* impressed? By anything? "I can do so many other things, too," the partner said. "And I will be able to do so much more once I gobble you up!" It reached out to Sarah with Altman's hands and then recoiled, biting back a scream. A flare of agony wreathed his fingers, wrists, and arms, like his bones had been replaced by molten metal. The pain faded slowly. "I don't understand," it muttered. "You have delicious power, but… I can't…"

"Our powers are intertwined, you stupid thing," the Warden said. "I am bound to protect the Order, and, for better or worse, Altman *is* the Order. But those bindings go both ways. You cannot harm me. You certainly can't consume me." She sighed. "Well done, Altman. You've allied yourself with some sort of monster that wants to consume magic instead of flesh."

"Oh, I'll eat flesh, too," the thing said. "There is power in meat and blood, soul-stuff, even in mortals." The partner receded, like a snake slithering into a hole, and whispered in Altman's mind: *I yield the floor.*

Altman whimpered and clutched his head. "That wasn't me, saying any of that."

"I gathered."

He moaned. "What have I done?"

"You made a new friend," the Warden said. "Just don't let it eat Sanford before he releases me from my oaths, all right?"

"Sanford." Altman looked up, momentarily distracted from the supernatural parasite within. "We found him, then?"

She nodded. "We were able to find traces of his body, bits of blood and beard hair, in the ruins in Arkham. Enough scraps to do a divination and trace him to Barcelona."

"Why would he go to Spain? Does he have allies there?" He looked out the window. "Here, I mean?"

She shrugged, radiating indifference. "Perhaps. The Ma– Sanford spent time in Europe tracking down relics, plotting his plots, making his plans. Though he was more often in France and Germany, I think. I wasn't privy to all the details of his comings and goings."

"I would prefer it if he were friendless and alone," Altman said.

Not me, the partner whispered. *I want to eat his friends, too.*

"We shall see. We enchanted a compass to pinpoint his location more precisely once we get close. I say 'we,' but of course I did it. You've performed exactly one rite of magic in your life, and that one filled you with a demon."

Altman ignored the barb. If you didn't ignore the Warden's barbs, you'd never have time to do anything but address them.

"See?" She reached into the leather bag at her side and withdrew a brass object slightly larger than a pocket watch. She opened the lid. It appeared to be an ordinary compass, but the needle pointed to the southeast. "Once we get closer to the city, we'll be able to ascertain Sanford's precise location with this. We can start our search on the outskirts of the city and spiral inward until we find him."

"And then?" Altman said.

Then we eat him, the partner said. *Obviously.*

Another shrug, this one a shade less indifferent. "Then we overpower him with your new friend's help and my hounds, and we force him to release me from my bonds, and to name you his official heir, in that order."

Altman straightened his spine. He'd been slouching abominably. "Why do your needs get attended to first?"

"If you want my help, those are my terms." She picked up the newspaper again.

He pushed the paper down, tearing it, and met her now-furious eyes. "I am the leader of the Order, and you are the Warden, and you *will* obey me–"

"I serve the Order itself, not you. If I were compelled to obey the leader of the Silver Twilight, I couldn't have turned on Sanford, could I? Since there is so little of the Order left, I have even more leeway than I once did regarding my actions. It's true I cannot harm you, and I might even be compelled to step in to save you if your death seemed imminent. But I can absolutely withdraw my active assistance. Given your recent tendency to drift in and out of consciousness, you'd likely end up in a Spanish prison cell or asylum without that help. Now leave me be. You grow tiresome. I've told you all this before." She went back to reading. Altman seethed.

I like her, his partner whispered in his mind. *I'm glad we didn't eat her. Sleep, now. You need your rest.*

I do not– he thought, then thought no more.

Altman fell asleep on that train and woke up sitting on a different one in an even smaller and dingier compartment, squeezed next to the Warden. There was only darkness outside. "What happened? Where are we?"

"Your new friend took over," the Warden said. "I am glad. Where you stumble, the beast strides. We had to change trains in Madrid. It was a hurried transfer, and we had no time at all to see the sights." She sighed. "I finally get to travel, after all those years trapped on the grounds of the Lodge house, and all I get to see is the inside of train stations. I wanted to visit the Prado." Her words were unusually petulant.

"The what?" he asked, baffled.

"It is a *museum*, Altman. It was founded shortly after the United States of America ceased to be a collection of squabbling colonies and became a new country. The Prado contains the art collections of queens and kings, on display for the public's enjoyment. They have *The Garden of Earthly Delights* there, Bosch's vision of hell. Sanford always said the original was remarkable, far more striking than any reproduction, and that he thought Bosch must have glimpsed the Dreamlands, given some of the striking similarities in the details."

Altman had never had much patience for art. Why hold up a warped mirror to life when life itself was all around you, true and undistorted?

Well. His life was fairly distorted at the moment. Thing, he thought. Are you there?

I am always here, his partner purred.

We made an agreement, didn't we? In that circle?

We did, it confirmed.

What were the terms of our bargain?

That I would help you achieve your goals, and in exchange, you would allow me the… occasional use of your body to achieve mine.

What are your goals?

Ha. Don't you wish you'd asked me that during the ritual, when I would have been compelled to answer honestly? But you were focused only on yourself. In your defense, there were some powerful hallucinogenic compounds in the smoke you inhaled. A certain degree of disassociation from reality is necessary to make your mind open enough for me to inhabit, but it does also have the useful side effect of impairing your judgment. You needn't worry about my goals. I'll see to them.

But you're taking control of my body so often! Just to change trains! Altman cried in his mind. Why?

I am helping you, Altman. As I promised. You cannot achieve your goals if you collapse into a gibbering heap and draw unkind attention. The truth is, your psyche is still fighting me; your mind doesn't much like having a roommate. Your feeble attempts to reject my presence take a lot out of you, and as a result, you're sleeping about sixteen hours a day now. I take over when you're unconscious to keep you moving forward, on toward your goals. Don't worry, you're becoming more accustomed to my presence. You used to sleep twenty-three hours a day. We'll have you down to, oh, twelve or ten soon. In the meantime, I will continue to act on your behalf.

That's all you're doing? The things I would do, if I were awake? Altman didn't believe it.

More or less. So far. We'll talk more later. For the rest of your life, actually. For now, I need my rest, too. Not as much as you do, but I get fewer opportunities. Toodle-oo.

"What kind of demon says 'toodle-oo'?" Altman said aloud.

The Warden examined her reflection in the window when she spoke. "Sanford used to say 'demons' were just paradimensional entities who intersected imperfectly with our reality. You can't really generalize about them. They all have their own hopes and dreams, goals and malices."

"What does *this* one hope and dream for?" Altman said. "You read the spellbook, didn't you? Why can't I remember it?"

"The demon is probably meddling with your memories," she said. "As for the creature's goals? We have no idea. The grimoire was damaged. There were large sections blotted out by ink and blood, pages torn out, other pages partially burned. The only bits that remained unobscured were the summoning ritual and the promises of power. All benefits, no costs." She shook her head. "It was almost like the last person to possess that volume wanted to obliterate any portions that might warn off potential petitioners and hosts. Which I took as more of a warning sign, but you believed the possible benefits would outweigh any costs. Perhaps they will." She smiled again, lips thin. "You'll be the one paying those costs, anyway, so I suppose it's fine. Just don't fall apart before Sanford releases me from my oaths."

Altman gritted his teeth. He felt more supported by the monster lurking in his brain. "How much longer until we reach Barcelona?"

"Many hours yet."

"Then I'm going to stretch my legs." He rose, surprised to find he didn't wobble and his legs weren't cramped from disuse. But they had been used – just not by him. He also noticed he wasn't hungry and didn't need to use the restroom; he felt, in fact, as physically good as he ever had in his life. Maybe even better.

The Warden didn't seem to think his comment warranted a reply. She turned her head again and looked out the window at the darkness.

Altman left the compartment, stepping into the narrow passageway beyond. He walked to the end of the car, past the closed doors to other compartments. He wondered how much money they had left. They must not be too close to the bottom of their coffers if they were traveling in private cars. There was a door here – this car was the last one on the train – and it opened at his touch.

He stepped out onto a tiny sort of balcony and into the cool night air. He stood and watched the rails unspool behind them. There wasn't much of a moon tonight, but he could see the landscape clearly all the same, everything touched with a silvery light. Was this exceptional night vision a gift from his new partner? It must be. He held out his hand and concentrated. A flame wavered into view, not as black or strong as before, but flickering red. That was something. He could access the powers even when his partner slumbered. He'd just need to learn and practice.

Altman patted his jacket with his free hand to see if he had cigarettes, thinking it would be amusing to light one from his own fire, but found nothing. This was all very strange, being on a long journey with no memory of either his preparations or most of the journey. He closed his fist. The flame was quenched.

Altman looked up at the sky, dotted with clouds, and at the stars. He had the strangest urge to climb. Why was that? There was a ladder here, beside the door, giving access to the roof of the train, but…

Before he knew it, he'd leaped straight up, easily ten feet in the air, and landed on the roof of the carriage. He straightened up, and despite the motion of the train, he felt entirely stable and sure on his feet. Altman laughed aloud, did a little jig, then crossed his arms and kicked out his legs like a dancing Cossack. He eyed the length of the car and flung himself forward, doing a cartwheel halfway down its length, and then spun. *This* was the gift of his new partner? Not just the parlor trick of conjuring a flame, but supernatural strength, supernatural grace, supernatural balance? What else could he do?

A long-mustached figure appeared at the end of the train, coming up the ladder, wearing a flat cap and scowling. He shouted, "Qué estás haciendo? Se supone que no deberías estar aquí! Bájate de ahí!"

What are you doing? You aren't supposed to be here. Get down from there! The words translated themselves quietly in Altman's mind, though he'd never learned much of the Spanish tongue. Another gift from his partner? He hadn't been able to read the Warden's foreign newspaper, but perhaps the demon – or "paradimensional entity" – could only render spoken languages comprehensible.

"Intenta detenerme!" Altman shouted back, delighted. *Try and stop me!*

The porter, or whatever he was, climbed onto the roof, crouching low. "Señor," he said, voice low and pleading. "Por favor. Es peligroso."

Dangerous? The partner was awake again, speaking in Altman's mind. Suddenly it felt crowded in there, like two people trying to share a cot. *Oh, yes,* the thing murmured. *Very dangerous. For you.*

Altman's limbs were no longer his own. Strength surged through him. When his partner was awake, he could do so much more. *Do you want to be present for this?* his partner asked. *It's apt to be messy.*

"What?" Altman said. "No, please–"

Very well. I don't like it when people watch me eat, anyway. Except for the people I'm actually eating. Sometimes I start with their feet so they can watch longer.

Smoke filled Altman's mind, obscuring his vision until darkness fully enclosed him. But it wasn't sleep. He was awake, aware, but simply closed off, unable to act or sense anything beyond his own thoughts.

When the clouds receded, Altman was back in their compartment, buttoning on a fresh shirt. "What happened to your old shirt?" the Warden demanded. "You came in here bare-chested."

"Oh, it got blood all over it." That wasn't Altman speaking. It was the thing, using Altman's mouth. Which, now that Altman thought of it, tasted distinctly coppery.

Did you drink that man's blood? he thought, aghast.

Of course not, the thing said. *I killed him and consumed his life essence as it escaped. I had to use your teeth to do the killing and a little blood inevitably got into your mouth, that's all.* A mental pause. *Well, not "had to," I could have snapped his neck, but it's so much more satisfying when they spurt. You should really keep your late brother's kukri in your pocket. It's a lovely blade, but it does us no good wrapped up at the bottom of your bag.*

Altman groaned and sat down, hard.

"What did you do?" the Warden demanded.

Altman laughed, hollow. "I didn't do anything."

"Are you going to be arrested for murder?" She sounded calm, like she could deal with that eventuality as long as she knew it was coming.

Altman slowly shook his head and both he and the voice decided not to tell the whole truth. "I don't think so. He was a night porter, and I cast him into the bushes on a lonely stretch of track. They'll notice he's gone in the morning, if not sooner, but there's no reason they'd suspect foul play."

The Warden tsked. "So, it's like the ship all over again."

Altman frowned. "What do you mean?"

"Two passengers and one member of the crew were lost overboard," she snapped. "Fortunately, you picked drunkards and people traveling alone. Everyone knew you were confined to your cabin with a terrible illness, so you were never suspected. I assumed you were responsible for their deaths, but I didn't know for sure, and you were hardly forthcoming on the subject. Do you mean to say you don't even remember what you did on that ship?"

Altman mutely shook his head.

She clucked her tongue. "Could you please ask your

passenger to refrain from killing anyone else unless there is a good reason?"

Altman listened and sighed. "It only says 'Shan't.' So. There we are."

"You made a deal with a devil you cannot control," she said. "Do you really think that's worthwhile? Even if it does help you get to Sanford?"

"We shall see." Altman turned his own gaze to the window. He'd killed people before, but he could remember killing every one, and he'd always had a reason for doing so, even if that reason was just "a government paid me to."

Hunger is a reason, his partner said. *So is boredom. If you want me to kill less often, do your best to make sure I don't get bored. I was* promised *a war with a magus.*

"You'll get your war," he murmured, and the Warden seemed to understand that he wasn't speaking to her.

CHAPTER EIGHT
Estrella, Monster Hunter

The soldier the Blood Moon inhabited was tall and strong, radiating more authority than the Moon's vessels usually did. He took Estrella by the arm and pulled her into the mouth of an alley where they could speak in private. "I have directions for you. Once you arrive at the house, make your way inside. You will find a … creature there. Not a man, however he may appear, but a foul thing that crawled up from the depths, a monster who means us all harm. Do not listen to its lies and blasphemies. Just remove the threat in your customary manner."

Estrella shuddered. "Must I do this? Is there no other way?"

"You have a great gift, my star. It is a sin to refuse to use a gift."

"But I feel so strange, afterward. Sort of hollow. It takes something out of me. It makes me ravenous and sleepy, but even beyond that–"

"If you run ten miles, you will feel tired and hungry, too, but it is a consequence of exertion, my darling. I know using your gift sometimes troubles you, but always remember, you serve a greater good. That means *you* are good, even if you have to do something that feels bad in the service of our work."

"That makes sense," she said. The Moon had taught her about the greater good, and making sacrifices, and the ends that justified the means. "I'll do it, of course, Moon. Anything for you."

"You are my right hand, my protégé, my heir. I could not be more proud." The soldier passed her a scrawled slip of paper, and she read the directions. Her destination wasn't far, and it was even on her way home. That was something, at least. Like running an errand, she thought ruefully. Just like stopping by the baker's shop on the way home for a loaf of bread.

The soldier saluted her sloppily, the Blood Moon not being the epitome of military discipline, and then returned to his own business.

Estrella walked south, past the imposing grandeur of the Museo Nacional del Prado. She'd once spent a whole day there in the company of the Blood Moon, who'd borrowed the body of a docent to give her a tour. They'd wandered the galleries and halls, and Estrella had marveled at the portraits of people in days past, royals in their great gowns, peasants laboring in the fields, the symbolic goblets and birds, fruits and skulls explained patiently by the Moon. She'd shivered at the works of Goya, images drawn from nightmares. Some of them could have been drawn from her own nightmares, in fact.

Oh, why had she thought of *those* dreams? Estrella did not sleep much, just a few hours a night – the Moon said it was because she was so young, but she knew other young people who slept much more – and what sleep she did have tended to be troubled. She dreamed often of black spaces dotted with stars, but the stars weren't always white. They were sickly yellow or hectic red. Sometimes the stars were black, and should have been invisible in the abyss of space, but instead they glowed, radiating a paradoxically visible darkness, and together formed a sort of black nebula.

At other times, the space she saw was filled with clouds, writhing and purple, flashing lights in what seemed like a pattern, but one that never quite resolved: an amorphous blight of bubbling confusion, with half-glimpsed shapes cavorting inside. There were howlings in that place, and even stranger, there was music, too: an eerie piping, as if a deranged flautist had been given free rein.

While she floated in that strange dream space, those dreams were not scary. They even seemed right. Like that place was her home, or at least more so than the orphanage or her bedroom in the house of her adopted parents.

When Estrella woke from one of those dreams, though, she shivered, sobbed, and she was afraid – afraid of *herself*. What was wrong with her to find such a horrible dream peaceful? To feel drawn to that airless, chaotic desolation? She wished she could dream of the better world she was helping the Blood Moon bring into existence. Why did that horror feel like home? Was there wickedness inside her? Was there *irredeemable* wickedness?

She hadn't ever told the Blood Moon about the dreams. To do so, she thought, would be ungrateful. How dare she have such vivid visions of cosmic chaos, when the Blood Moon had worked so hard to give her a good, meaningful life? She was not ungrateful. She knew what the Blood Moon had done for her.

And she knew what she would do for them.

So Estrella took a right turn a few blocks past the Prado into narrow and winding streets, walking past apartment buildings and shops, feeling separate from the strolling people running errands. She took the turnings indicated in the instructions, frowning because some of them required her to double back over paths she'd already followed, but she obeyed them strictly. Soon, she found herself alone in a warren of small alleys she did not recognize, though she was sure she'd walked nearly every inch of this city on her various errands for the Moon.

The walls towered over her, though the buildings that pressed in were more worn down and decrepit. Ornamental stonework on the walls depicted snarling inhuman faces, and puddles of black slime shimmered on the cobbles. The alley grew narrower until soon she had to turn nearly sideways to progress. The sky above darkened, some smoky cloud obscuring the setting sun and turning the light that strained through a poisonous yellow.

Estrella stepped at last into a courtyard with a black stone fountain in the center and stared, aghast. In the middle of the fountain twisted a statue with long limbs and talons, an elongated skull, and large teeth holding aloft the headless body of a human like a trophy. Water fountained from the stone corpse's neck like blood and flowed down into the basin.

"This is not Madrid," she murmured. At least, not the Madrid *she* knew. This sort of thing had happened in the past when the Moon sent her to deal with the irredeemably wicked. Some of their foes lived in pockets of stolen space, carving out rooms, basements, or even whole street blocks from conventional reality. The Moon said that in the past some powerful people could fold space that way, steal geography and hoard it for themselves, but that few possessed such abilities now. More often, those hidden places, abandoned now by their makers, were discovered by other creatures who infested them, like squatters in a condemned house or rats in a basement.

She skirted around the fountain, the stench of the rotten water making her shudder. Blank and broken windows looked down at her from the buildings that hemmed in the plaza, but she didn't get the sense she was being watched. She had a sense, instead, of desolation, that this was a place once thriving but now bereft.

Good. Any creatures that gathered around a fountain like that must be foul, and she would not wish to meet them, although she'd met and dispatched many unsavory creatures on the Blood Moon's behalf.

Estrella followed the directions out of the plaza into another alley, and then to a wider, cobbled street. The cobblestones here were a strange yellowish ivory and very rounded. When she knelt down to look at them more closely, she gasped and stumbled away. The stones were skulls, hundreds of them, maybe thousands, set into the ground. Like something from a catacomb, but blasphemous: you should not tread on the bones of the dead. Estrella tried to walk on the narrow stone sides of the road, horrified when she had no choice but to step on a skull's rounded dome. She whispered apologies for the disrespect as she went.

Her destination was just off the street of skulls, a tall, narrow house wedged between what seemed to be derelict warehouses. The stones of the house were cracked, but the windows were intact and even had blood-red curtains hanging inside.

Estrella steeled herself and went up the stone steps to the imposing front door, carved with the cavorting shapes of creatures that were like a cross between humans and hounds. More skulls and grave markers were carved there, too, the further details too hideous to dwell upon. She rattled the doorknob and found it locked.

She took a breath, reached for the power within her, and *shoved*. The door burst inward with a splintering of wood as the force of her blow tore the lock out of the jamb.

Such strength was one of her "gifts." But in many ways, it was the least of them.

The entryway beyond was dim, lit by flickering candles set on the floor. There *was* someone in here, then. Perhaps the last denizen of this rotten cavity hidden away in her beloved city. She strode in, carrying no weapon but her own will. "I bring greetings from the Blood Moon!" she called.

"Come closer." A croaking, rasping voice drifted down from the shadowed stairs ahead of her. "I would speak with you. I would tell you all about this Moon of yours."

Don't listen to its lies. Estrella flitted to the stairs, moving faster than ever allowed out in the world where others might see. The Moon had bestowed so many gifts upon her. They'd taken an ordinary, orphaned girl and imbued her with extraordinary powers. This was done for a purpose: that she might better serve the Moon and the world. She used those powers now and flashed up the stairs, her feet barely touching the treads, until she reached the upper landing.

There were more candles here, and lanterns flickering on the wall. The lamps stank, burning unclean oil – was it pig fat? Or something fouler? Closed doors lined the hall, the wood speckled with mold, along with paintings grown dark from long exposure to the dirty smoke.

"Do you like the pictures?" The voice seemed to come from nowhere – or else from everywhere, emerging from the air itself. A petty trick of obfuscation, one that would not fool her long. "The painting behind you is an original Pickman. Do you know his work? He still makes art, now that he lives in the Dreamlands, but he uses different sorts of paint." The voice tittered.

Despite herself, Estrella looked at the painting. It was a night scene and depicted a small church standing in a graveyard, with monuments of crosses and crouched angels in the foreground. A crowd of figures spilled out of the church, but these were not solemn worshippers or the faithful coming from midnight mass. They were inhuman things, bent and hunched, leering and snouted, fanged and dressed in rags.

"It's called *The Congregation at Midnight*," the voice said. "One of his early works, but I'm fond of it."

"Come out and face me, foul thing!" Estrella called. She turned and kicked in one of the doors. Her boot tore through the wood like paper. The space beyond was derelict with a broken bookshelf resting face down on the floor. She kicked the next door in, too, and found the remnants of a washroom, a porcelain basin shattered on the floor. The final door, at the end of the hall, took two kicks to destroy, and when she burst in, she found … nothing. A moldering mattress full of bugs and piles of books that fell apart when she nudged them with her toe, the pages gummed together with rot. She whirled around, clenching her fists. "Where are you hiding?"

"With creatures like myself, you have better luck searching below ground than upstairs." The voice spoke right in her ear, from behind her, and she spun, furious. There was no one there. This creature was taunting her.

She went downstairs, searched the kitchen, turning away in horror from bones and rotten meat on the countertop and the flyblown innards that filled the sink. She'd seen terrible things, but God, the *smell*. She stumbled to a corner and vomited.

While she was wiping her mouth on her sleeve, she noticed a small half-sized door in the corner, slightly ajar. She eased it open and looked into what was originally a storage cubby, but the floor was gone, revealing a wooden ladder that disappeared into a dim subterranean space.

"My ancestors took over and remade this whole neighborhood, street by street," the voice said, emerging now from the dark hole. "They were organized, then, and employed by a sorcerer who offered them refuge in exchange for certain services. Until he asked too much and they ate him. At first, they tried to live in the apartments as the humans did, but my people aren't comfortable so close to the light and open air. Instead, they hollowed out the earth below and returned to their beloved caverns. My forebears thrived here for many years, venturing out to find sustenance or to place our babies in human orphanages, to learn the ways of humans. No, no, you are not one of ours. You are… something else." The voice sounded curious. "Other times, we would steal away human infants and bring them back here to raise as our own. Some of them, anyway. Oh, those glory days, before the colony fell."

"You are wicked," Estrella said. "You steal *babies*?" She started down the ladder, furious. She was no longer at all conflicted about destroying this creature.

"We act as our nature dictates, child," the voice said. "Are we wicked? Yes, perhaps. But do you eat beef? To the cow in the slaughterhouse, *you* are most wicked."

"A cow is not a person! People think and hope and dream!"

"Who knows what a cow dreams? Certainly things other than people can hope and think. I do. Everyone in my colony did, too, before they were taken. Do you know why this place is so desolate, child? Why when I returned recently from a long sojourn to the Dreamlands, I found my home annihilated? The one you call the Blood Moon did this. Killed them all. Eradicated the whole colony."

"Good." Estrella looked around the bare dirt of the tunnel, rounded like it had been excavated by a burrowing worm of enormous size. "I am sure that went a long way toward making the world a better place."

"Oh, little girl, the Blood Moon feeds you lies." The voice drifted down the tunnel. Which didn't mean much, since this creature could manipulate its voice, but she'd checked the rest of the house and there was nowhere else to go. She wished for a light, but only for the comfort it would bring. She could see just fine in the dark. That was another of the many gifts the Moon had given her.

She walked along the uneven ground, wrinkling her nose when her foot struck tangles of old bone and dry cloth – nothing like the meat upstairs. "You're the liar!" she shouted. "You pour poison into my ears, but I will not believe you!"

"You are not in the Blood Moon's thrall," the voice called. "You have your own mind. Which must mean you are immune to the Moon's powers, somehow. How has the Moon convinced you to serve? Don't you know what they are?"

"My parent, savior. My teacher, mentor. That is what they are. Do you know what *I* am? The Moon's protégé. The Moon's heir."

Another titter. "Foolish child. The Moon wants to live forever. The Moon's crown imparts the power to control humans, and their scepter gives them long life. I know – I was there when my people breached the tunnel and found the barrow where those artifacts were hidden in the grave of a great and terrible king of antiquity. A king who oppressed his people and died, not of old age but in a war against beings from below, inhuman beings that his crown could not command. Would you believe I was once not like this? Would you believe that the Moon – who was once friend and family – laid hands on those cursed objects and changed? That power gave them new ambitions and turned the Moon away from whom we served. The Moon only worships themself now. They abandoned our colony with plans to make a *new* colony, one filled with human thralls, unquestionably obedient–"

"The Blood Moon made their crown and scepter using their wisdom and art!" Estrella shouted. "They didn't find them in some grave! And they will pass those regal accoutrements on to *me*, when it is time."

"You believed such fairy tales when you were little, of course," the voice said. "But aren't you too old to believe them now?"

"Shut up!" Estrella raced down the tunnel, seeking the voice.

It taunted her as she followed the curve of the corridor deeper into the earth. "You were sent here to kill me because the Moon knows if they sent human thralls into this tunnel, I would kill them, put them in my larder, and eat their flesh. He sent you because you are something else, not a ghoul, but *something*. Why do you think you have these powers, this speed, the ability to see in the dark, whatever else makes you confident that you can best me in my own lair?"

"The Moon gave these powers to me so I could better serve."

"Ha. The Blood Moon claims all great and good things flow from them, but the Moon is a thief. They only take, girl. They don't *give*. You have these powers because they are *yours*. You were born with them. The Blood Moon has only claimed credit and tricked you into using them for–"

Estrella finally saw the glow ahead: an aura of black light, the telltale sign of supernatural power. This was a feeble flame compared to the great tower of the Moon's strength, but it was enough to identify the hiding place of her target. The enemy of the Moon, this whisperer of lies, was hidden away in the dirt, concealed behind the wall of the tunnel. She plunged her hands into the damp earth, seeking that light. She clawed forward, shoving her arms in past the elbows, and then she felt something – flesh, cloth – and wrenched it from the wall, flinging it onto the floor of the tunnel along with clods of wormy soil.

The thing before her scrabbled back. It was a little smaller than Estrella, dressed in dirty robes, its long face doglike. The thing pulled itself upright, snarling. "You don't have to do this." Now its voice came not from the empty air or into her ear, but from the figure before her. "The Blood Moon is using you. Tricking you, because they cannot compel you. The people the Moon sends you to kill are the ones the Moon cannot control, don't you understand? Their powers of compulsion and possession only work on humans, so they send you to kill the inhuman, any of us who possess power sufficient to threaten the Moon's plans."

"I don't kill anyone," Estrella said. "The Moon gave me these powers so I don't have to."

The ghoul faltered. "You don't kill? What do you mean?"

"You will see. You are wicked." She took a deliberate step forward. "You want to destroy the future. You have to be sent away."

"Listen to me, girl! If the Moon has kept you alive, it is only because you're useful and obedient! If that ever changes, they will kill you, too! These powers are *yours*, not a gift. The Moon doesn't give gifts! They are a heretic! My people worshipped Umordhoth, we feasted and fed for its glory, but the Blood Moon doesn't want to serve a god, the Blood Moon wants to *be* that god–"

"Then I will be heir to a god." Estrella took another step. Close enough.

She closed her eyes and listened for the void. That place she dreamed of: the purpled dark, the clouds of stellar dust and lightning, the eerie piping. She could hear that faint piping now, as if drifting from a room far down a long hallway. She breathed deep and opened herself. She *opened.*

"By the blood and by the bones," the ghoul murmured. "What *are* you, girl? There are portals hidden in so many dark places, but I have never seen one hidden inside a–"

Then the ghoul screamed. Purple light flared beyond Estrella's closed eyelids. In all the times she'd opened herself this way, she'd never looked. She was too afraid of what she'd see. The monster's scream didn't cut off, but instead slowly diminished, as if the creature was rapidly moving a very long way away.

Estrella didn't kill people. She didn't even kill monsters. Instead, she *sent them away.*

She exhaled, and the light faded. The open feeling in her chest closed down, and she felt like herself again, except for the ache beneath her breastbone, like she had a void where her heart should have been.

Estrella opened her eyes. The ghoul-thing was completely gone. She trudged back to the ladder and climbed up to the filthy house. This one had been very bad. Other creatures had threatened her, snarled at her, tried to attack her, but none of them had made such outlandish claims, told such terrible lies, tried to make her doubt the Moon.

Aren't you a little old for fairy tales now?

She whirled, thinking the ghoul had somehow returned to whisper to her again, but then she realized that voice had come from her own mind, instead.

Estrella left the house and hurried out of the desolate quarter, following the Moon's directions in reverse, until she finally emerged back into the ordinary world where humans dwelt.

A girl, a year or two younger than Estrella, hurried up to her as soon as she reached the street that led her home. "Did you find the wicked one?"

"Of course, Moon," she said.

"Did it speak to you?" the Moon demanded.

Estrella didn't hesitate. "No. Not really. I surprised it, took care of it, before it could say much."

"You sent it away, then? Good. Good."

"Where do they go?" Estrella asked. "When I send them away, where am I sending them?"

"I've told you," the Moon said, a little querulous. "They go to a place where they cannot harm anyone but can live out their lives in peace."

"That's what you told me when I was small," Estrella said. "But it's the way parents tell a child, oh, your pet isn't dead, it went to live on a nice farm, where it can run and play. Please, Moon, I'm old enough to know the truth."

"Fine." The voice was stiff and cold, suddenly as remote as the actual moon. "I have no idea where they go. Just that they never come back. And that's good enough for me. It should be good enough for you too."

"But… you lied to me," Estrella said, feeling so small and incredibly hurt.

"Only to protect your beautiful heart. There is no harm in a comforting lie, my star." The girl reached out and patted her on the cheek.

"I suppose not," Estrella said.

But that was a lie, too.

CHAPTER NINE
The Knight in the Tower

Sanford returned to his hotel after meeting with Thorne, mulling over his options all the way. There was someone he knew in Madrid who might be able to give him insights into the magical community there. She was a bookseller with an expertise in occult volumes, someone he'd done a great deal of business with over the years and even shared memorable experiences with. Her rapacious desire for the rarest texts put her in contact with all sorts of arcanists, archivists, and cultists, so she might have picked up useful information over the years. The only problem? He was fond of her, and he was fond of few people in the world – really, only Ruby these days – and bringing her into his mission would, inevitably, put her in danger. Better, perhaps, to put off contacting her until he ran out of other options.

At any rate, the most pressing issue was to discover the whereabouts of the Blood Moon's lair, and she wouldn't know that, anyway. The next one after that was figuring out how to get close enough to the Blood Moon to dispatch the creature without falling under the sway of their powers. According to Thorne, the Moon used blood magic to control people at a distance, but could directly compel those in their immediate presence. How could you gun down or stab someone who could seize control of your mind and limbs the moment you got too close?

Sanford had some ideas about how to solve that problem, though. Not a plan, yet, but certainly the broad *outlines* of a plan. Achieving success would depend on some of Sanford's enemies displaying a certain degree of basic competence, but he could count on them for that much, couldn't he?

Pleased that he'd planned as much as he could, Sanford went to sleep content. He had a goal, now, and that was a great comfort to him. There'd been entirely too much idling in recent months. Tomorrow he would take the first step on a long journey: defeat the Blood Moon, join the Red Coterie, seize control of their organization, use their resources to hunt down and destroy Tillinghast, restore the Order of the Silver Twilight, and come home to Arkham triumphant. Since he'd once spent months traveling through the nightmare realms of the Dreamlands on foot, such long journeys were hardly intimidating.

When he woke, he went down for breakfast in the *desayunador* – they really did have the most delicious ham in Iberia, he had to give them that much – only to be accosted by the clerk at the front desk. "Señor Phillips! I have another message for you, sir."

Sanford schooled his countenance to placidity as he padded over to the desk. "Oh, thank you so much."

"This one was delivered in person, by an older gentleman, *muy elegante.* I think it is not meant for you, but perhaps a friend of yours?" The clerk handed over a creamy envelope and Sanford glanced at it, nodded his thanks, and headed on to the dining room for breakfast.

Once he had a cup of coffee before him, he took up the envelope again. "Mr Carl Sanford," it read, "Care of Mr Phillips," followed by his suite number. Could it be from Thorne? Unlikely. Last night's parting words had seemed quite final. He wouldn't expect to hear from the fellow until he had the Blood Moon's head in a bag. But who else in Spain knew his true identity?

He broke the seal with his thumbnail and pulled out the single sheet using a fork. The message was brief:

I wish to assist with your plans to conquer the Moon. If you are interested in my aid, meet me this afternoon at 3PM at the Sagrada Familia, at the top of the St Barnabas Bell Tower. I trust that reaching such heights unobserved will prove no great difficulty for one of your talents.

Yours most sincerely,
TOK

TOK? Was that a name, or someone's initials? Either way, it meant nothing to him. Given the looping scrawl of the author, he might not even be reading it correctly. That O could have been a D or even a sloppy C, easily.

A meeting at three. Prime siesta time. Perhaps his correspondent wasn't local.

Sanford sighed and put the letter in his jacket pocket. It might be a trap, but he'd walked into plenty of those over the years. If you were properly prepared, no trap could hold you, and springing one was usually the easiest way to find the trapper. Sanford had some hours yet before that meeting. He went to make his preparations.

• • •

The Sagrada Familia was an astonishing achievement, even only partially built. The center of the grand cathedral was more or less complete, at least in structural terms, and masses were regularly held inside, even in the midst of eternal construction. Sanford had gone inside the building once and marveled at the beauty of the columns, the stained glass, the gentle curves and fluted shapes meant to evoke forests and the natural splendor that Gaudí believed was God's greatest aesthetic achievement.

The outside wasn't as beautiful, yet, bristling with scaffolding and bare stone waiting to be decorated, but the sweeping Gothic arches had an undeniable grandeur, and the towering spire dedicated to the Virgin Mary was a clear pinnacle of human endeavor. There were going to be more spires, lots of them, but the only other one finished so far was the Saint Barnabas bell tower on the Nativity façade and it was only recently completed.

The central spire and the Saint Barnabas tower were the only ones the cathedral's visionary architect had lived to see finished. Now that Antoni Gaudí was dead, struck down in the street by a trolley of all things, it was hard to imagine how the Sagrada would ever be completed. But even if he'd avoided the traffic, Gaudí was already quite old, and would never have lived to see his life's masterwork even half-finished. The Catholic Church was good at managing projects across generations. The nature of the basilica might shift away from Gaudí's vision over time – such things were inevitable – but his imprint on this building, and the city that surrounded it, would remain, indelible. Sanford expected he would leave a mark on the world just as profound, if likely more subtle.

For now, though, Sanford had to reach the top of the tower.

The public was most assuredly not welcome to ascend the bell tower, so he didn't bother to seek entry inside. He hated to expend any of his power on reaching a meeting in such a pointlessly whimsical place, but he recognized that this was a test of sorts. If he couldn't get to the meeting, he wasn't good enough to *be* at the meeting.

Or else, yes, it was a trap, and making it more difficult to enter the trap was just a misdirection to make him think it wasn't. Sometimes having a mind convoluted enough to properly deal with the jagged edges and curlicues of reality could be quite wearying.

Sanford opened a leather pouch, shook the contents into his palm, and sprinkled a bit of the clumpy dust over himself. He shivered as a wave of cold passed through his body. He'd sourced the ingredients from a local herbalist and made certain modifications using an alchemical process he'd learned from a blind monk dedicated to a dead god. Ironic, in a way, because what this concoction did was hide you from sight. There were other, arguably better, ways to go about unseen, such as becoming one with the shadows; or making it impossible for people to remember you so it didn't matter if they saw you in the first place; or simply making yourself easy to ignore. But he didn't have the resources to conjure any of those alternatives. His wonderful storehouse of supplies and spells had burned to the ground in Arkham. So he made do.

At least the dust wasn't glittering.

Invisible, Sanford moved to the base of the St Barnabas tower, avoiding the construction workers, clergy, and other personnel. They couldn't see him, but they would notice if he jostled them, and he didn't want anyone alarmed or shouting about ghosts.

He craned his head back and looked up, and up, and up. The peak of this tower was more than three hundred feet above the ground, and this was going to be one of the *shortest* spires on the church, once they were all finished. Gaudí didn't lack for ambition. Sanford was sorry he hadn't had the opportunity to meet the man. He might have been able to suggest a few small improvements.

Sanford pulled on the same gloves he'd used to scale the walls in the Gothic Quarter and then reluctantly set his walking stick aside, leaning it against the stones. He'd clambered up a few stories with the stick clamped under his arm last night, but this was more of an undertaking. He needed total mobility.

No matter. He would be fine. What terror did great heights hold for him? He'd once jumped out of a window on the upper floor of a hotel in Arkham. Of course, he'd had a charm to prevent him from dying then, which he didn't have anymore, but he would be fine.

He began to scale the tower, reaching for outcrops and handholds, tiny imperfections in the stone as useful to him as rungs on a ladder. Even with magic, scaling the wall was still hard work. It took tremendous effort to haul his body weight along, supporting himself by his hand- and finger-grip. He relaxed from time to time, but then his weight hung painfully from his wrists, a bit like being manacled to a dungeon wall, and goodness, he wished he didn't know that from personal experience. Though his muscles burned, he pushed himself to climb quickly. The sooner he reached the top, the sooner he could properly rest.

The first part of the climb went well enough. But the tower's layout changed into smooth stone now dotted with windows partway up, every one of them narrowing his path. The stone began to curve, making handholds trickier, and the surface gradually became more and more irregular and ornamental. It was all very pretty, but a devil of a thing to ascend.

Sanford also hadn't properly considered the wind. It was much more powerful up here than on the ground, whipping around the corners of the tower and across his body, every gust shoving him like a giant's hand. One particularly brutal windburst came while he was reaching with his right hand, so strong it tore his left hand free, and he wobbled, then plunged, reaching desperately for the wall, a scream blurting from his throat. He was going to *fall*, he would *die*, he would be *splattered*.

His mind, inanely, recalled an article he'd read recently by the biologist J.B.S. Haldane, "On Being the Right Size." It was an intriguing piece, largely about how, in nature, the size of a living creature dictated certain necessities regarding its form and function. Sanford had wondered how those principles applied to shoggoths and some of the other creatures he'd once housed in his lost menagerie.

The portion of the essay that came to mind in his current straits was an observation about the impact of size on, well, impact. Haldane had written: "You can drop a mouse down a thousand-yard mine shaft and, on arriving at the bottom, it gets a slight shock and walks away. A rat is killed, a man is broken, a horse splashes."

The wall climber Harry F. Young had certainly broken. Sanford did not wish to follow suit.

He scrabbled at the wall, hoping to slow his descent, and after a dozen feet his hands caught a hold. He dug his toes in and then clung to the wall, his face pressed against the stone like a baby to its mother's chest. He slowed his breathing, holding still, willing his legs to stop shaking. His long trek through the Dreamlands had hardened him, but he'd spent too much of the time since on ships, trains, and in hotels, eating and drinking and recovering from his ordeal. That had left him ill-prepared for new ordeals.

He clung to the wall, unmoving, like a barnacle or a limpet, until his heartbeat settled. Safe enough for now, but he had to keep moving, didn't he? The meeting time approached.

Sanford crept further up the wall, sliding his hands up the stone, scraping the toes of his shoes the same way, even though such treatment would scuff the leather. When the wind burst with particular vehemence, he stopped, clinging tight, eyes shut. He soon discovered there was a loose pattern to the arrival of the gusts, and from then on he moved only when they ebbed.

Finally, after what seemed a trembling eternity, he reached a round opening that led inside the tower to the bell itself. He hauled himself through the window and fell to the narrow platform surrounding the bell, shaking and sweating and entirely too aware that he was still more than three hundred feet from the ground. He wasn't at the top of a thousand-foot mine shaft, no, but there was still plenty of distance to fall and be broken.

"It's a lovely view from up here," a gently French-accented voice said.

Sanford turned his head, annoyed. He shouldn't have been visible to anyone! That was the reason why he'd been comfortable sweating on the floor in the complete absence of his customary dignity!

Sanford struggled to his feet and faced the stranger, and felt even more undignified, for this old gentleman was the very picture of elegance. He certainly hadn't climbed up here like a fly on a wall, or if he had, he'd found it no great challenge. The man was older than Sanford by a few years, his white hair swept back, with serious eyes regarding him over an elegant, aquiline nose. He wore a red ascot, and his identity clicked in Sanford's mind. Not TOK at all, but TCK.

"The Claret Knight, I presume," Sanford said with all the bland calm he could muster, trying not to pant from exertion. He didn't know much about the Claret Knight, but he was said to be one of the more peaceful members of the Red Coterie, likely part of Thorne's faction, if they truly were even organized enough to have proper factions. The Knight was rumored to be French nobility, and he was either centuries old, or simply the latest in a long line of Coterie members who shared the same sobriquet.

The Knight looked at Sanford and blinked. "Hmm? Oh, yes, quite, I am he. But come, Mr Sanford, and take in the view."

Sanford joined him by a window, gazing down at the city sprawled beneath them, the broad avenues and dignified buildings, the parks filled with trees and fountains, the orderly interruptions of plazas and squares, and in the distance the gentle hills. The city really did look beautiful from up here, where you couldn't see any of the monsters or the blood. "It's extraordinary," Sanford murmured.

"I haven't been to Barcelona in nearly thirty years," the Knight said. "The Sagrada Familia has come a long way since then, but there's oh so far yet to go. Still, all this time, effort, and money channeled toward a singular creation… you have to admire it, don't you?"

"I am certainly an admirer of great human achievements," Sanford agreed. "What brings you to the city after so long away?"

The Claret Knight gave him a kindly look. "You do. I was in Marseilles, so it was easy enough to travel here once I heard from Thorne about your… conversation last night."

"You chose an unusual place for our meeting."

"I cannot give you long," the Knight said. "I have affairs to attend to in my own territory and being in the Blood Moon's sphere of influence is unpleasant for me. I wanted to see the view from this tower before I left the city and thought it sensible to combine my tasks. I do hope coming here was no hardship. I thought a magus of your renown could easily attain such heights."

"I find myself a bit under-resourced at the moment," Sanford said. "I suffered some trouble back home. But I managed well enough, as you can see." He straightened his crooked tie.

"Indeed. I won't keep you in suspense regarding my intentions. Thorne and I are allies in certain regards, and while I would have liked to join that meeting, clearly Thorne preferred to take your measure privately."

"And you want to take my measure now? How many other Coterie members can I expect to snap their fingers to summon me?"

The old fellow chuckled. "I don't think you'll find your calendar too crowded. We in the Coterie generally stick to our own territories. Even those who distrust the Blood Moon might be troubled at the prospect of one Coterie member sending an assassin after another. It's not the sort of information Thorne wants to spread."

Was the Knight troubled by the prospect? Did he intend to do something about it? Honorable people could be so tiresome. Sanford was always prepared to fight, in theory, but hoped it wouldn't come to that; at least not until he'd had more time to recover from the climb. "How do you feel about my mission?"

"Conflicted," the Knight said. "You should know that Thorne thinks they've sent you on a fool's errand at best, and a suicide mission at worst."

Hearing it so bluntly put didn't even sting. Much. "Do you share that opinion?"

The Knight drummed his fingertips against the wall. "I endeavor to be an optimist, Mr Sanford, even against the experience of a lifetime. Like Thorne, I have grave concerns about the Blood Moon's mysterious yet seemingly ever-increasing power. Concerns strong enough to warrant extending you support, which is more than Thorne is willing to do."

"A company of armed men, say?"

The Knight smiled faintly. "Something more subtle, but as valuable in its way. You must understand: the Moon is a member of the Coterie, in name at least, but even by the admittedly loose standards of our association, they stand apart, secretive and sly. To my knowledge, none of us have received any communication from the Moon since before the Great War. I personally believe they joined our group only to make sure the rest of us wouldn't meddle inside the Moon's territory. I said as much when we first considered their membership, but I was overruled. The Moon and I never got along particularly well, I suspect because their power wouldn't work on me, and they don't like people with immunity. There are hardly any such individuals left in Madrid. They've all been driven off or disappeared."

"I understand the Moon's powers work on all humans. You

aren't human, then?" The Knight looked ordinary enough, but Sanford knew that didn't mean much.

The Knight held out a hand and wobbled it back and forth. "I… differ from the everyday run of humanity in certain crucial ways. One needn't be fully inhuman to resist the Moon's power. To be imbued with the touch of the supernatural is enough. That doesn't mean the Moon can't harm me. If he directed a mob to tear me limb from limb, I would probably survive, actually, but it would be quite unpleasant. There are some two billion people in this world, and the Moon's power works quite well on ninety-nine percent of them."

"Would they work on me, despite my long association with magic?" Sanford said. It would be nice to hear they wouldn't.

"You *use* magic, Mr Sanford," the Knight replied. "But you are not magical *yourself*. Do you see the difference?"

"I do indeed," Sanford said. He'd deliberately avoided altering himself the way some magi did, because the cost-benefit analysis had never swayed him. Yes, he could acquire great power by becoming something less than human, but there were tradeoffs and side effects, usually severe and permanent.

"Your humanity will make it more difficult for you to fight the Moon, but I gather you are a resourceful man," the Knight said.

"I have some notions for how I might succeed despite my limitations."

"Good," he said briskly. "I trusted you would. As mentioned, I wish to offer you a bit of help, Mr Sanford. I cannot be seen moving directly against another member of the CCoterie, even one as isolated and unpleasant as the Blood Moon. But I can offer this." The Knight reached into his pocket and withdrew a small pair of collapsible folding opera glasses, plated in gold and elaborately filigreed. The lenses were pale red.

"Rose-colored glasses?" Sanford said. "It's been quite some time since I looked at the world through those."

The Knight chuckled. "Likewise, sir. I have enchanted these glasses. They will allow you to perceive the presence of blood magic. If you look through these at someone who is bound to the Blood Moon, their allegiance should be apparent."

Being able to identify and avoid the Moon's thralls would be a great help. Sanford had dealt with hidden enemies often in his life, most recently the Cult of Cain, murderous creatures capable of mimicking the forms of their victims and stealing their lives and identities. Being attacked by people he trusted, or strangers he assumed were harmlessly mundane, had proven deeply irritating. Not that he trusted anyone anymore, as a rule. Not since the Warden had betrayed him, anyway. Still, being able to differentiate real threats from innocent bystanders would make his life easier and cut down on unnecessary collateral damage. "What will I see? An aura, or something?"

"No, it looks more like a tether extending out from the victim's body and trailing off through the air. Those tethers stretch back to wherever the Blood Moon sits and pulls their strings."

Could this be a solution to his greatest problem, then? "Indeed? If I can find one of the Blood Moon's victims, I can follow their thread back to their lair? But no. Surely one of you would have done that by now if it were that easy. Then, you could have simply told me the location."

"We would have, yes. In fact, we tried to do as you suggest, as soon as I made those glasses. That is the only reason we know the Blood Moon is currently in Madrid – we followed threads from all over Europe, and they converge there. But we cannot narrow the Moon's location down to an area smaller than five miles in the city because the Moon has taken steps to obfuscate their location. When you get to Madrid and look through these glasses, you will see what I mean."

"You could bomb those five square miles," Sanford mused. "Or rain down some magically destructive equivalent. If the Moon is such a profound threat to Europe and to the world, such an act would be defensible."

The Knight's mouth became a moue. "The option has been discussed, but the loss of innocent life would be vast. And we couldn't be certain such an attack would even kill the Moon. *I* could certainly survive a bomb blast, if the need arose. Couldn't you?"

"With the proper resources," Sanford said. "But I see your point."

"That's why we're exploring other avenues. The Blood Moon won't know you're coming. They have no reason to know you even exist."

Sanford wanted to object – he was hardly unknown to practitioners of magic! – but he held his tongue.

The Knight went on. "You have the element of surprise. You're highly motivated to succeed since membership in the Coterie will help you achieve your own goals. Of course, there's still the matter of a Key, since I don't think we'd be comfortable giving you the Blood Moon's artifacts…"

"The situation with my Key is well in hand," Sanford lied. It wasn't much of a lie. He had most of a plan to make sure it would be true, when the time came. "I should have it in my possession shortly. By the time this business with the Blood Moon is wrapped up, anyway."

The Claret Knight shook his head, almost fondly. "I have seen great things in my very long life, many of them were dreadful, but to live without hope is worse than no life at all. If we can't imagine a better world, how can we ever hope to create it?" He put a hand on Sanford's shoulder. "So I say truthfully that I hope you will succeed."

Sanford couldn't decide if that was comforting or not.

He considered asking the Claret Knight how *he'd* gotten up to the tower and then decided that would be worse than returning the way he'd come. So he bid the old man farewell, clambered out of the window, and made his way down the side.

Descending was easier, because as he went along, he had progressively less far to fall, which was a great comfort psychologically. *Killed, broken, splashes.* Once he reached the bottom, he would head to his hotel, secure his belongings, and proceed to Madrid on the next train.

And he would pause at the front desk on his way out, to tell the clerk that if anyone came looking for him, he should feel free to acknowledge that he'd been a guest. No reason to let his trail grow too cold. He wouldn't inform the clerk of his next destination, however. He was looking forward to a reunion with Altman and the Warden, but there was no reason to make things that easy for them.

If they didn't have to work a little to track him down, they'd get suspicious and realize he *wanted* them to find him.

But only once the time was right.

CHAPTER TEN
Vocera

While Sanford was at breakfast reading his invitation to visit the Claret Knight, Akh and Fantasma were on their way to the backwater neighborhood of La Ribera, down by Barcelona's waterfront.

Once, the area had been a thriving place, home to grand palaces and mansions, various markets, and lively bars, populated by sailors and shipping magnates. But all that had changed more than two hundred years ago, when Spanish forces arrived to crush the Catalans and impose the will of their government. The whole area was razed to construct a formidable citadel in order to make sure the will of the Catalan people *remained* crushed.

The fortress was gone now, apart from a few picturesque ruins, transformed into the enchanting Parc de la Ciutadella, for a long time the only expanse of green space in Barcelona. There was a fine old church here, too, the Basilica de Santa Maria del Mar, and some palaces remained along Carrer de Montcada, but the district was essentially a backwater now, a sleepy neighborhood far from the center of the city and burdened by bad memories. There was a mass grave near the church, holding the bodies of the Catalan soldiers who fell in 1714.

History could be a terrible weight, which was why Fantasma preferred to look forward.

He wound through the medieval streets until he found the building he wanted, a tall, narrow, run-down structure dotted here and there with chipped mosaic tiles. The entryway door was swollen and stuck, so he hit it with his shoulder and popped the jamb free. The lobby was dusty and littered with trash. The people who lived in the tiny apartments in this building were mostly old and without much in the way of family and friends, so the landlords had no interest in doing more than the bare minimum required to keep the structure standing and the meager rents flowing.

Akh followed Fantasma inside the lobby despite seeming too large to fit through the door. His body was fleshy, filled with strange fluids and malleable voids, and he could squeeze through surprisingly tight spaces – an ability which had led to the discoveries of some gruesome bodies left behind in seemingly inaccessible locales over the years.

Fantasma climbed up the warped and creaking stairs to the third floor, his brother floating invisibly behind him. There were two apartments on that floor, one on the left and one on the right. He rapped on the leftward door with his knuckles, waited, and knocked again. Impatient, he considered a shout or kick to the door, but the person inside the apartment wasn't someone he dared offend.

Or, rather, he didn't dare offend the person *inside* the person within the apartment.

The door finally creaked open, and an older woman with bright red hair looked at him through pale blue eyes. "Oh.

It's you." She wore a black silk dressing gown patterned with yellow flowers, and her voice was flat and lifeless. "Were you summoned?"

"Madame Navarro," Fantasma said with as much warmth as he could muster. He swept off his hat and gave a deep bow. "It is so good to see you again. I trust that you are well–"

"I persist." She sniffed and looked him up and down, but didn't invite him in. "You *weren't* summoned?"

"I need to get in touch with our… mutual friend. I have information they will find of great interest."

"Are you sure? If you waste their time, there is nowhere you can hide from them. No way to escape their wrath."

"Have I ever let them down before?"

"I have no idea," Madame Navarro said. "But I suppose not, since you still draw breath. Come in, then." She turned and shuffled into the apartment, and Fantasma joined her. Akh stayed in the hallway, keeping watch. If this conversation did go badly, there might be danger to watch for.

Madame Navarro had been an ingénue in the French theater, a long time ago, and had come to Spain to study flamenco. She'd performed at some of the most renowned flamenco houses in Madrid, making a minor name for herself in the process. At some point, she'd become acquainted with the Blood Moon, or more likely one of their thralls, entered their service, and been assigned to Barcelona as a dedicated liaison – or "vocera," as such individuals were called. It was a post she'd held now for decades.

The job didn't seem to pay very well, or else Navarro's lust for life had diminished. The apartment was cramped and dusty, the furniture worn and sagging, the only decorations framed posters for shows featuring Madame Navarro in her younger days. There was no trace of any Monsieur Navarro, if he'd ever existed.

Madame Navarro sat on a small couch, sinking into an indentation that fit her perfectly. She gestured vaguely at an armchair covered in horsehair upholstery, and Fantasma perched on the edge of the seat. She might have offered him tea, at least, but she never had before, and she didn't now. "Let me see if the Moon is available," she said, and then stared into the distance, her breathing slow and steady in the still room.

Then she jolted, like she'd been startled awake, and blinked rapidly before turning her head slowly toward him, without moving the rest of her body at all. Her blue eyes were brighter now, more alive, and she smiled wider than seemed possible, showing off teeth marred by stray lipstick marks. "Why, if it isn't Fantasma! I hope you haven't come to the home of my *vocera* to ask for a job. If I want you, I'll contact you." She – they, it, the vessel that carried the voice – leaned forward and put a hand on Fantasma's knee, gripping too hard. "You should know that I despise ambition and personal initiative."

The voice was still Navarro's, a once-elegant contralto turned raspy with time, but now it boomed instead of whispered, hale and strong. The thing using Navarro's mouth to speak had a lot more energy and enthusiasm than the host did.

"No, not at all, Blood Moon!" Fantasma said, hurriedly. If the Moon wanted him dead, he could call up hordes to hunt him down… assuming he didn't just use Navarro's body to get the job done. Fantasma could easily overpower an old woman – as he had done to many humans in a quest to quench his thirsts – but when that old woman didn't feel pain, and didn't care if her body was destroyed in the fight, success became a less certain proposition. "I have come to bring you valuable information."

"Oh, really? Do you expect to be paid?"

Being paid would be wonderful, but Fantasma was in this for vengeance. He couldn't move directly against Sanford, but he could make the bearded bastard's life harder. "I am here as a" – not *friend*, the Blood Moon didn't have *friends* – "a respectful admirer. When I heard someone intended to do you harm, I knew it was my duty to warn you."

"Who could possibly do *me* harm?" The Blood Moon sounded far more amused than angry.

But Fantasma knew his next words would make an impression. "My brother Akh recently witnessed a meeting between a foreigner and the one they call Thorne."

Navarro's face went slack for a long moment, seemingly empty of consciousness – the Blood Moon's or any other. Then her eyes narrowed, and that booming voice became low and far more menacing. "I see. Who was this foreigner and what was the nature of this meeting?"

Fantasma recounted everything he knew – from the first approach by Sanford, the subsequent brush-off, the man making a nuisance of himself, passing the message to Thorne, and on through the meeting last night. He even mentioned the humiliating parts, because he knew that made the whole story more convincing. Fantasma reported almost everything Akh had heard, too.

"Mmm," the Blood Moon said after the recitation ended. "You have been an intermittently useful associate of the Red Coterie. Surely you realize this treacherous act by Thorne indicates deep divisions within my group?"

"Yes, of course."

"Then why have you chosen my side? Because you must realize, you *are* choosing sides, now."

Fantasma chose his words carefully. "Two reasons. First, I think Thorne's assessment is correct. You *are* incredibly powerful and dangerous. If there is a conflict to come, I believe you will be the one to win."

"Very astute. The other reason?"

"This Carl Sanford humiliated me and stole my ability to seek retribution personally. I asked Thorne to free me from the bindings, but he said as long as the magus lives, I will be under his compulsion, and that it serves me right for failing to kill him."

"Thorne and I agree for once!" The Moon tittered. "But yes, I can see why you'd want me to slaughter the fellow."

Fantasma winced, a pain lancing through his head. He hadn't strictly violated the restriction against causing Sanford to come to harm, since he hadn't actually *asked* the Moon to do anything, but he was walking the line. "I… never… asked… for that. Please… don't… hurt… him."

The Blood Moon chuckled. "Oh, I understand. You can't bite the hand that leashed you. Fine, Fantasma. I appreciate your reaching out. As a personal favor to me, I'd like you to keep a watch on Mr Sanford's hotel. Let me know when he leaves town. I assume he'll head for Madrid soon. But keep watching after that, too. I want to know if anyone else comes looking for this Sanford – members of the Coterie, other allies, or anyone. Information is power, after all. Let Madame Navarro know if there are any developments."

"Should I follow Sanford to Madrid?" Fantasma asked, visions of at least getting to see Sanford killed dancing in his head.

"That won't be necessary. I have agents in place who can

track his progress. If your information turns out to be true, Fantasma, I'll see that you're properly rewarded. Farewell." Madame Navarro's eyes rolled back, and then a moment later, her head lolled forward, chin resting on her chest.

Had the strain of hosting the Blood Moon's consciousness finally killed her? Fantasma started to rise to leave, and the woman's head snapped up. She looked at him through narrowed eyes. "Fool," she hissed. "Why did you warn the Moon? I could have been free!"

Fantasma stared at her, astonished. "Free? But you're the Blood Moon's *vocera* in Barcelona, their agent, you work for them."

"What work? The Moon provides enough money to keep me from starving and freezing, but that is all!" She shook her head furiously, red hair flying around. "I did not choose this! Someone pricked me with a needle at a show in Madrid many years ago, and then that horrible voice was in my head, and sometimes in my limbs, and sometimes in my body! Don't you know what the Blood Moon *does*?"

"I thought… I thought the *vocera* were different, a higher order of being, more respected, with more privileges–"

She laughed, low and nasty. "The Moon likes beauty and talent. I was beautiful and talented. So, they made me a *vocera*, yes, their face in Barcelona, their point of contact. They moved me to this apartment, away from my friends and my husband, but I am just as much a possession as the hordes of street urchins the Moon controls. I will pay for this outburst, too, because the Moon is always listening. I will be forced to hurt myself, in places that don't show. But I don't care anymore. You *fool*. You could have let the assassin creep up and saved hundreds of us, or perhaps thousands."

She rose and looked down at Fantasma – despite being only five feet tall, she could do that, while he was seated – and then astonished Fantasma by spitting in his face. A wet glob hit his cheek. "*Your* kind, the Blood Moon pays, because you are not human, and so he cannot possess you directly. He has to buy you. But me, and the other *vocera*, and all his thralls? He simply *takes* us." She pointed a finger at the door. "Get out of here. Out of my home, which is not my home, which I did not choose, where I am forced to wait in case anyone wishes to speak with my *owner*. Go and enjoy your freedom."

Fantasma took a handkerchief from his pocket, wiped his face, and then dropped the sullied cloth on the carpet. He stood, straightened his jacket, and then drew back his hand to slap Navarro.

She lifted her face, smiling, daring him. He lowered his hand. To strike Navarro, a *vocera* of the Blood Moon… no, he didn't dare. The Moon might take it as an insult. "You dwell only on the negatives, madame," Fantasma said. "But remember, the Moon protects you as well. If he didn't, I would be drinking your blood right now."

"Without the Moon, I would never have even crossed paths with filth like you. Go."

Fantasma went to the door, wondering if he could engineer a fire in this building to kill the old woman or send Akh to get rid of her discreetly, but that was too dangerous. The Blood Moon could not dominate Fantasma's mind or steal his body, true. But they could take revenge in so many other ways.

As long as the Moon killed Sanford, Fantasma was content to suffer some small indignities in the process.

• • •

"Estrella! There you are."

She stopped mid-stride and turned to look down at a beggar sprawled against the base of a wall, stick-thin limbs poking out of ragged clothes, face a smear of ash and stubble, age impossible to guess.

"Did you speak to me, sir?" she asked. She knew it must be the Moon, but she didn't want to talk to her mentor right now. She was still sorting through the strangeness of her experience in the ghoul quarter, trying to sift truth from lies – if there *was* any truth. The creature in the hidden quarter had been objectively monstrous, an admitted thief of children and eater of human flesh, but it hadn't tried to deceive her about any of that. Couldn't a monstrous voice tell the truth, just as a kind one could lie?

"It's me, little star," the man said. "The Moon in your sky. Ugh, this vessel is filthy. It's useful for me to have eyes and ears among the worms of the Earth, but it's so unpleasant to inhabit such a wretched one."

The poor man seemed more unfortunate than wretched to Estrella. "You could have someone buy him fresh clothes, and give him money, and let him find a room to wash up," she suggested.

"What a good idea!" the Moon replied brightly. "I'll see what I can do. I'm just so busy, lately… and that means you're busy, too, little star. I've had my eyes open for you all morning, and I'm so glad I caught sight of you." The Blood Moon had eyes everywhere, and no one could stay hidden long in Madrid, even if they wanted to. Which Estrella didn't. Of course.

"I was going to check in with you this evening as usual." Estrella was running errands, buying produce and conserves for the old couple who lived upstairs from the Gullettes, since they had trouble getting around these days. This was one of her rare free days… or so she'd hoped. *Please don't send me after one of the wicked.* Not again, not so soon. Her dreams of the churning, violet-tinged void became so much stronger in the days immediately after she opened herself that way.

There are portals hidden in so many dark places, but I have never seen one hidden inside a– Inside a what? Inside a girl?

She shook off those thoughts and asked, "Has something happened?"

"Something *abominable.*" The beggar beckoned and Estrella crouched down, putting her basket on the pavement beside her. "One of my associates in the Coterie is trying to kill me! More than one, probably. A whole conspiracy of them."

Estrella gasped. "But why?" She didn't know much about the Coterie, just that they were the Moon's allies in the quest to make a better world, off pursuing their own related projects all over the globe.

"Jealousy," the Moon said promptly. "The ones who have set themselves against me thrive on chaos and misery, and they don't like my plans to create a peaceful, orderly society. What place would lovers of disarray have in a world free of war and strife? They have dispatched an assassin to kill me, an American sorcerer named Carl Sanford. Tall, slim, dresses well, a neat silver goatee, tends to carry a walking stick. I'll see if I can get a sketch drawn up. He's coming to Madrid, and he means me harm. If we see him, we need to capture him and explain to him the error of his ways."

"Will you send the family to trap him?" She had a sinking feeling that she knew the answer to that.

"Mmm, well, my star, this Sanford is a sorcerer of great

repute," the Moon said. "I'll try it that way, of course, but it's possible he'll prove too formidable for the ordinary members of the family. But *you*, with your special gifts, your speed, strength, and resilience, you would be more than a match for him. That's why I gave you those powers in the first place, to deal with threats like Sanford."

You don't even know where I send people when I open myself, she thought. Wouldn't you know if you were truly the one who'd given me these powers? "I don't like using my abilities, Moon."

"I know, my dear." The beggar reached out and patted Estrella gently on the arm. How many times had the Moon touched her to comfort her, using how many hands? Innumerable. "Believe me, love, it grieves me to ask these things of you. The day will come when you no longer need to do such things. Once we usher in our golden age, such actions will be unnecessary. But for now… you remember when we talked about how sometimes ugly things must happen, in order to achieve beautiful things?"

"We have to drain the pus," she said. "Burn away the dead wood. Like that?"

"Yes, exactly, Estrellita. And you are my lance and my flame! You will help prepare this world for glory."

"Why capture this Sanford? Why not just… send him away?" She shuddered even to suggest it since using her Moon-given gifts in that way was so unpleasant, but at least when she sent people elsewhere, they were just *gone*. It was clean, in a way. Cleaner than holding someone down while they struggled, knocking them out, dragging them off somewhere for who knows what unpleasantness to follow.

The Moon knew. But she didn't want to ask.

"There is a conspiracy afoot, Estrella. Forces are moving against me. This Sanford may know details. He may know which other members of my Coterie have turned against me. I need to talk to him before we do… anything more permanent."

"Are you going to kill him when you're done?" Estrella didn't like it when the Moon killed people. It was even worse than what she did, because killing was so final and absolute. She'd never really understood how you could build a better world on a foundation of corpses.

The beggar shook his head. "I certainly hope not. I don't want to kill him *or* send him away. He may not be irredeemably wicked, after all. If there is any goodness in his heart, then I will let him live, and more, I will bring him into the family to join our great cause."

"I hope you can. But… I could never be an assassin. To kill people for money?" She shook her head. It was bad enough to get rid of people for noble reasons. "But you can fix him. Correct his mind and his heart." The Blood Moon had never inhabited Estrella's body, never entered her mind or taken her blood, because, they said, she didn't need correction: she was already perfect, a little star.

She didn't feel perfect, most of the time, but the Blood Moon knew better than her, didn't they? The Moon had the collective wisdom of their whole family to draw on, and their family was growing and growing, and someday it would encompass all of humankind, bound by blood.

"I hope so," the Blood Moon said. "Some people don't want to be fixed. But this Sanford is worse than a mercenary. He hasn't agreed to kill me for money. No, the Coterie has promised that if he destroys me, Sanford can take my place.

They would have him take up my crown and scepter to rule Spain. Can you imagine what a hired murderer would do with my powers? And an *American*? I shudder to think of the dark purposes he would turn my family toward."

Estrella frowned, nodding. That made sense. Such a usurpation would end all hope for the golden age and usher in an age of darkness. "We cannot allow this to happen." She pushed her doubts aside. Why should she let the words of a filthy inhuman monster trouble her? The Moon had always taken care of her, and she owed him whatever protection she could provide. A lifelong family relationship, however unorthodox, should mean more than a single brief exchange in a dirty hole in the ground.

"We won't," the Blood Moon said adoringly. "We will vanquish Sanford with our love."

The Warden, Altman, and his lurking partner arrived in Barcelona midmorning. Altman practically bounded off the train, carrying all their luggage. He thrummed with energy stolen from the unfortunate night porter. Altman was troubled by the dietary habits of the entity inside him, but it was impossible not to be cheerful when he felt this *good*.

Barcelona Sants station was as grand as anything Altman had encountered in the States, and he marveled at the modern architecture as they navigated through the concourse and made their way out onto the street. The Mediterranean sun was bright and hot, the streets bustling with Spaniards out and about on their business. Altman was jostled several times as people streamed in and out of the station. Such casual disrespect normally outraged him, but his disposition was too positive to be easily dislodged.

"What day is it today?" Altman asked.

"It's Tuesday," the Warden said, frowning down at the compass in her hand.

"All right," he said amiably. He'd been more curious about the date – he wasn't even certain about the month, frankly –

but then again, what did it matter? They were in one of the great cities of Europe, he was flush with power, and his quarry was near. They would track Sanford to his lair, and beard him there, and force him to do their bidding. *Perhaps Sanford can even rid me of the thing inside me once I don't need it anymore,* he mused.

I can hear you, you know, his partner murmured. *We have already settled on the terms of my tenancy, Altman. I am not open to renegotiation.*

What were the terms? he wondered. *Precisely? You were vague about the details.*

Don't worry about all that. His partner was constantly forbidding him to worry, which only had the opposite effect. *I'll make sure our agreement is followed to the letter. Strict adherence to bargains is in the nature of creatures like myself. We can only take that which has been freely offered. I can no more break a contract than you can fly to the moon.*

That's beyond your power, then? Altman thought, amused. *You can't take me to the moon, like Cyrano?*

Maybe if I ate enough people first, the thing replied. *Why, did you want to go?*

"Never mind," he muttered, and the Warden looked at him sharply.

"What?"

"Nothing. Talking to myself."

"Very poor company, I'd imagine. We have a problem."

"Oh, only one?"

"Very droll." She held out her hand to show him the compass. "The needle is spinning, pointing first one way, and then another. Which could mean Sanford has been chopped into pieces, and those pieces have been scattered around the city. But I think it's more likely he's done something to manipulate his precise location."

He took the compass so he could look at it more closely. The needle didn't whirl wildly but would instead point in one direction, then abruptly move and point in another, before shifting position again. He watched the needle complete a full circuit and then sighed and snapped it shut, handing it back. "Do you think he knows we're coming?"

"I can't imagine how he would," she said, "but this is the Order of the Silver Twilight Lodge's magus we're talking about. I wouldn't dismiss any possibility when it comes to him."

Altman scowled. "Sanford isn't so formidable. Tillinghast bested him easily enough."

The Warden gave a razor-thin smile. "Do you think it was easy? I was down there in the deep basements when Sanford released his menagerie of monsters, when the ceilings came tumbling down and the conditions of reality were stretched, twisted, and torn. I thought you were there, too, but perhaps you've got more holes in your memory than I realized?"

"I remember it all well enough," Altman grumbled. "Sanford has his tricks, I admit, but his 'all-knowing, all-seeing, unflappable expert at everything' pose is mostly smoke and mirrors."

"Mmm. Do you really believe that? Don't pretend you aren't afraid of Sanford. You invited a monster to share your body before you'd risk facing him. That's how afraid you are of the magus."

Altman ground his teeth, but arguing with the Warden was pointless. She said vicious, stinging things, but if you tried to sting her back, she took absolutely no notice at all. Sparring with her verbally was like sparring physically with a brick wall: you wouldn't hurt the wall, but you might break a few bones in the process.

Oh, we could hurt a brick wall, his partner assured him. *Punch a hole right through it. Give it a try if you like.*

Altman shoved his fists into the pockets of his military greatcoat. It was far too warm for that garment here – Spain in whatever month this was turned out to be much warmer than dreary old Arkham – but Altman wasn't uncomfortable. He suspected his partner was regulating his temperature. That would have been useful on some of those freezing nights in Kandahar. Still, the coat was a bit of a problem. "We should probably dress more like the locals do, so we can blend in."

The Warden wore the same sort of gray, ankle-length dress she always did, her long dark hair pulled back severely, her face stern but unlined. "No one will take any notice of us, Altman, unless we want them to or we make our presences aggressively known. My powers are protective, and that includes protecting members of the Order from unwanted scrutiny. Dress however you like."

He forgot, sometimes, that she wasn't just an ill-tempered traveling companion, but a powerful force of magic. "Ah. Yes. Of course. Good of you. So, then. Where do we begin?"

"I suspect Sanford has created magical doubles of himself," the Warden said.

"What, there are a dozen copies of Sanford wandering around?" Altman hadn't been present for the tussle with the cult of doppelgängers who'd attacked Arkham, who'd copied and then killed his brother, and he found the idea of such creatures repellent.

"No, no," she said. "At least, probably not. It's more likely he fashioned bundles of his blood and hair, enchanted with sympathetic magic to make the part seem identical to the whole, and scattered them around the city. That would serve to baffle our divination spell. But making copies wouldn't stop the compass from pointing at his real body, too, so… let us eliminate each possibility until we find our true target." She glanced around, then clicked her tongue. "Here, girl," she murmured.

A hound emerged from the shadows at the base of the train station wall, even though the shadow was far too small to hide the black mastiff, which might have been mistaken for a small bear at first glance.

What is that? his partner asked, inner voice full of dark wonder.

The Warden can summon hounds, he thought. Or things that look like hounds, anyway. She used them to defend the Lodge house from intruders in the old days.

Van Shaw knelt before the slavering beast and rubbed her face affectionately. That was one of the few affectionate things Altman had ever seen her do. She held out the compass toward the hound, flat on her palm, and to Altman's surprise, the hound *ate* the thing, gobbling it up in a single gulp, then licked her chops. "Good girl," the Warden said. "Follow the scents to their sources, one at a time."

The dog set off, trotting along the street to the northeast, and Van Shaw strode after it, leaving Altman to hurry after her a moment later. "Where are we going? Why did you feed that animal the compass?"

"She's not an animal," the Warden said absently. The hound glanced back at Altman, disturbingly directly, and seemed to swell, like a black balloon, bulging and rippling with extra muscle. The hound's eyes briefly flashed red before turning her gaze away.

"The compass was useless to us. The needle didn't point in any direction long enough for us to follow it to a particular signature. But my hounds have special properties, including excellent tracking skills. By merging their magics together, I transformed her into a blood magic hound. She will follow the trail to each blood signature, one by one, until we find the magus himself." She sighed. "That's the idea, anyway. I know Carl Sanford well enough to predict what he'll do. But what if he's even better at predicting *me*? I always got the sense my hounds unsettled him, so perhaps he doesn't have a full understanding of their capabilities. We can hope."

"Imagine you, being hopeful!" Altman said.

"It is not in my usual nature," she said. "But then, I never hoped to see any of the great cities of Europe, either, and that came to pass."

They walked for some miles along a broad avenue lined with trees, passing occasional plazas beautified by sculptures and fountains. The tall buildings on either side of the thoroughfare seemed to mingle offices, residences, and businesses indiscriminately, and their architectural styles were just as jumbled. "I'd gotten too used to Arkham," Altman said, trying to make conversation, though the Warden was one of the world's worst conversationalists. "Where most of the houses and buildings look more or less the same."

"Nonsense," the Warden said. "Back home we have Colonials, and Cape Cods, and Tudors, and even some Greek Revival architecture, in the grander houses. Here, though … yes, here, the history is much deeper." She pointed, seemingly at random as far as Altman could tell. "We have old

Roman styles there, and Renaissance, even some Modernism beginning to crop up, and yes, there are some Art Deco touches, too."

To Altman they all just looked like buildings, some more encrusted with pointless geegaws, and others less so. *Philistine*, his partner murmured.

"This city is *old*," the Warden went on, warming to her topic. "It began as a Roman colony called Barcino, before the birth of Christ. There are still remnants of that original city visible here. And there." She gestured in some seemingly arbitrary direction, as if that gave Altman any useful information. "Later, rule of the city passed from Christians to Muslims and back again. The Bourbons invaded. The local Catalan people were brutalized by their oppressors. Then came a long period of decline for Barcelona, but the textile industry has led to booming times recently, and there are construction projects all over the city now, not least of all the Sagrada Familia. This city is becoming a true jewel of Spain. I wouldn't be surprised if someday it overshadows Madrid."

"Why do you know all this pointless trivia about a foreign city?" Altman asked. "Have you been here before? I thought you hadn't left Arkham in decades?"

"Oh, it's been longer than that," the Warden said. "Longer than I wish to contemplate. That's the *reason* I know so much about Spain. About France. About Italy. China, Japan, the Middle East, Africa. About almost everywhere." Her strides were long, keeping pace with her trotting hound, but her voice turned contemplative. "I don't sleep, you know, not really, not when the Order is healthy. That's part of the spell that binds and empowers me: you can't be eternally vigilant if you spend a third of your life unconscious. On those long and quiet nights, I would stay up in my shed on the grounds of the Lodge house, burning a lamp, and what else was there to do, really, but read? Sanford had his scouts all over the world searching for rare tomes and forbidden volumes, and as a favor to me, they also brought back traveler's guides and memoirs of various expeditions. I learned many languages, so I could read more of the books people brought me. I traveled vicariously through those volumes, from the jungles of Africa to the river basins of South America, from the snowy heights of the Himalayas to the frozen tundra of the Arctic. I have seen the great cities, felt the breath of volcanoes, watched the shimmer of the Northern Lights. But only up here." She tapped the side of her head. "And my memory… it is not like yours, Altman, all full of smoke and fog and chasms. I remember everything, because it's important for a protector to remember everything. So, yes, I could lecture you all day on the architectural styles of Barcelona. But I won't. Don't worry. Your incuriosity about anything that doesn't directly serve your ambitions is one of your animating qualities. But I'll be glad to answer questions if you ask them."

I am increasingly glad I didn't eat her, Altman's partner said. *None of my hosts ever brought me to this part of the continent. I'm practically as ignorant as a* human *here.*

What happened to your other hosts? Altman asked.

Ah, well, they're mortals. Even with my protective influence, their bodies don't last forever.

Altman shivered. *Their bodies,* it said. Not *their lives.* He already knew the thing inside him could use his body as its own. Would it continue to use his body even after he died? Just walk around in his soulless corpse, imitating him, performing atrocities and besmirching his reputation?

Though Altman knew his partner could discern his thoughts, it made no reply regarding his speculations.

"Oh, would you look at that," the Warden murmured, jostling Altman out of his dark thoughts. They'd moved off the street into a park with winding paths among the bushes and trees and small statues – no, wait, that was a public water fountain, with a sculpture of a fox or something on top. He considered getting a drink but wasn't thirsty. That was a bit disconcerting. They must have walked several miles already in the heat, and he was in an overcoat, but he wasn't thirsty, or even sweaty.

You're welcome, his partner said.

Altman shook off his preoccupations and tried to see what the Warden was looking at, and once he did, he took an involuntary step back. There was a gargantuan building across the street, one of the largest structures he'd ever seen, a cathedral that dominated the view like an elephant in a room full of house cats. The building was still under construction, covered in scaffolding, swarming with workers. A single tall tower on one side of the church pointed into the sky like an accusing finger.

"The Sagrada Familia," the Warden said. "Cathedral of the Holy Family. I've read about this place. It's an audacious combination of the Gothic and Art Nouveau styles."

Altman grunted. "I'll take your word for it." But he couldn't help but be impressed.

The Warden stood with her hands clasped before her, gazing rapt at the building. Her hound sat on her haunches, staring at the cathedral, teeth bared, silently snarling. Was it *actually* a hound of hell? Would going into the church make it burst into flames? He didn't think things were that simple in the supernatural world, but there had to be some truth to those old stories.

The Warden lapsed into her tour-guide tones. "The architect, Antoni Gaudí, died recently, but his apprentice has stepped in to take over the work. Gaudí knew he wouldn't live long enough to see the Sagrada completed, of course, though I think he expected a few more years." The Warden's head tipped back as she looked up at the single spire. "There will be more towers when it's all done, of different sizes. A dozen for the apostles, four for the evangelists, one for the Virgin Mother, and the tallest, of course, for Christ himself."

"That sounds like a staggering amount of stone to lift into the air." Altman had never been religious, but he found this monumental construction rather awe-inspiring regardless, as a testament to what humans could accomplish. He could, admittedly, think of better ways to channel all that effort and energy (and money), but the Catholic Church hadn't asked his opinion. "When will it be finished?" he asked.

"I'm not sure. They began construction in 1882, and Gaudí took over the next year, when the original architect resigned."

"They've been working on this for more than forty years?" Altman exclaimed.

"And will for another forty," Van Shaw said placidly. "Or eighty. Or perhaps a hundred."

"They might not finish this thing for another *century*? No one alive today will be around to see it completed."

Speak for yourself, his partner murmured.

Van Shaw huffed. "It's a church, Altman. They're concerned with the business of eternity. What's a century or two out of infinity? That's why the Order was founded, too, you know. It was meant to outlast Sanford, for its work to stretch into the future indefinitely."

"It did outlast Sanford. It's in my hands now."

The Warden merely sniffed. Her dog shook and began to pace around impatiently, circling her legs. "Let's go. Sanford isn't in there."

"He probably thinks the cathedral should be dedicated to him," Altman said. "He'd find it insufficient for his own splendor, though, I'm sure."

"The magus always did have a good sense of his own worth," Van Shaw said, and set off after the hound.

They roamed all over Barcelona that day, stopping half a dozen times when the hound indicated that they'd arrived at their latest destination, going stiff and pointing like a hunting dog. They wandered the twisting streets of the Gothic Quarter where Van Shaw shared historical facts, despite the fact that Altman never asked, and viewed a grand statue of Christopher Columbus. In both places they uncovered little jars of filth and magic, planted by Sanford to deceive them.

"But perhaps this wasn't done to trick us, specifically," Altman said. "We don't know what Sanford has been up to since he left Arkham. He could have made other enemies, or attracted unwanted attention, and hid these decoys as a preventative measure. There's no reason to think he knows *we're* here."

"Believe what you like," the Warden said. "I will proceed under the assumption that he knows we're coming and plans to ambush us at the most devastating moment. It's safer that way."

They continued their search and spent longer than necessary in a place called Park Güell, designed by that

Guadí chap again, apparently. He was a busy fellow, or he had been, until a trolley car mowed him down. The Warden shared *that* tidbit without Altman asking, too. The Park was actually more of a garden city, in the English style – a satellite community encircled by greenery – though rather more baroque than the usual sort. There were colorful mosaics everywhere, and staircases that seemed more ornamental than functional, and residences that blended almost seamlessly into their natural surroundings. The Warden lingered, exclaimed, and paused for a long time to look at Gaudí's own home, only recently left untenanted. The Warden claimed they were looking into every nook and cranny in case Sanford was hiding out here, but Altman could tell she just liked the place and wanted to explore it. The environment was rather more beautiful than the weeds and dying trees that made up the grounds of the Silver Twilight Lodge where she'd lived.

Altman was less enchanted by the Park and tried to hurry the Warden along, but she was impervious to chiding. Since Altman had recovered his strength, the Warden had grown commensurately more powerful, too, and as a result, she was even less tractable than usual. He finally dragged her away, arguing that it was getting late and they needed to either find Sanford or secure accommodation so they could resume the search tomorrow.

She sighed. "I don't sleep, but I suppose you sleep enough for the both of us. I could search without you through the night…"

"No," Altman said, but at her severe look, he held up his hands. "I'm not ordering you. I'm asking. I want to be there when you find him. We'll stand a better chance of…

persuading him to help us if we present a united front, anyway. Two against one and all that."

Three, his partner whispered.

Van Shaw's scowl softened. "You are not wrong. For once. Very well. Unlike you, I still get hungry, so I will want to eat at some point. They take their evening repast quite late here, just so you know."

"I've heard," Altman said. "Spaniards sleep all day and dance and feast all night, and never do any work at all."

"You just watched an army of workmen climbing all over a cathedral," she pointed out. "How can you say they don't work?"

"An American crew could have finished that cathedral in ten or twenty years, I bet," Altman said, which made the Warden stomp off in irritation, following her hound.

The creature led them to Las Ramblas, a wide bricked thoroughfare that ran down to the sea, or bay, or whatever body of water this city butted up against. Altman didn't share the Warden's interest in the culture and history, or even the geography of foreign lands. Most of his experiences abroad had involved long stretches of boredom and brief intervals of stabbing people or being shot at.

Stabbing, you say? his partner piped up, but Altman ignored it. He *was* doing better – he'd remained conscious and in control during this whole long endless trek and didn't feel tired, though his descents into sleep had been rather sudden lately, so perhaps that didn't signify much.

The hound trotted straight into the lobby of a white hotel and then up a staircase. The Warden whistled and she came back, though she was definitely eager to climb. Another of Sanford's little jars was hidden up there, no doubt. Altman had given up on hoping they'd find the magus today. Sanford might not be as clever as he thought he was, but that didn't mean he wasn't clever at *all*.

"We should speak to the front desk," the Warden said. "In all the other places we've visited, we found traces of Sanford outdoors, where he hid his jars. But this… he might actually have stayed here. There's a possibility he's up there right now." She gazed at the stairs.

"Good point." Altman strode to the front desk, where a thin young man leafed through a ledger. "You there," he said. "I'm looking for an American chap, about so high, neat silver beard, probably in a suit."

The Warden stepped up beside him and elbowed him in the side. "Hola," she said.

"Hola señora," the clerk replied cheerfully. "Le puedo ayudar?" He didn't seem to notice the hound at all.

Altman's partner translated in his mind as the Warden continued. "We're looking for an old friend. He told us he was going to be staying here and we wondered if he's checked in yet?"

"What is his name?" the clerk asked.

"Ah, well, you see, he's a very important American businessman and sometimes he travels under an assumed name, so stock speculators won't get wind of his movements. I'm not sure what name he might have used." She sounded so cheerful and apologetic. Altman had never realized Van Shaw was such a gifted actress.

The clerk frowned. "I am unsure how I can help, then."

"We have a photograph." She reached into her handbag and withdrew a small framed portrait. Altman tried not to goggle. She'd brought a photo of the magus? What, had she kept it in her shed on the Lodge grounds, next to the straight-backed wooden chair she had in lieu of a bed? God, she probably had.

The clerk leaned forward obligingly and peered at the photo. "Ah, yes, Mr Phillips! He was indeed staying with us, but I am afraid he checked out yesterday. You just missed him. How unfortunate."

"Oh dear," the Warden said. "Did he happen to say where he was going next? His itinerary wasn't finalized the last time we spoke and I'm afraid we might have missed a telegram during our travels."

"Oh, I am afraid not. He did not share his plans with us." The clerk smiled brightly. "May I be of any further assistance?"

"We need a room and a meal," Altman said.

"Yes, of course, we have rooms available and our lounge will be serving dinner in a few hours."

"Could we have the same room Mr Phillips did?" the Warden asked, a little too sharply.

The clerk cocked his head. "Pardon me?"

"We want the same room," Altman said. "Mr Phillips always gets the very best, you see, and we try to follow his example in all things."

The clerk shrugged, then leafed through a ledger. "I believe that particular suite has been reserved by another party."

The Warden reached into her purse, withdrew a sheaf of bills, and set them on the counter. "But there must have been some mistake. I'm quite sure *we* reserved that suite, before the other party did."

The clerk looked at the pile of bills, looked at her, looked at Altman, looked around, then neatly swept the cash off the counter and made it disappear. "Ah, yes, of course, I see it here." He spun the ledger around. "Just sign in, please. I'll have someone carry your bags up."

"No need," Altman said. "Just hand over the keys, por favor."

The Warden signed them in under the names Mr and Mrs Greene as Altman took the keys, and then they headed for the stairs. "Where did you get all that money?" Altman asked.

She looked at him sidelong as they ascended. "I got it from you, Altman. I didn't care to inquire about where *you* obtained our travel funds. You and the beast within went out, several days before we left Arkham, and returned with enough for us to get by. Though I changed much of it for local currency in Madrid."

What did we do to get that money? he inquired of his partner.

We didn't do anything. You slept through the whole thing. I had a very enjoyable time, though. Isn't it nice when pleasure and profit go hand in hand?

Altman was traveling with the two most annoying conversationalists in the world, it seemed.

The hound trotted toward the suite they'd rented and scratched at the wood, its claws lengthening as it did so, scraping curls of wood away from the door. The creature seemed to change every time Altman looked away from it. Sometimes it shrank to the size of an ordinary hound to slip into tight spaces, but other times it grew to something closer in stature to a black bear, constructed of shaped midnight.

I wonder what it tastes like, his partner mused sleepily.

The Warden unlocked the door, and even knowing Sanford wasn't really inside, Altman tensed as if for a confrontation. The magus *had* been here, just days ago. They were so close! Perhaps Sanford was still in the city.

The suite was nice inside, but that wasn't what Altman noticed at first, or the Warden, either. "The walls are covered in sigils!" he said. "Is it some kind of trap?" He hunched his shoulders, expecting to burst into flames or be pummeled by invisible fists or frozen alive.

"You can see the sigils?" the Warden said. "That's new. You used to be as ignorant as any ordinary mortal to the presence of invisible runes. And yes, it is a trap, but not for us." She looked back at her hound, who stood outside the room threshold, haunches up, bristling. "It makes my hound uncomfortable, though." She waved her hand and the beast melted away back into the hall. The Warden shut the door after it, then peered around. "There might be something here that could trouble your passenger, too."

A portion of the wall flared into burning brightness briefly, then subsided, leaving only scorch marks behind. "Not anymore," the thing said through Altman's mouth. "Those markings weren't meant to bind me, specifically, or I couldn't have destroyed them, but they were… a little too close. Suitable to entrap a cousin of mine, you might say, and enough to make me itchy."

"You seem to love destroying property," the Warden said. "We're going to have to pay extra for that damage, you know."

"Just hang that ugly picture of a sailboat over the scorch marks," Altman said, his voice his own again. He looked at the Warden. "Can you tell? Whether it's me talking, I mean, or… the other thing?"

"Of course," she said. "You sound like you. Your *partner* sounds like… snakes hissing in a drain."

"Really?" Their voices sounded exactly the same to Altman's ears.

"I'm sure most people don't hear it that way," Van Shaw said. "Illusions don't work well on me, that's all. I'm not fully impervious to them, but I'm more resistant than most. All part of my complement of powers. I couldn't let someone walk into the Lodge just because they'd glamoured themselves to look like a member of the Order."

"Part of my powers now, too, apparently," Altman said. "What else can I do, I wonder?"

Isn't half the fun finding out? his partner murmured.

Someone knocked on the door. Altman raised one eyebrow at the Warden, then went to open it.

Ooh, can I eat whoever that is? the beast asked.

The front desk clerk stood on the other side of the door, holding an envelope. "Just after you checked in, someone brought this letter and asked me to deliver it to your door."

"Was it Mr Phillips?" Altman asked.

"No, no. He did not give his name. A pale man."

The Warden glided over, took the letter, and slipped the clerk a tip, as if they hadn't paid him enough already. Altman had never been rich, and he resented the Warden splashing his hard-earned money around, even if he didn't remember what he'd done to earn it.

The clerk departed. Altman shut the door. The Warden opened the envelope and read the paper inside. Her expression revealed nothing regarding the nature of its contents.

"Well?" Altman demanded. "What is it?"

"It seems we've been invited to a midnight rendezvous," she said.

CHAPTER TWELVE
The Bull and the Matador

Sanford was in no great rush. The Warden and Altman were coming for him, yes, thank you for the warning, Ruby. Without a body to prove his death, they would inevitably worry, investigate, and learn the truth. They had sufficient resources to do so, and Altman wouldn't rest while the former leader of the Order still lived. That would be like having two popes. On the rare occasions when *that* happened, the consequences were inevitably schism and sectarian violence.

Not that Sanford was comparing himself to a pope. Sanford hadn't waited around for some conclave of old men to elect him to power. He'd simply seized power for his own.

He'd expected them to come for him, even counted on it. But he would choose the ground for their reunion. He had time to prepare while they chased his false trails around Barcelona. If he timed things right, they would find him established in Madrid, and at that point, their arrival would be less of a problem, and might even be the *solution* to a problem.

While his erstwhile allies were in pursuit, Sanford was packing his valise and departing his hotel. He took a taxi to Barcelona Sants and bought a ticket for the next train to Madrid, which was departing shortly. While he waited until it was time to board, he strolled around the concourse, leaning on his walking stick, and generally presenting a frailer version of himself to any watchers. He found a shadowy corner, between a support pillar and a wall, and eased back into the dim, leaning against the wall as if taking a rest. No one took any particular notice of him.

He reached into his jacket pocket and withdrew the opera glasses the Claret Knight had given him. When closed, the glasses resembled a golden cigarette case, but when he released the hidden spring, the case sprang open, revealing the ruby lenses. Sanford put the glasses up to his eyes and looked through them.

There were two strange things. The first was that, despite the red lenses, the view wasn't rose-colored at all. The glass might as well have been clear, but they enhanced his vision better than any binoculars he'd ever used, rendering everything unnaturally crisp and detailed. He could read not just the headlines of the papers displayed at the newsstand across the way, but even the fine print of the articles. Sanford's vision was perfect, or so his physician had assured him the year before when he still had a physician – when he still had lots of things he'd subsequently lost – but these opera glasses gave him the eyesight of an eagle, beyond peak human capability.

He slowly scanned the crowd at the station, wondering idly if he could put these lenses in a less ostentatious setting without spoiling the magic. They would be more subtle as a pair of shaded spectacles, perhaps, or he could remove one lens and use it as a monocle, to go with the other lens he used to detect illusions. Back at the Lodge, he could have tasked one of his underlings with the job, but here on his own, without proper tools, he couldn't risk breaking the glasses and losing his advantage. He'd just have to be an eccentric expatriate instead.

He didn't see anything unusual and was about to fold up the glasses and make his way to the train platform when something caught his eye. At first, he thought it was some sort of cable strung along the ceiling, but the wire undulated. It was even brighter and more vibrant than everything else seen through the glasses. The cable was also very red.

Sanford squinted, wishing he could get a closer look without giving up his position in the shadows. He looked over the glasses case and noticed a small wheel on top, the sort used to adjust focus. Perhaps it had a different function here. He fiddled with the wheel, looked through the glasses, and was gratified to see the magnification changed, images leaping twice as close. Further adjustments magnified the view four times, then eight or ten, and that seemed to be the limit.

That was close enough, though. He could see the pulsing wire was no wire at all, but something alive, like a skinned snake. Sanford rolled the magnification back, and then tried to follow the bloody thread to its point of origin. One end vanished right through one of the station walls, to the southwest. Toward Madrid. Ah ha.

He reluctantly stepped out from behind the pillar to better trace the thread the other way, watching it dip down from the ceiling and disappear into a crowd on a train platform.

His platform. How interesting. He strolled onto the platform, moving swiftly among the waiting passengers, occasionally putting the glasses to his face to check the position of the cord. He angled around the platform carefully until he was able to trace the line to its owner. Or rather to the person who was *owned*.

The cord emerged from the base of a small man's neck. He was dressed in a faded brown suit, holding a battered briefcase, with a homburg hat shoved down tightly on his head. He looked like a minor clerk or functionary, the least threatening creature in the world, which was always a good appearance for an operative.

Hmm. Was Sanford leaping to conclusions? Just because one of the Blood Moon's thralls was here didn't mean he was here for *him*. The Moon reportedly had minions scattered all over Europe, with the highest concentration by far in Spain. Even if the Moon's lair was in Madrid, it made sense they'd have a significant presence in Barcelona, too, and running across a thrall here was probably an inevitability.

Still, it would be nice to be sure. The element of surprise the Claret Knight had mentioned was one of the only advantages Sanford possessed. He folded up his glasses and slipped them into his jacket pocket, then strolled idly to the edge of the platform, like someone pacing to pass the time, and made a point of crossing the man's eyeline without paying him any apparent attention.

He saw the man jolt in his peripheral vision. That was interesting… and troubling. The Blood Moon shouldn't even know Sanford existed. If they did know Sanford existed, they shouldn't know what he looked like, certainly not well enough to recognize him at first glance.

Fantasma. Sanford suppressed a groan. Of course. He'd talked to Fantasma in the first place because of rumors that the creature did odd jobs for the Coterie. That meant he knew Thorne, but it could mean he also knew the Blood Moon. Fantasma had facilitated Sanford's meeting with Thorne and given him directions to the meeting place. He could have easily crept, or more likely dispatched, his invisible brother to surreptitiously observe the meeting and Sanford's movements, and then turned around to sell or trade that information to the Blood Moon. Or *gift* it to the Moon, in revenge against Sanford for binding him and besting him.

Sanford based much of this on seeing a small man in a homburg hat twitch briefly, but the scenario felt terribly plausible, and he decided to proceed as if the Blood Moon knew he was coming. Excess caution wouldn't do him any harm.

How irritating, though. Sanford had been nice enough to let Fantasma *and* his hideous sibling Akh live. This was the thanks he got? No one had any sense of proportion, anymore.

All right, so he'd lost the element of surprise. That was a shame, but how long could he have hidden his intentions in Madrid anyway, a city full of mind-controlled – or at least mentally influenced – spies? Sanford could adapt to this new situation.

He moved along the platform, asking a few people if they spoke English, only to get one blank look, one hostile look, and one murmured "No, lo siento." Then he sidled up to the small man and said, "Pardon me. I'm terribly sorry. Do you happen to speak English?"

The diminutive Spaniard looked at him with an expression of stark terror, as if Sanford were death himself, come in black robes to collect souls with a swinging scythe. But then his expression changed, the eyebrows going up and the mouth opening in a smile. The man's eyes changed, too. They didn't turn black or flash red or anything so obvious, but they became merry, sparkling. "I *do* speak English. Forgive me, my skills are very poor, but I welcome the opportunity to practice!"

"You speak very well, to my ear." Sanford was fairly sure

he was talking to the Blood Moon now. Certainly, that antic tone was not in keeping with the general mien of the person who spoke it, and Sanford had some experience conversing with the possessed. He'd spent enough time with the Scholar who'd lived in his basements for all those years: the body of a woman inhabited by the mind of an alien creature from deep time.

The question was, should Sanford let the Blood Moon know that *he* knew, which risked exposing the fact that he could recognize the thralls? No, no. Information asymmetry was a powerful thing. Sanford was happy to know anything his target didn't. So, he simply said, "I'm new to the country and want to make sure I'm going the right way. Is this the platform for the train to Madrid?"

"Si, yes, that's right." The minion of the Moon pointed along the tracks, where a locomotive was coming into view. "That is our train."

"Capital," Sanford said. "I appreciate the guidance."

"It is my pleasure," the Moon said. "You are American, yes?"

"A Bostonian, in fact," Sanford replied. "Have you ever been to Boston?"

"No, never to America at all. What brings you to our country?"

"Oh, I am eager to see the bullfights!" Sanford said. "The test of wills, the artistry, the cunning of man set against the brute strength of a beast, the triumph of the underdog, it all speaks to me. Do you like the bullfights?"

"Oh, yes," the Moon said. "I saw the great matador Joselito gored to death not so many years ago." Those eyes positively danced. "It was a profoundly moving experience for me. Joselito was a prodigy, he even fought the bulls as a child, and by the time he was twelve, he was a respected professional. Not like these matadors nowadays, who root themselves in place and depend on the picadors, pah, no. Joselito moved like a dancer of ballet, no, of flamenco! He was grace incarnate."

"Your English really is marvelous," Sanford said. The train was grinding into the station and people picked up their bags in preparation. He'd never set his own bag down, or loosened his grip on his stick, either. "But despite all this grace, Joselito was killed?"

"Ah, yes. He fought the bull Bailador, not a particularly challenging foe, but Joselito forget the bull was *burriciego* – you would say, hmm, not blind, but with poor vision, yes? So when Joselito raised the red flag and waved it to distract Bailador, Bailador could not see the flag. He was not distracted. He tore poor Joselito open, right there in the arena." The man took off his hat and clutched it to his chest, revealing a thinning, wispy head of hair. "They say that moment was the end of the golden age of bullfighting. But you will still find much to enjoy, I am sure."

"It seems as if there could be some sort of lesson in the story you told me," Sanford said. "But I'm afraid I lack the necessary wisdom to truly comprehend your intention."

The man, or the Moon, shrugged. "It is not a parable. It is just something that happened. There was a man who fought beasts for a long time, and he was clever, smart, and quick – but when you put yourself over and over again in the path of danger, you are certain to fall, eventually."

"Now that *does* sound like a parable. Or perhaps a fable? I get them confused."

"Me too," the Moon said. "As I mentioned, my English is very poor. Our train is here." He put his hat back on, took a step away, and then stumbled. He glanced back at Sanford and his face changed – afraid again – and he rushed onto the train car, shoving others aside in his hurry.

Sanford took his time finding his own compartment, a private one, small but well-appointed. He didn't have access to his former wealth, alas. Tillinghast had successfully forged a will to seize that wealth for himself, but Sanford had smuggled numerous jewels out of Arkham along with some other treasures from his vault, and the proceeds from selling a few sparkling gems afforded him a life of adequate comforts, if not his preferred luxury. He shut the door of the compartment and considered his options.

The Blood Moon was toying with him. They'd seen right through Sanford's pretense of ignorance and mocked him with that story about the human being torn apart by the raging bull. Or was Sanford supposed to be the bull, blindly rushing forward, unable to see red flags? The whole thing was a bit semantically muddled, but it was definitely some sort of insult, warning, or threat.

Sanford put the Claret Knight's glasses to his face and looked out the window. He saw no other red threads on the platform, and thus, no other thralls boarding the train. That was good. He suspected he could handle the man in the homburg, if it came to that. Before going to see the Claret Knight, he'd been prepared for the possibility of walking into a trap and made preparations to defend himself. Those preparations would work equally well against a minion of the Blood Moon.

Still, better always to be safe. He licked his fingertip and drew a symbol on the inner door of his compartment, something to make it stronger, denser, and nearly immovable for any hand but his own. No one would be able to burst in on him unawares now.

No one tried. The train trundled along, making numerous stops along the way, and at every platform Sanford looked through the glasses. He saw a few red threads here and there, but none boarded the train. Hmm. Perhaps he'd been mistaken and the Blood Moon hadn't realized Sanford recognized them inside their thrall. Maybe the Moon just enjoyed being enigmatic and strange for their own sake.

Or maybe the Moon was waiting for him to get to Madrid where it would be easy to capture or kill him, so close to the center of the web with more nodes in the graph of connections, lending the Moon greater power.

Or maybe something else entirely. He didn't know his enemy well enough yet. Normally he would bribe – or threaten, or cause to be seduced – associates of the Moon, trying to find out more about his foe, to probe for vanities, habits, preoccupations, any weak spot he could exploit to his own advantage. But did someone who trafficked in mind control even *have* associates? Sanford thought again of his bookseller colleague in Madrid and the light she might shed on the situation. That was a place to start, anyway, even though he was loath to bring her into it.

Darkness fell. Sanford went to the dining car, wondering if the thrall would be there, but there was no sign of him or his thread for that matter – he must be up ahead, his blood tether stretching the other way through the train, off toward Madrid in the distance.

He sat alone and ate a perfectly adequate meal, admiring the brass lamps, the cloth napkins, the crystal glasses, the porcelain dishes, the silver cutlery, the white coats of the servers. The trains in Europe really were quite nice. He then returned to his compartment and considered closing his eyes, just for a while. He'd done a lot today – he'd climbed an entire tower! His compartment was a sleeper with a little bed as neat as the bunk on a sailing ship, and his door was defended against intrusion.

But allowing himself to rest didn't feel right. Sanford's mind raced as he tried to put himself in the Blood Moon's position. If he knew an assassin was coming for him, what would he do? Why, either set a trap close to home, or dispatch operatives to remove the threat before it drew near.

The answer was simple: Sanford would do both. If the advance operatives failed, then the trap would be there waiting.

So Sanford drifted but mainly stayed awake as the rest of the train slept, and then, deep in the belly of the night, they pulled into a sleepy country station. He would have expected the platform to be nearly empty. They weren't very far from Madrid now, only a few stops away, and unless you needed to arrive there with the dawn, there was no reason to book a ticket on this train.

Yet there were easily twenty people on the platform patiently waiting to board. All of them were young and looked fit – no elderly people, no children, no pregnant women. None of them had any luggage at all. He lifted the opera glasses to his eyes and they turned the night scene into something as bright as daylight. He could see clearly, all shadows banished.

Every person waiting on the platform had threads stretching from the backs of their heads or necks, extending off into the darkness, tangling together into a knotted cable that stretched west toward Madrid.

Sanford watched the thralls as they boarded the train, stroking his chin. Twenty of them, eh? Twenty-one, counting the man with the homburg hat. Could he defeat twenty-one people? Perhaps, since the confines were close here, and they wouldn't be able to bring their advantage in numbers to bear the way they would in an open field. But it would be wearying to fight that many people, and even if Sanford succeeded, when they pulled into the next station there would be screaming, police, and a lot of dead bodies. That would definitely put a crimp in his plans.

There was a good chance the authorities would include thralls of the Blood Moon, too. Certainly, if Sanford had the power to control bodies and minds via blood magic, he would make a point of acquiring blood from as many people with guns and badges as possible. Even Sanford would have a hard time escaping from a situation like that.

He watched as the last of the thralls boarded the train. They'd come for him quickly, he assumed. They'd want to take him while most of the train was asleep.

So, he slid open the window, wishing it was larger, and shoved his valise through the opening. It fell to the ground with a thump. Then he pushed his walking stick through, and it clattered on impact. He began to edge through the window just as the train started to crawl forward.

He swore, planted his feet against the side of his bunk, and shoved himself forward, shooting through the window while scraping his back and stomach and tearing a button off his shirt in the process. He tumbled down and out, hands outstretched, and tried to tuck and roll when he landed, but mostly succeeded in scraping himself on gravel.

He lay sprawled on his back, aching, looking up at the sky,

then turned his head to watch the departing train until it vanished into the night. Sanford got to his feet, bruised and sore, and limped to gather his valise and walking stick. He peered through his opera glasses – they hadn't broken, thank all the gods for fine magical craftsmanship – and took in the view. There was no sign of thralls, no red threads stretched across the station toward Madrid, so he made his way toward the puddle of light.

There was one employee on duty, some combination of night stationmaster and security guard. He spoke slightly less English than Sanford spoke Spanish, but with considerable effort and goodwill on both parts, and the offering of considerable dinero, they determined that Sanford *could* get a taxi to Madrid, since he'd just missed his train. Or, if not precisely a taxi, at least a ride with someone who had a reliable car and bills to pay.

That was how Sanford ended up in the back seat of a 1910 Packard with no springs to speak of and a yawning driver who didn't seem to speak a word of Spanish *or* English, driving along country roads in the general direction of the great city of Madrid, deep in the small hours of the morning.

Sanford settled down in the uncomfortable seat and closed his eyes. *Better luck next time, Bailador,* he thought. *This matador can still dance.*

Then he drifted off to peaceful sleep, or something quite like it.

CHAPTER THIRTEEN
The Fortress on the Hill

While Sanford was on a train, waiting to see what dangers the night would bring, the Warden and Altman were doing some waiting of their own for the meeting with their mysterious letter-writer.

Altman slept through the evening, mostly, though he wasn't sure what his body was doing in the meantime; his partner would only promise to relinquish control to Altman in time for their midnight climb up the hill. He returned to consciousness standing outside the hotel, leaning against the wall, a toothpick in his mouth and shreds of meat in his teeth. Altman didn't want to think about what *kind* of meat, and he flung the toothpick away in disgust while his partner chuckled in his mind.

The Warden emerged from the hotel's front door moments later, dressed in a long camel-colored overcoat. The nights here were rather cooler than the day, but Altman's comfort neither increased nor diminished with the lower temperature. Weather was beginning to be something that happened to other people. At least he still enjoyed how he looked in his overcoat.

"The castle is only a couple miles away," she said. "We may as well walk, so we can speak freely. But the going will be quite steep near the end."

"A long walk into a trap?" Altman grunted. "How wonderful."

The Warden ignored him. The letter they'd received was brief, just a few words scrawled in English: "I know where you can find Carl Sanford. Meet me at Montjuïc Castle at midnight." All they knew for sure was that it wasn't Sanford's handwriting, both acknowledging that he could have faked it. They'd debated about whether to obey the letter or not, but it wasn't as if they had any other leads worth pursuing, and neither relished the idea of spending another day on a treasure hunt for jars of hair and blood.

So they set out walking without a hound to lead them this time – though the beasts were surely lurking, incorporeal, waiting for the Warden's call. There were many people out and about on the streets despite the lateness of the hour. Not at all like sleepy Arkham, where the good citizens were tucked up securely soon after sunset and the bad citizens safely ensconced on the outskirts. Their route gradually took them away from the most bustling areas, moving into narrower, steeper streets, at first lined with homes, and then only with trees. There were hills in the southeast of the city, overlooking the sea, and they were going to climb all the way to the top.

"Go on then," Altman said, wanting a distraction more than experiencing real curiosity. "Tell me about this castle. I know you're dying to."

"If you've seen castles elsewhere in Europe, this one is unlikely to fill you with wonder," she said. "It was built in the 1600s as a simple fort, just sturdy walls with a good view of the sea on one side and the city on the other. It was the site of a battle during the revolt in 1641."

"The locals, yes? Catalans fighting for independence from Spain?"

"So you *have* read a book at some point," the Warden said.

"Sometimes the smarter soldiers would leave books lying around the barracks, and once I realized you couldn't eat them, I asked someone to show me what they were for." His partner and the Warden chuckled almost simultaneously.

The Warden gestured in the air. "The fortress was built up further after the revolt, with the addition of bastions and battlements, and became something like a proper castle. The British took control of the site in the 1700s and laid siege to the city from here. Like a hermit crab crawling into someone else's shell."

"A lot of blood must have been spilled there over the years," Altman said approvingly. This kind of history was at least interesting.

"Historically, the castle gained one hundred and twenty cannons. The French army captured the place during the Napoleonic wars. Those cannons have been turned on Barcelona more than once. You'd have to look up the details for yourself. Military history isn't my main interest."

"And here I thought we finally had something in common."

"Perish the thought," she said. "Late in the last century, the castle was used to imprison and torture anarchists and other enemies of the state. Some consider that the darkest part of its history."

"Really. Are there soldiers garrisoned there now?"

The Warden shrugged. "I'm not sure. But the city is trying to change its reputation, it's safe to say. This whole area is being redeveloped. See?"

They stood at the base of a steep hill, and though no builders were present at such a late hour, the signs of their efforts were everywhere: neat stacks of bricks, heaps of stone, and literal tons of other building materials staged all around. The ground was churned up by all the vehicles that had gone up and down the hillside, hauling materials. "What are they building here?"

"Many things, but the grandest structure will be the Palau Nacional, a museum and cultural center. I've seen the designs – it looks like a palace from a fairy tale. They're also building a grand fountain and a miniature Spanish village, all in preparation for the International Exposition in a few years."

"Just a few years? They're cutting it a bit close. Judging by what I've seen of Spanish workmanship, they should have started building a hundred years ago if they wanted to finish in time."

"I'm glad you amuse yourself." Van Shaw trudged up a pathless section of the hillside away from the work site and into the darkness of the trees. "We should skirt around the construction. We don't want to stumble across any security guards. I don't have many spare clothes, so I'd rather not get blood on these."

Altman followed her. They made their way up across uneven ground and in near total darkness. Neither of which bothered her, or, amazingly, him, either. His steps were sure and his sight was clear, if a bit monochromatic. There were definite advantages to renting out his body. There were disadvantages, too, but why dwell on those? His legs did not ache and his lungs did not burn. He could take pleasure in that.

You're welcome, his partner practically purred.

They finally crested a ridge, and the Warden nodded. "There. The castle."

The first thing Altman saw was the watchtower, thrusting high into the dark sky. He followed the line of that structure down to the high walls that concealed the interior. "Do you think there's someone up there watching us?" He pointed to the spire.

The Warden considered. "It's a telegraph tower now, but it's possible. Woe betide anyone who tries to play sniper with me, though." The Warden had nothing to fear from bullets.

Neither do you, anymore, the partner murmured.

"There's been a watchtower of one sort or another here for a thousand years, watching for trouble from the sea. On the other side of that wall there should be a parade ground, a huge square, with a pedestrian arcade around it. There are also sentry boxes at each corner, see?"

He nodded, but they didn't appear to be manned, and no one had fired on them. "Do you think our mysterious friend is waiting patiently inside?"

"I'm not sure," the Warden said. "Let's get closer and see what we can discover." Two hounds came out of the shadows, briefly twined around her legs, then trotted toward the walls, sniffing as they went. One of them stopped, pawing at the ground and whining. The other hound loped over to join its fellow and the whining became a chorus. They moved forward, heads low, as if following a trail.

"They smell something unnatural," the Warden said.

"What does 'unnatural' mean in this context?" Altman demanded.

Things like me, his partner chimed in. *Only not as interesting as I am, of course.*

The Warden ignored his question and followed the dogs, forcing Altman to hurry to catch up. The dogs wound their way toward the fortress and stepped onto the bridge across the moat. The gates stood open, an invitation surrounded by imposing battlements. "Do they leave the place wide open?"

Altman asked. "They don't mind people wandering in and out?"

"No, there's magic here." The Warden sniffed, and her dogs lifted their noses at the same moment, making Altman think briefly of Cerberus, the three-headed hound that guarded the gates of Hades. "There's a spell on this place to keep mortals away, to make them get lost and walk in circles, and cause them to forget what they were doing and wander off."

"A spell wasted on you because you aren't mortals," a voice called from inside the gates. "I could smell *you* right away. Your Sanford, he's only human, however smart and formidable he might be, but the two of you, you're something else entirely. Or a couple of something elses."

The voice was lightly accented, though Altman wasn't sure if it was Spanish – "European" was the best descriptor he could come up with. He couldn't see the figure, either, even with his preternatural vision. Their new friend might have been hidden behind one of the doors or manipulating his voice.

"You're something else yourself!" the Warden called. "My hounds can tell. Stop wasting our time. What do you know about Sanford?"

"Come inside, downstairs, and we'll talk about it."

The Warden strode onward, and Altman grabbed at her sleeve. "We can't just charge in there. It's certainly some kind of trap."

"Then let's spring it, and deal with whoever set it." She shook him off. "I am the *Warden*, Altman, and you have … your beast. The likes of us don't skulk around in the dark, afraid. We are the things in the dark that make *other people* afraid." Van Shaw snapped her fingers, summoning two more black hounds from the shadows, and all four streamed through the open gates. "If someone intends an ambush, the hounds will show them the true meaning of harm." She cocked her head for a moment, then said, "All clear." They walked in.

The interior of the castle was dominated by an open parade ground, though it looked like renovations were happening here too, with building supplies staged in neat piles. Were they going to turn this into some sort of museum of atrocities for the International Exposition? Altman wondered. Or make it into a monument commemorating the might of the Spanish armed forces, despite all the times it had been seized by enemies? The latter seemed most likely in a nation ruled by a military dictator.

The dogs now arranged themselves in a line and walked slowly toward the seaward side of the fortress, then down a sloping tunnel that descended to a lower level. "We're bound for the dungeons, I think," the Warden said.

"Oh, how cheerful."

The dogs went first, and they followed down a dark path – or a path that would have been dark, if not for their superior vision.

This is very exciting, the partner said. *I love dungeons. The psychic residue is like gravy in the bottom of a bowl, I can just lap it up.*

The dogs began to growl, and that same friendly voice called up from the darkness: "What big hounds you have! Are they friendly?"

"Try to pet one of them and find out," the Warden said. The path terminated in a black iron door, standing halfway open, and she pushed it wide with a scrape and a squeal.

The dungeons were surprisingly small, just a handful of cells on each side, with a walkway between them. The cells were composed of thick, if rusting, crisscrossing iron bars on three sides, while the stone of the fortress provided their back walls. Torches burned on the walls and every surface was liberally scrawled with graffiti in a variety of languages, doubtless left by generations of prisoners. The cell doors all stood open, and a red-haired man sat on a wooden stool in the empty space between them, the dogs arrayed around him and more monstrous than usual, like hunting dogs who'd found prey. The stranger seemed untroubled by their presence, which suggested he was either mentally unstable or a very good actor.

Altman frowned. The clerk had described the messenger as pale, but this man was positively ruddy. In fact, there was something distinctly *off* about him, his face bloated and fleshy in a manner that made Altman think of a blood-filled tick. No, this couldn't be the person who delivered the letter; that must have been some underling.

"Greetings," the stranger said. "My name is Fantasma." He gave a little half-bow from his seated position.

He isn't going to introduce us to his friend? the partner said.

What friend? Altman wondered, looking around the space. There was nowhere for someone to hide. There wouldn't be, in a dungeon.

My apologies. I forget how limited you primates are. Allow me to further adjust your perceptions. Please try not to scream and give the game away.

Why would I scream–? Altman thought, then had to bite down on his tongue to keep from doing just that. He forced himself to stillness, and though he credited his own willpower for succeeding, he could admit that his partner was probably also lending some glandular stability to keep their shared body from trembling.

In the cell to the right of Fantasma, there lurked a monster. From this angle, Altman could only see parts of it through the open door. It shimmered as if viewed through wavy glass, but he had the impression of a fleshy floating orb, tentacles dangling from the underside like catfish whiskers, body studded with oozing eyes and drooling mouths. He shifted his stance for a better look and noted a distressingly human-looking face on top, rather like a mask perched on top of a rotten pumpkin. Its body looked horribly *soft* – fungal, or tumorous. He realized that without the intercession of his partner, Altman never would have noticed the thing at all.

You wouldn't see it, but you'd experience a mysterious discomfort, his partner described. *The hairs on the back of your neck standing on end, a sensation of being watched, all those prey-animal feelings that arise in the presence of a true predator. But direct observation is better, isn't it? I am here to help.*

The Warden didn't appear to notice the monster, and while her hounds were agitated, they weren't paying the occupied cell any particular attention, either. Altman smiled. Finally, he was better than her at something.

"Fantasma," the Warden said. "How do you know Sanford?"

The ruddy man preened. "He hired me to assist him with certain matters while he was in the city. I was something of a local guide for him, introducing him to the finest people."

"I see," Van Shaw said. "Did Sanford tell you to look out for us? Is that why you reached out?"

That was an interesting question, Altman had to admit.

"No, no. I heard you were making inquiries and thought I might be able to assist you." He touched his chest and smiled, radiating modesty. "I have eyes all over the city."

Not as many eyes as your friend has all over his body, I bet, the partner said, and Altman almost tittered. He should have been terrified. He was within three strides of an invisible abomination with enough mouths to eat a rugby team. But he wasn't scared. Why not?

Fear is in the glands, mainly, his partner said. I have adjusted yours. I haven't turned your fear responses off entirely – fear has its uses as a diagnostic tool – but you have a higher threshold for horrors than usual now. Don't thank me. I just don't want to deal with you gibbering and clawing your eyes out and going mad all the time.

I wasn't *going* to thank you. Altman couldn't help but scowl.

"Where is Sanford now?" the Warden demanded.

"You Americans are so forthright," Fantasma said. "Blunt, even. Brusque. Dare I say… rude?"

"Rude? I could have my hounds eat your fingers and toes," the Warden said. "Giving you a chance to answer me first is more than just being polite, it's being generous. Tell us where Sanford went, and we'll be on our way, and even leave you intact by way of payment."

"Why do you want to find him?" Fantasma asked. "You can't expect me to share that information when I don't know your intentions."

"You'll share whatever I–"

Altman put a hand on the Warden's arm. "Let's not make violence our first choice," he said, and she shook his touch off. He gave Fantasma his best smile, which wasn't much, but surely the effort would count for something. "We're old friends of Sanford's," he said. "Associates from back home. He's gotten into a sticky situation and needs our help. He won't mind if you tell us where to find him. Indeed, I daresay he'll reward you. He's more… generous than my associate here."

"Is that so?" Fantasma said, and the metal door behind them slammed shut with a clang. The man rose, mouth widening unnaturally, revealing teeth sharp as spearheads. "Sanford cast a spell of binding on me. That wasn't very *generous*. He forbade me from harming him. Of course, that didn't stop me from informing certain interested parties about his plans, so they can do the harming instead. And it won't stop me from harming *you*, either, to cause Sanford further trouble. I don't like being bound. I am, in fact, very peeved. I'm afraid I'm going to take that out on you."

The huge thing in the cell drifted toward them like a flesh balloon.

"Oh, this is absurd," the Warden said. "We aren't Sanford's friends, this fool was lying to try and ingratiate himself with you. If you hate Sanford, we have common cause. I'd like to beat the man with iron rods until he releases me from an oath I've come to regret."

"Hah. Should I believe what you say now, or what he said before? Decisions, decisions." Fantasma tapped his forefinger on his chin, pivoted on his heel, and observed them each for a moment in turn. "I think I'll–"

Oh, let's just eat them, the partner said.

Altman thought, Agreed.

The beast inside Altman allowed him to retain his awareness of its actions this time.

First, everything around him slowed down: the hounds, with their hackles raised, moved by barely perceptible increments toward Fantasma. The Warden lifted her hands like a maestro about to conduct a symphony. The endless bulging, writhing, and undulation of the thing in the cell became comically exaggerated.

Altman dashed past Fantasma and straight into the occupied cell, but from the perception of these slowed-down people around him, he must have flitted like a hummingbird. He drew his kukri, the curved blade he'd inherited from his late brother, one of the most adept killers Altman had ever known – and he'd known many.

Up close, the monster did not come into any sharper focus, but remained hidden behind a shimmering veil. Altman could smell it now though, like yeast and rancid meat.

Delicious, his partner said. *Cut us off a slice, would you?*

Altman – or, more accurately, Altman and his partner working in perfect synchronicity – swung the knife, slicing at the nearest dangling tentacle. They severed the wrist-thick pseudopod cleanly, but it hung in the air, falling with imperceptible slowness as he danced around the monster. Next, they plunged the knife into a dozen of its varied eyes and lopped off at least as many protruding tongues, then hacked in a general way at its odious body. When they slashed across the thing's central mass, fragments of gray matter sprayed out like a mushroom expelling spores, but they dodged the mess easily.

They must have spent ten minutes of subjective time cutting into the monster, Altman choosing the attacks while his partner consumed the dying creature's essence, or drank its soul, or stole its breath. Altman grew stronger, and time moved even more slowly as he inhaled those foul but life-giving miasmas.

When he grew weary of slashing and stabbing, Altman simply leaned his shoulder against the monster's battered, oozing form and shoved it toward the nearest barred wall of the cell. It was like pushing a well-loaded cart down a dirt track. Altman pressed, thrusting its great soft body against the bars, relentlessly forcing its abused flesh through the metal grate like garlic through a press.

The end result was a messy heap of filth on the stones both

inside and outside the cell, and the complete ruin of Altman's overcoat. He removed the besmirched garment and dropped it on the floor of the cell in disgust. The monster was dead, and in death, that obscuring, shimmering veil vanished, rendering the creature entirely visible – if no longer recognizable as anything but a shambles.

Wasn't that nice! his partner said. *A true collaboration, eh? All right, I'm going to ease you back into a normal tempo. Do try not to fall over, it can be a bit of a jolt.*

Altman stumbled as the ordinary flow of time returned, catching himself on the bars of a cell. Fantasma spun, looked at the mess on the floor, and screamed, "Brother! Akh! No!"

Brother? Hmm. I smell the resemblance, now that he mentions it.

"Your little ambush didn't work." Altman started to come out of the cell, but Fantasma drew a pistol and fired at him, sobbing as he did so. The first two shots went wild, sparking off the iron bars, but the third caught Altman in the shoulder and spun him around, making him fall halfway in and out of the open doorway.

Altman had been shot before, twice in fact, but it wasn't the sort of thing you ever got used to. He whimpered, pushing himself upright with his undamaged arm. He knew, after the initial shock, that a wave of pain would come… but it didn't. His partner must have prevented that, too. Thank you, he thought, and the voice replied, *Think nothing of it, all part of the service.*

Fantasma advanced on him, pistol wavering but pointed down more or less at Altman's head. The surviving brother was close enough now that he couldn't possibly miss his shot. Could the partner save Altman from *this*?

He never had to find out. The Warden hadn't moved from her

position, but she didn't need to: her hounds leaped at the man, or whatever he was, one clamping its jaws around the forearm that held the gun and pulling it down, the others attacking his legs and pulling Fantasma to the ground just outside the cell.

The Warden stepped closer, plucked the gun from the floor, emptied the chambers, then tossed the pistol onto the stinking pile of Fantasma's dead brother.

The hounds held Fantasma down on the floor, one stationed at each ankle and wrist, teeth gripping him tightly. He was spread-eagled and helpless, but he kept shouting the name "Akh!" over and over, as if the mess on the floor could ever answer him.

"Let me look at your shoulder," the Warden said, crouching before him, but Altman shook his head.

"I think the bullet is coming out… yes." He could feel the slug moving inside him, shifted along by minute contractions in his flesh. His partner could control Altman's body completely, it seemed, to the most precise degree.

The deformed bullet fell out of the hole in his shoulder and bounced on the stone floor. His flesh itched abominably as it knitted itself up, but in a moment, there was no sign of any wound. When Altman experimentally shifted his arm, he felt not even the slightest pang.

"I suppose drinking the essence out of that abomination gave you plenty of energy for healing," the Warden said. "I'm glad the monstrosity was good for something."

"You killed Akh," Fantasma screamed. "You killed my brother. I will peel your flesh and violate your–"

The Warden snarled and leaped on top of Fantasma, landing on his chest with her knees and driving the wind out of him. "Knife," she said, extending her hand.

Altman passed her his stained and dripping kukri. The Warden pressed the blade to Fantasma's throat. "Where is Carl Sanford?" the Warden hissed at Fantasma as she smeared the remnants of his dead brother onto his skin with the kukri. "Speak, creature, or you have no value to me, and I'll end your life now."

"He went to Madrid," Fantasma spat at her. He struggled, but the dogs holding his limbs in their jaws growled until he subsided. "But you won't be able to help him. He's drawn the attention of the Blood Moon. *No one* can win against the Blood Moon."

"We don't want to help Sanford." Altman squatted on his heels beside the pinned man. "That was the truth. But we can't let someone else kill him, not before we settle a few things first. Who is this Moon person?"

"Person?" Fantasma scoffed. "I don't even know if they *are* a person. No one has ever seen the Blood Moon. At least no one I've heard of. I only speak to their messengers, their proxies… their puppets. People say they live somewhere in Madrid, but their territory covers the entire Iberian Peninsula, with tendrils extending far beyond that. They are the spider at the center of a web of power, money, and influence. The Blood Moon whispers in the ear of Primo de Rivera, and the Sanjuanada only failed because of the Blood Moon's informants hidden in the ranks of the plotters and the court of the king."

"I don't know what any of that means," Altman said.

The Warden sighed. "Primo de Rivera rules Mexico, Altman. He took over as military dictator in a coup a few years ago, with the tacit support of the king of Spain, who doesn't wield much in the way of real power these days. The Sanjuanada was a recent attempted counter-coup against Primo de Rivera by other members of the military. Around and around it goes." She poked Fantasma in the cheek with the point of the knife. "So this Blood Moon meddles in politics? What do they want with Sanford?"

"Sanford met with members of the Red Coterie, who hired him to kill the Blood Moon," Fantasma said.

Altman sighed in irritation. The red what? All these cults had ridiculous names. That wasn't the most baffling part of the statement, though. "*Hired* him? Has Sanford really fallen on such hard times, that he'd work for someone?"

"It's a fool's errand anyway. Sanford can't win. He annoyed the Coterie by trying to join them, so they sent him to his death instead, promising him a place if he can do what no one can."

"Ah, so he's looking for allies," Altman murmured. He didn't know what the Red Coterie was, but if Sanford wanted to join them, they were probably a dangerous bunch.

"Sanford might surprise you," the Warden said. "Or, well. He might surprise the Red Coterie. You won't be around to be surprised at that point." She glanced up at Altman, or perhaps at the thing inside him. "Did you want to eat this one too?"

"Don't mind if I do," the partner said through Altman's mouth, and reached out.

Fantasma screamed, thrashed, cursed, and promised vengeance.

But not for very long.

CHAPTER FOURTEEN
Let There Be Lightning

Morning came, and Carl Sanford arrived in Madrid, waking when the driver reached back and gave his knee a shove. "Thank you, my good man," he murmured, straightening up and looking out the window.

His first sight of Madrid wasn't particularly inspiring. His driver had clearly brought him to the outskirts, a region of warehouses and waste ground, but Sanford was cheerful enough anyway. He was rested, now, his aches and pains vanquished, and he didn't mind the idea of walking for a bit. He clambered out of the car with his valise and his stick, bid the driver good day, and set off toward the taller buildings looming ahead on the skyline.

At first, he walked along cracked streets, but gradually the quality of the pavements improved, and the warehouses gave way to apartment buildings, many with balconies overspilling with potted plants in Mediterranean fecundity. He had no particular destination in mind, but reasoned he would find both food and lodging closer to the center of the city. He would let whim and happenstance guide him; if even Sanford didn't know where he was going, his enemies wouldn't be able to anticipate his movements, either. The city woke up around him as dawn slid into early morning, and people spilled out of their buildings and began to maneuver through the streets.

Madrid was qualitatively different from Barcelona, perhaps because it was the capital, perhaps for other reasons of history or civic character. Sanford sensed a greater degree of industry and bustle. The buildings were grander, especially as he approached the city center. Overall, Barcelona had the sleepier aspect of a seaside town, but Madrid was the center of business, of art, of everything. It seemed a colder city in some ways; if not precisely unwelcoming to a visitor like himself, then at least too busy to pay him very much attention.

Madrid differed from Barcelona in another way that impacted him more directly: there were thralls of the Blood Moon everywhere. He occasionally ducked into the shadow of a column or the recessed doorway of an apartment building to survey the crowds through his opera glasses. There were red threads everywhere. Oh, it wasn't as if every citizen was in thrall to the Blood Moon, but perhaps one in twenty were. And with a population that surely numbered in the hundreds of thousands, that added up to a lot of thralls.

He suppressed a shudder. Even at its height, the Order hadn't boasted so many members, and his underlings could be a fractious and quarrelsome lot. To have that many followers, all obedient and unquestioning… someone with vision could do amazing things. Or horrible things. Or both. To go up against that army, essentially alone, was a daunting idea even for Sanford.

Sanford told himself the Moon couldn't be controlling, or even passively observing, all those thralls at any given moment; even a powerful sorcerer didn't possess infinite attention. Most of the people trailing red threads were going about their ordinary business, waiting to be activated. Even so, it was still best to avoid them. The man on the platform in Barcelona was proof enough that the thralls were actively looking for him.

He sighed. That meant he should change his appearance, didn't it? How it grieved him to meddle with perfection!

Sanford walked until he stumbled into a few blocks blissfully free of red threads, then checked side streets until he located a suitable gentleman's clothing shop and stepped inside. The elderly salesman spoke English, and when Sanford explained that he'd taken a fall and ruined his suit, the old man clucked his tongue in sympathy. "We can have something new tailored for you in a few days, sir."

"I'm afraid I'm traveling light and have nothing suitable to wear in the meantime," Sanford said. "Might you have something I could wear out of the shop today? Something casual would be fine."

And so, after a bit of tutting, rummaging and negotiating, Sanford departed without his torn suit, dressed far less formally than he preferred in a linen shirt with no vest or jacket and loose-fitting trousers. He wore a white fedora, too, the sort of affectation that he would have sneered at, but it would do well to conceal his regrettably handsome and memorable face.

More walking brought him to a fine hotel with a liveried doorman outside… but he sighed, and stepped into a newsagent's instead, and inquired about more "affordable lodgings." Which was how he found himself on a narrow side street some blocks away, standing before the scratched door of a traveler's hotel of the sort frequented by students and artists. The stringy-haired malcontent at the desk inside seemed bemused by his presence but made no comment. Sanford paid a premium for a single room – he could not relinquish *all* his dignity – though the bathroom was shared with other residents on the same hall, a situation frankly too hideous to contemplate for long.

Sanford stowed his valise and walking stick under the narrow bed in the shabby room, then took his toiletries bag to the bathroom, a dingy affair that would have been more at home in a train station than a place where people lived. Fortunately, at midmorning, the bathroom was deserted and he was able to shave in peace.

Oh, his beautiful beard! He'd cultivated it for ages and hadn't seen the bare skin below his nose in many years. Being clean-shaven was admittedly more fashionable nowadays. The soldiers in the Great War had been encouraged to shave every day so their gas masks fit more securely, and many of them had kept up the habit after hostilities ceased. Sanford ran his fingers across his smooth chin and gazed at himself in the spotted mirror. He looked younger, vulnerable, less dignified, and honestly a little *soft* without his beard. He no longer resembled himself, at least at a casual glance. The change in his appearance might not fool any particularly sharp-eyed minions of the Blood Moon, but it should buy him a little time at least.

After washing up, he found a stairway that led to the roof. The door to the outside was locked, but Sanford hadn't been troubled by ordinary locks in a very long time; one of the various rings he wore had a charm inscribed on its inner surface that made such barriers spring open at his touch.

Sanford walked across the dirty, tarred roof to the edge and took in the view of his surroundings. This wasn't the tallest building in Madrid, not even close, and the vista hardly rivaled the one he'd seen from the St Barnabas tower in Barcelona, but it was sufficiently elevated to give him a sense of the neighborhood, at least.

Sanford put the opera glasses to his eyes, slowly walked around the perimeter of the roof, and tried to count the thralls below.

There were so many of those pulsing red threads visible from up here. The scarlet cables emerged from the walls of buildings, connected to people inside. They extended from the heads of people walking on the streets and emerged from the roofs of passing cars. A few even rose up out of the street – were there sewer workers down there, or underground tunnels, or just basements?

All the red threads led off in the same direction, back to their source, presumably the Blood Moon, gradually converging into a single tangled rope that stretched off to the south.

The Claret Knight said tracing the Moon to their lair by following the threads was impossible, but Sanford wasn't in the habit of taking someone else's word for anything. He returned to his room and gathered a few useful trinkets – leaving his walking stick with reluctance because it was one of his more identifying accoutrements – and then set out to see the problem for himself.

He kept to the side streets, where logic dictated there would be fewer minions of the Moon, keeping his hat low and his pace casual. He occasionally glanced through his glasses, making sure he was still following the threads streaming through the sky. When he neared large intersections, he risked a peek through the glasses, and inevitably noted thralls posted like sentries. They were doing the bare minimum to blend in with the crowd – leaning against walls, sitting on steps, lounging by fountains. All of them watched the passing crowds, their eyes constantly scanning. The Blood Moon knew he'd escaped the train. They surmised he was here. They were on the hunt, but they didn't need to stalk the streets for their prey. They could act as ambush predators, waiting for their prey to pass them.

With Sanford's altered appearance, some of them might miss his presence, but could he be lucky hundreds of times? When necessity required passing near any of the watchers, he would hover in the shadows and wait for a group of people to walk by, and then insert himself near the back of the crowd. If they were looking for a lone man, he would do his best to avoid being one. Perhaps he should hire a companion...

He soon realized he'd put himself in danger for nothing. The Claret Knight was right. His search for the lair was futile, at least while following these clues. Perhaps a mile from his hostel, the threads changed their behavior. Instead of streaming off in a single direction like a guideline, they abruptly rose high into the sky. Sanford stood by the trash cans behind a restaurant and stared upward.

The threads flowing from all directions in the city converged above him in a great messy tangle, knotted together and looped back on themselves, forming a cloud that resembled looping lines of red ink scrawled all over a piece of paper, or a nest of snakes. The writhing cloud was vast, extending for miles, like a permanent bloody thunderhead. Some obfuscating magic to stop people from doing exactly what Sanford was trying to do. The Blood Moon's lair was probably somewhere under that cloud, but where?

Sanford walked until he reached the Prado, wishing he had time to explore the museum. He'd never been to Madrid before and considered himself a connoisseur of fine art. Ah, well. Once he defeated the Blood Moon he could explore the city to his heart's content, couldn't he? The territory would be his. He didn't particularly want to be the secret ruler of Spain, but, well, it was a good start and the first step to gaining the necessary power to get back home. For all the cosmopolitan pleasures of the Continent, the home of his (admittedly thorny) heart was New England, specifically Massachusetts, more specifically the city of Arkham, a place he'd helped shape and nurture and a place that, by all accounts, had suffered grievously in his absence and needed to be saved. He missed the grand buildings, the haunted and stony riverbanks.

There was a sprawling park near the Prado, rich with ornamental lawns and ornate gazebos, trimmed hedges and placid ponds, and Sanford found a secluded bench where he could sit and contemplate his situation. After determining that he remained unobserved, he looked up and through the opera glasses. The cloud was thickest here, so dense in the center that individual threads could no longer be discerned, seen as a great red stain upon the heavens. To his unaided eyes, the sky was blue and clear, but seen through the glasses, the red cloud blotted out the sun, casting the entire park – indeed, the entire center and oldest parts of Madrid – under a deep shadow.

Sanford shivered, taken by a chill that wasn't entirely physical. No central conduit descended from that cloud conveniently pointing to a lair. The ultimate connection to the Moon was hidden, just as the Claret Knight had promised. Blood magicians were often a sneaky sort. For good reason, too. People got upset when you used their bodily fluids against them.

Ah, yes, that reminded him. Sanford reached for the vial of the hotel clerk's blood around his neck, plucked it free, and dropped it on the ground, crushing the delicate glass beneath the heel of his shoe. Once he did that, his etheric signature was no longer hidden, and the decoys he'd hidden in Barcelona would be fading in efficacy by the moment.

The Warden and Altman should be able to track him now. He was almost ready for them.

First, though, he needed to ascertain the precise whereabouts of the Blood Moon. Madrid's territory representative was surely somewhere in the city, probably in the shadow of that cloud, but there were a million hiding places not even taking into account the possibility of folded space.

What were his options? Normally, if he wanted to track down a rival sorcerer, he'd seek out an employee or associate of his target and force them to reveal the location. But the Moon's employees and associates were often unaware they were associated with the Moon at all. None were likely to know his true location, anyway.

Hmm. But Sanford had run a large network not so long ago, and though his Order had plenty of ignorant Initiates suitable for fetching and carrying, he'd also had a few trusted – or, at least, *relatively* trusted – lieutenants to perform more complex tasks. Surely the Moon couldn't handle everything on his own? He must have at least a few people capable of independent thought and action, who could improvise and respond to threats in real time without waiting for instructions from central command. If Sanford could track down such a lieutenant, he might get useful answers. But how could he find them, assuming they even existed?

Perhaps the time had come to seek out local advice after all. Sanford knew the address of his bookseller friend's shop. They'd met in person twice over the years, once at a public book fair in New York and once at a secret auction in the catacombs in Paris, and they'd corresponded frequently. She would be, if not delighted to see him, at least not hostile. More importantly, she was a curious person, so she'd be *interested*. For the time being, he moved about the city undetected. If he proceeded carefully, he might be able to get useful information from her without putting her in the path of the Moon's wrath.

And it would give him the opportunity to check that she wasn't a thrall as well.

He glanced around, noting a few red threads rising from the heads of thralls in the park, but not many and none close by. He risked walking to a corner and hailing a taxi. The cab slid up to the curb, and though the driver spoke no English, he understood the address Sanford gave well enough. His destination wasn't far away, if he was remembering the geography of the city well enough, but it was safer to travel obscured in a car.

They drove around the glamorous edifice of the nearby royal palace of Madrid. Was the king in there, Sanford wondered, or was he off somewhere kissing the boots of the general who ran his country now? The cab stopped behind two other cars at an intersection near the palace to wait for a crowd of pedestrians to cross, and then the driver shouted out the open window and waved his arms. Sanford turned his head away from the glittering windows of the palace to find the source of the commotion, and his heart sank straight down into his belly.

The pedestrians on the intersection weren't crossing.

Most of them were blocking the way despite the shouts of the drivers. Two dozen other people stepped into the street, streaming around the cars on both sides. Sanford fumbled for his opera glasses and looked through them, already knowing what he'd see.

Every pedestrian obstructing the road had a red thread rising from their head or neck and vanishing into the clot of bloodied filaments overhead.

Some unusually observant thrall must have seen him on the street, watched him get into the cab, and mobilized the others. If those people were all connected, then it made sense that they could share information quickly, perhaps even instantaneously, with this many nodes so close together. Was the Blood Moon directly controlling all these people? Or were they simply following their orders? If so, what were those orders? To stop Sanford, to capture him, or to kill him?

None of those were desirable outcomes. He needed to lose them. Sanford scrambled out of the car. The driver shouted at him, cursing him for not paying his fare. Sanford fled across the lanes of traffic before the thralls could reach him. He needed to break their line of sight.

Madrid was home to innumerable narrow streets, alleys and plazas, offering ample hiding places, but the Moon's minions were everywhere. With every glance Sanford stole through the glasses, he saw the threads emerging from walls, drifting down from the sky, thickening, converging as every thrall in the vicinity joined the search. He cursed himself for not putting the lenses into a pair of spectacles after all, so he could see his pursuers without fumbling the glasses up to his face again and again.

Sanford fled, dipping down alleyways, watching for threads,

taking turns that led him away from the thralls, looking for a bolt-hole and then walked into a dead end. He'd run into another of the city's plazas, but this one was a cul-de-sac and the only way out was behind him. There weren't even any doors he could slip through: the plaza was surrounded by the backs of three-story buildings with just a few high windows, not easily accessible. Could they have deliberately driven him here by closing off his other avenues of escape? Were they adept pack hunters as well as ambush predators?

He turned to consider his chances of racing back down the way he'd arrived, but thralls began to stream into the path. They were a perfect cross section of the people of Madrid: students, old men, laborers, soldiers, police, businessmen, flower-sellers, even a few tourists who must have been pricked by the Blood Moon in anticipation of spreading his taint to other countries.

Well, there were a lot of them, perhaps thirty, but they were physically only human, and *he* was Carl Sanford. He didn't have a way to make himself invisible just now, having used the last of his reagents during his meeting with the Claret Knight, or he could have vanished and strolled right past them. Stealth wasn't an option, but there were other ways to escape from mortals.

Sanford pulled on his special gloves and began to scale the nearest wall. He'd clamber up to the roof, scout the clearest route, and flee to freedom.

A hand grabbed his ankle and he froze. He was ten feet up the wall – how could they possibly have reached him? Did the Blood Moon employ giants, or cat burglars?

He looked down, trying to shake his leg loose, and gasped. The Moon's horde crowded against the base of the wall in a single mass. The smallest and nimblest of the people were climbing the others, standing atop the shoulders of their fellows to form a human pyramid, reaching for him. Such was the power of a single mind directing the actions of thirty bodies: they could act as one and be a greater whole than the sum of their parts.

He kicked the grasping hand away and kept climbing but feared he wouldn't be fast enough to escape. When he looked down next, he saw a limber young man scrambling up his fellows with a knife clenched in his teeth.

Of course! They wanted his blood! If the Moon acquired a sample of his blood and took it back to his lair, there would be no need to mobilize the hordes to capture Sanford's body.

The Blood Moon would control Sanford's *mind*.

He couldn't permit that. These people were innocents, but they were also his doom. This wasn't his fault; it was the Moon's fault for putting them in his path. "I am giving you one chance!" he shouted. "Send your people away, Blood Moon, or they will die!"

The horde below spoke all at once, together, in a single voice, like a horrible chorus: "I have more people. More and more. There is no escape."

Ah, well. He'd made the effort. Sanford tore off his right glove with his teeth, clinging to the wall with his left hand, uncomfortably flashing back to that moment of terrible precarity on the tower: *Killed, broken, splashes.*

He wouldn't be the one broken today. He'd brought along several enchanted rings once stored in his vault, some of the last of his accumulated magic, and he was loath to use any of them now, especially against people dragged into this conflict against their will, but he had no choice.

The ring on his right index finger was thick and black, patterned with what looked like silver tree roots or branches, but the image was actually that of a Lichtenberg figure. The German physicist Georg Christoph Lichtenberg had discovered those patterns could be etched onto surfaces by electrical discharge, and indeed, some people who were struck by lightning were marked by a "fern tattoo" in the same design, permanently imprinted onto their skin.

Sanford reached down and pressed the tip of his index finger into the forehead of the uppermost figure of the human pyramid just as the poor fellow reached up with his knife. Sanford turned his head away, snapped his eyes shut, and murmured, "*Fiat fulgur.*"

Let there be lightning.

Sanford's ring contained the compressed fury of a thunderstorm, and even through his closed eyelids, everything lit up with white brilliance the moment he spoke.

The people below him screamed in a unified voice. When he looked down, all thirty or so of them were lying in a heap, unmoving, their clothes smoking. I've never killed more people at once than I could count at a glance, Sanford thought. The electricity had arced through the thrall Sanford touched and then flowed into the others, their bodies pressed so closely together that the lances of energy found ample targets. Sanford's finger tingled, and when he clenched his hand into a fist, the ring crumbled into black dust, its power spent.

After a glance detected no approaching red threads, only those of the dead slowly drooping and disappearing, Sanford descended the wall, angling away so that he could touch down apart from the heap. Killing them was bad enough, but stepping on them would be tantamount to rudeness.

Sanford needed to go, but he stood for a moment first and looked down at the massed dead. "It didn't have to happen this way, you know."

Someone in the pile groaned and Sanford moved toward them. They must have been far enough from the initial contact to survive, but he doubted they'd live much longer. The survivor looked like a young woman with long brown hair pulled back in a jaunty yellow band. She crawled a little way away from the pile and rolled over onto her back, then stared up at Sanford. There were Lichtenberg figures climbing up her neck and onto her cheeks.

"You can't escape," the Blood Moon said with her mouth. "Do you think this diminishes me? These people are like fingernail clippings. They are insignificant. My body is vast."

The magus crouched. This next move might be unwise, but it might also unsettle his enemy, and an unsettled enemy was a careless one. "There *are* an awful lot of you, La Luna. But do you know what's interesting?" Sanford smiled. "I can *see* you. It may surprise you to hear you've made a lot of enemies, and some of them offered me the gift of true sight. I can see the filthy tethers that connect you to your thralls. Oh, how interesting, they dissolve away when your hosts die." He couldn't see the tethers now, he didn't want to reveal that he needed the opera glasses to do so.

The woman's eyes went wide and then narrowed.

"There are a lot of your thralls in Madrid," Sanford continued, "but as you can see, I'm not averse to killing them. Your bodies are not infinite. You've heard of me, clearly. You looked me up. Surely you must know I've killed more men in my lifetime than the Spanish Flu."

Well, hardly. He had some blood on his hands, but he

preferred subjugating to killing whenever possible. Still, what was the point of having a fearsome reputation if you didn't *use* it? "Keep sending your minions against me and I'll keep right on killing them."

"You will be mine!" a voice cried behind him, and Sanford spun just in time to see the smoking, staggering figure of a policeman lunging toward him with a knife. Sanford stumbled back as the dying woman on the ground cackled with her last breath. But he couldn't avoid the knife, which sank into the side of his belly, before being yanked out again – not a killing blow, just a wounding one. The point was not to kill him, but to *control him*.

Sanford reached for the man's throat and squeezed. In his panic and agony, he wasted the power of one of his other rings, yellow gold etched with the image of a sunburst.

The policeman's head burst open like a watermelon stuffed with dynamite, and the body fell.

Groaning, Sanford stumbled away, then knelt when his knees went weak. The knife, the knife! He couldn't leave it here for another thrall to retrieve!

He found the weapon on the stones and dropped it in his pocket, then cursed. Blood dripped all over the courtyard. Hissing, he sliced off a good chunk of his new shirt, and made a hurried bandage to press against the wound.

Then he wasted another ring setting the bodies in the courtyard on fire, so they'd burn up along with any drops of his blood he'd left behind on the pavement.

He staggered away from the inferno, fumbling the opera glasses to his face with one hand, escaping the cul-de-sac. He saw no nearby threads, just distant ones rising from beyond the buildings, but they were heading his way. Sanford lurched along, keeping to the shadows and alleyways, hoping the pad pressed against his body wouldn't drip, or if it did, that none of the Moon's minions would notice and collect his precious scarlet leavings.

Sanford gritted his teeth and trudged on until he reached his destination a few blocks away. He'd approached through an alley, to the back entrance, but the address was right. He hesitated – this was most *definitely* bringing trouble to an old friend's doorstep, and he didn't have old friends to spare. But what alternative did he have?

Sanford pounded on the rear door, then leaned against the wall, one hand pressed to his belly, his strength ebbing away and darkness gnawing at the edges of his vision. What if she wasn't here, but out running an errand, or worse, off in London or Paris on a collecting expedition? What if she was here, but was already in thrall to the Moon? What if–

The door opened. Sanford staggered back in alarm, sitting down hard on the pavement, releasing a hiss of pain.

A familiar, but astonished, woman's face gazed down at him from the open doorway. "Carl Sanford?" she said.

"Anna Elizabeth Waite," he answered, and then consciousness fled.

CHAPTER FIFTEEN
The Desolation of Desire

Before they set off on their long trek down the hill and back to their hotel, Altman and the Warden climbed up to the top of the fortress and stood at the battlements. She gazed, rapt, at the view of the vast dark ocean, doubtless thinking of all the unvisited countries beyond, feeling the pinch of her essential captivity, aching for freedom.

Altman wasn't aching for anything. "I feel like I could eat the world," he said, positively thrumming with power. He wanted a brandy and a cigar.

"That may well be the goal of the thing inside you," the Warden said. "Such beings never make a bargain unless they get ten times more than they give."

"It is heartbreaking to witness such cynicism in someone so young," the partner said aloud.

"I am not that young," Van Shaw said.

"Oh, well, but consider your age from my perspective." The partner receded, but having his voice stolen yet again put a damper on Altman's good mood. He was a monster slayer, yes, but he'd been forced to become a monster to do it.

Altman cleared his throat, spat over the side of the battlement, and said, "So Sanford is in Madrid. He could have been in Madrid when we changed trains there!" Something occurred to him and he turned to the Warden, frowning. "Why didn't you check the compass when we stopped there?"

"I did," she said, as patiently as if talking to one of her hounds. "I checked the compass constantly. The needle never wavered away from Barcelona. Sanford didn't just scatter decoys of his etheric signature all over this city. He disguised his own signature, too."

"How did he do such a thing? I didn't even know that was possible!"

The Warden sighed. "In such matters, the limits of the possible tend to fluctuate. Sanford knows more about the art of magic than I do. More than most people do."

"If he is in hiding, then how will we find him?"

She shrugged. "There are ways to find people without recourse to blood magic, Altman. We can make inquiries when we get to Madrid. We will take the ma– Sanford's photo to clerks at the better hotels. We still have funds and might be able to cultivate local contacts, or even hire detectives to search for us."

Altman didn't like the idea of involving others in the search. It felt like admitting weakness. "If this Blood Moon gets to Sanford before we do… if he dies… what will happen to us?"

"If Sanford dies without showing me how to release the spells that bind me, my fate remains tied to that of the Order, which means my fate is tied to yours, which means I am doomed."

Altman's hackles rose. "Don't say that. Even if you remain tied to me, I will make the Order great again. You *will* reap the benefits. I will take Sanford's head, treasures, and his endorsement – I suppose not in that order. I have the power now, thanks to my… partner. Power to impose my will on those schismatic heretics back home."

"Since your partner's strategy is limited to 'eat absolutely everyone,' I'm not sure how much help it will be in managing a disorganized organization. Sanford ran the Order of the Silver Twilight through a combination of fear, bribery, manipulation, promises, and trading favors. You don't have much to offer except the fear part."

Organizing is not my strength, his partner admitted. *Conquest, yes. Tearing things down, absolutely, but building something up? A bit outside my skillset, old chap.*

Dissent and argument from all sides! Altman seethed and then deliberately forced himself to be calm. If he was going to run the Order, he did need skills other than anger and knifework. "Warden. Van Shaw." He paused. "Sarah." She looked at him, eyes narrowed, and he held up his hands, placating. "We have had our differences. But we are united in our goal, yes? To find Sanford and bend him to our will? We both bring resources to this effort. Even weakened as you are, your magics are still incredibly formidable, your wits are sharp, and your will is iron. I like to think my skill at soldiering complements my… newfound gifts of violence, too. We are in this together. I apologize if I've taken you for granted. I value your contribution. I hope you come to value mine."

Her expression didn't exactly soften, but at least it didn't get harder. "Apology… accepted," she said. That was clearly as much sentiment as Van Shaw could indulge in, because she turned away and stared implacably at the sea again. "How do we proceed in our shared mission, then?"

"If we just turn up in Madrid and cast around like we did here in Barcelona, I don't have much hope." Altman leaned on the battlement and scowled at the indifferent ocean. "There must be some way to track Sanford down, some thread we can pull. You know the man. Can you think of anything?"

"Hmm," the Warden said. "Madrid. Yes. You know, there was a book dealer in Madrid Sanford often corresponded with. He mentioned her to me, because she always had interesting travelogues and would often throw one in for free when he bought something valuable from her, and then he would pass the volumes on to me. That small kindness made me fond of her, as fond as you can be of someone you've never met or spoken to, anyway."

"Do you think Sanford might look up an old friend while he's on a mission to assassinate someone?" Altman asked.

"Does that seem so strange to you?" Van Shaw asked. "Sanford is a sociable man. Well, he enjoys having an audience and someone to listen to his various witticisms and bon mots, anyway. I should think you'd know that; you were his chauffeur, once. He must have bent your ear often enough."

"I was his bodyguard and drove him as part of those duties," Altman said, trying to maintain his newfound calm. "I wasn't a *chauffeur*."

"That's a shame. You'd look much more fetching in a little cap."

He stared at her. "Was that a joke?" Maybe she *had* softened toward him.

"Evidently not, if you needed clarification. I am not as humorless as people think, Altman. I just don't find many things funny."

"You find me funny, though?"

"I find you to be a great many things." She tapped a fingertip against her lips in thought. "I don't know if Sanford would contact the bookseller or not. But I remember the name of her shop, and it's a place to start, which we otherwise lack. We'll take the first train to Madrid in the morning."

Altman woke up on another train and groaned. "I grow weary of this."

"Weary of what?" The Warden was reading another newspaper, this one in Spanish.

"These gaps in my memory!" he said. "The last thing I remember, we were walking back from the fortress, and now, what, we're on a train heading west to Madrid?"

"Madrid?" The Warden was incredulous. "We've *been* to Madrid! We found Sanford, we bent him to our will, and his severed head is stowed in your luggage! That was all weeks ago!"

Altman gripped the armrests of his seat on the train and whimpered. *So much time–*

Then his partner chuckled in his mind and he noticed Van Shaw's smirk. He bared his teeth at her. "You're toying with me! Making a mockery of my… my condition!"

"I told you I have a sense of humor. Ha. Your 'condition,' you say. Like it's something that *befell* you, instead of something you performed a complex ritual to deliberately achieve. Calm down, Altman. You didn't lose much time. We've only been on the train to Madrid for an hour."

"I just want to know what happens when I'm… away. What did I do? Or rather, what did *it* do with my body?"

She looked back at her newspaper. "I couldn't tell you. We got back to the hotel, and you immediately went out again and didn't return to our room until just before dawn. And what a return – you climbed up the wall of the hotel like a spider and came in through the window."

"This is intolerable," Altman said.

It is important for you to rest, his partner said. *Your mind can't cope with my presence, not constantly. I am preserving your sanity.*

So you say! How can I believe you?

I don't suppose you can, his partner said cheerfully. *But in a gesture of goodwill, I can give you access to the memories of how I spent my time…*

Altman winced as his head filled with overlapping visions of blood splashing on stone, dizzying views of Barcelona as he leaped from rooftop to rooftop, and his own voice laughing as he drowned someone in a fountain. "Enough!" he shouted, and the Warden cocked her head. But the visions faded.

Just let me know if you'd like to see more.

"Why did you go out hunting?" Altman whispered. "After Fantasma and his horrible brother Akh, we were so *full*. We had so much energy. Why did you hunt more and kill those people?"

His partner answered, and Altman shivered.

"Well, don't leave me in suspense," the Warden said. "You asked the question aloud, so you may as well share the answer aloud, too."

"It said…" Altman swallowed. "It said I misunderstand. It doesn't hunt to gain strength. It gains strength so it can hunt better. The hunting is the… whole point of the exercise."

"Demons." The Warden clucked her tongue. "They're simple creatures. Not unlike you, Altman. You've never once told me about your grand vision for the restored Order of the Silver Twilight. You don't want power so you can *do* anything. You just want power to have it."

"The point is, once I have it, I can do *anything*," he said.

"Hmm. Do let me know when you figure out what 'doing anything' actually entails."

"Well, what do *you* want freedom for?" Altman said. "You want to break your oaths and sever your connection to the Order, but why?"

"So I can see all the places I've only read about," she answered promptly. "And go as long as a week, perhaps, without seeing someone's blood and brains dashed out all over the ground. *That's* my dream."

That sounds dreadfully dull, Altman's partner said.

They passed the next hours in mutual silence, the Warden reading while Altman gazed out the window at the passing scenery. The landscape held no wonders for him: golden Mediterranean hills, copses of trees, blue skies, occasional villages, all tedious, just empty space he had to traverse to reach his target.

About halfway to Madrid, the train slowed to a halt, pulling into a small station. They sat there for a long time and finally a conductor rapped on the door of their compartment, wrenched it open, and stuck his head inside. He rattled off rapid Spanish, translated by the thing in Altman's head. There was a problem with the train, a maintenance issue, so they'd be stopping here for another couple of hours. If they wished to disembark to stretch their legs or get something to eat, they were welcome.

I could eat, the thing in Altman said.

"I am fine here," the Warden said, eyeing him as he stood up. "Don't do anything that will get you arrested, please. We have work to do." She went back to her newspaper.

Altman joined the small crowd of people departing the train, stepping down onto the platform of a small station made of weathered wood. This little town had a name, probably, but Altman didn't know it and didn't endeavor to find out. There were stalls around the station, selling sweet sausages and thin slices of ham and bread, but none of those appealed to him. Which was strange as he'd always enjoyed a good meal, but now he simply had no desire for food at all. No longer needing sustenance was one thing, but surely he could still enjoy the taste?

Mortal food is a distraction, his partner assured him. *We hunger for other things now. I don't want you to get confused about the nature of your appetites.*

A beautiful young woman, dark-eyed and dark-haired, walked past him in a clinging blue dress, spinning a parasol, and gave him a distinctly meaningful look. Altman did a brief threat assessment, saw nothing about her to worry him, and turned away, walking across the platform toward the station proper to see if there was a tobacconist inside… but he didn't actually want to smoke, either, did he? He'd reached for cigarettes once or twice on this trip, but reflexively, not from any real desire. Even that brief wish for a cigar and brandy the night before had been a habitual response to the aftermath of a good meal, not an impulse born from a true craving, and he'd done nothing to gratify it.

And wait, that beautiful woman had given him a flirtatious look, hadn't she? Why hadn't he at least smiled back at her? Why hadn't he at least *desired* her?

Altman veered off course and sat down on a wooden bench, then leaned forward, clutching his head in his hands. All my appetites? he thought. You've suppressed all my appetites?

Not at all! You still want vengeance, violence, and power. But sex, alcohol, food… why waste your time and energy on those when your efforts can be more meaningfully directed elsewhere?

But these passions are part of who I am, Altman protested.

You say that, but they're mostly glands, just like fear. Though I suppose glands are a large part of you. I've freed you from those silly concerns though, Altman. You're a new man. A focused man. A man destined for greatness.

But without appetites, what did he even want those powers *for*? Surely the point of power was to gratify desire. Was the Warden right? Was he a fool, chasing an arbitrary goal without meaning or reason? What was he–

Now that's interesting, his partner said. *Some of the people boarding the train here have these threads extending from their heads. A bit like the silver cords that attach people to their astral bodies, you know, but those emerge from the navel and, well, they're silver. These are… here, look, I'll tweak your perception so you can see.*

Altman lifted his head and frowned. There were four people boarding the train carrying small bags, giving every appearance of ordinary travelers: two men, two women, a couple of them dressed smartly, the others dressed in a more casual fashion, none of them paying attention to one another, seemingly unconnected in every way. Yet they all had these *things* emerging from the back of their necks or, in one case, from the top of their head. The things did look like threads, or thin ropes, but they were strangely liquid, undulating gently, dark red in color.

They looked like parasitic worms made of blood.

Altman followed the threads with his eyes to see where they originated, but they extended off to the west until they vanished into the distance. As the people boarded the train, the threads emerged through the walls, moving slowly as the people inside moved, their substance and direction unimpeded by gross physicality. "What are those things?" Altman asked.

The indication of some kind of blood magic, if I had to guess, his partner said. *But I don't know exactly what sort. I've never seen anything quite like it. I wonder what those people taste like. If I devour one of them, I might be able to understand the nature of the magic.*

You can't eat one of them! Altman objected. The train is full of passengers and it is broad daylight. Even if we get one of them alone, we don't have a way to dispose of the corpse.

You should let me worry about those things, his partner said. *It's more my area of expertise than yours. Oh, I've rifled your memories, I know you've concealed a few murders, but really, I'm a walking massacre. I won't do anything to jeopardize your mission. Though it's worth pointing out, no prison can possibly hold us anyway. Not if there are other prisoners for me to feast on when I get peckish.*

Altman shivered. "And then have the entire Spanish national police force hunting us down? We'd have a bit more trouble with them."

I don't see why, the partner mused. *The number of policemen in this country is large, but it is not infinite. The more they send, the more I eat, the stronger I get, the more I can eat, and so on. I was once responsible for the extinction of an entire language group, did you know that? Oh, it was a small, isolated civilization, but I erased their whole culture. Don't underestimate me, Altman.*

Destroying the Spanish people is not our goal, Altman thought sternly. We need to find Carl Sanford.

We can do both. But fine, I'll accept your priorities. Still, we should investigate these strangers. Perhaps the Warden has some ideas about them. She's a fount of unusual knowledge.

Altman grunted begrudging agreement, then pushed himself up from the bench and returned to the train. The bloody threads extended down the aisle at head height, all four clustered close together. He couldn't suppress a shudder when it became necessary to walk *through* them, their presence unavoidable even with his head tilted to one side. He couldn't feel them at all when they brushed his cheek, not even a sensation like walking through a spiderweb, but he still imagined them fouling his face and infecting his brain.

Altman paused outside his compartment. Three of the threads continued along the passageway, extending farther into the train, the people they were connected to out of sight… but a fourth one veered off, right through the closed door of his compartment. One of them was *inside*. He reached into his pocket for his kukri, then shoved the door open.

A young woman dressed in a white peasant blouse embroidered with flowers around the neckline sat in Altman's seat, smiling at the Warden, and then she turned that smile on him. "Please, sit down," she said. "We have much to discuss."

"Do we?"

"You might as well," the Warden said. She held Fantasma's pistol in her hand, partially hidden beneath her newspaper, but pointed at the woman's midsection.

Altman sat down on the seat beside the Warden, facing the woman. She wasn't visibly armed, but who knew what powers she might possess?

"Hello," the woman said. "I am the Blood Moon's *vocera* in Madrid – their voice, their herald, yes? I understand we have a common enemy. If you bring Carl Sanford to my master, they will reward you beyond measure."

CHAPTER SIXTEEN
Life Is a Series of Negotiations

Carl Sanford was sprawled on a mattress, dressed only in his undershirt and shorts, staring at a large reddish stain on the ceiling in confusion. How did that stain get there? It wasn't there last night. Did someone conduct a ritual in the room above me? Something bloody? No, the Warden wouldn't allow such a thing. Drat. I'll have to call someone to tear out the ceiling and replace it. It's not enough to paint over the mess, stains like that always bleed through...

He turned his head, setting off black fireworks behind his eyes, and groaned. He groped blindly for his glass of water on his bedside table, but instead his knuckles struck a wall. Who moved the bed? he wondered, furious. His bedroom, like his office, was inviolate, a part of the Silver Twilight Lodge where he would not permit trespass—

No. Wait. The Lodge was gone. Caved into a sinkhole, the remnants burned. He'd looked at the ruins once from the shadows before he left home. This wasn't his room. This wasn't his bed. This wasn't even his city. Or his *country*.

"I was stabbed," he murmured and touched his side, wincing. Yes, his abdomen was quite tender and his midsection tightly bandaged. This must be what wearing a girdle felt like. He tried to sit up and then thought better of it when his head swam. To think, not so long ago he'd been scaling walls and fighting thirty people at a time…

The bedroom door opened, and Anna Elizabeth Waite entered. Sanford felt an unexpected surge of affection. He'd last seen her in the dank tunnels beneath Paris years ago, and she hadn't changed. It was nice to think that some good things in the world stayed the same. Waite was a tall woman in early middle age and had the look of a kindly librarian – a deceptive appearance, since in matters of business she possessed the vicious acquisitiveness of a magpie. That commonality of ambition was one of the reasons they got along so well. They understood each other. Waite was American by birth, a New Yorker in fact, but had been raised all over Europe with her professor parents and spoke more languages than the Warden. She sat on the edge of the bed gently, so as not to jostle him. "I see you're awake."

"My dear Anna," he croaked. "It's so good to see you."

She snorted. "I wish I could say the same. You look terrible."

"I'm sure I feel worse than I look. If it's not too much trouble, could you tell me where I am?"

She raised an eyebrow. "Madrid. Specifically, my spare room above my bookshop, which fortunately is open by appointment only, so no customers watched me drag your bleeding carcass up the stairs. I did my best to tend to your wound. Given the way you arrived, I thought you might object to a trip to the hospital."

"Quite right," he murmured. One of the Moon's pet nurses could have drawn his blood openly, and that would be that.

"You're lucky I'm good at sewing, Sanford. You're also lucky that you mainly incurred a flesh wound. I didn't smell anything unpleasant from the injury and you don't have a fever, so you may recover. I'm not a doctor, though, just a frequent reader of anatomy texts."

Sanford groped for her hand and clutched it in his own. "I thank you for saving me." He despised needing help but understood the importance of showing gratitude when help had been required and received.

She gave his hand a perfunctory squeeze. "Several months ago, someone told me you were dead. I thought, that's impossible, Carl wouldn't *die*, he hasn't collected all the books in the world yet. I'm glad I was right, but you do seem rather determined to die. Were you mugged or was this assault more targeted?"

Sanford sighed. "I seem to have drawn the attention of an individual who goes by the *nom de guerre* 'The Blood Moon.'"

Anna Elizabeth tore her hand away. "Are you *serious*?"

"You're familiar with this character, then?"

She barked a laugh. "I've heard stories from my elusive contacts. You know, it's necessary to mingle with those robes-and-chanting types to track down the best volumes. I assumed the Moon was a myth. Are you telling me otherwise?"

"Why don't you tell me what you've heard?" The Blood Moon enjoyed spreading rumors and confusion, and according to Thorne, sought to increase their own legend. It didn't shock him that someone as connected to the occult world as Anna would have heard a few.

She waved a hand. "Oh, I've heard the Moon called a crime boss, and a minor deity. I've even heard they're an ancient sorcerer, or that the Blood Moon is actually the name of an organization with an imaginary figurehead. I've heard they dabble in politics. Some say the Moon is involved with funding and arming revolutionaries, republicans, separatists, anarchists, or monarchists, stoking conflicts to profit from them. I will say, there are fewer interesting cultists in the city in recent years, and I've gotten the sense the Moon is the reason why: you're forced to join them, or you aren't welcome here. Fortunately, I'm a neutral party and haven't been approached, but I'm not interested in getting involved."

"The Moon is worse than all that," Sanford said. "They're a blood magician, a user of blasphemous and insidious power. They collect blood and dominate your will, forcing you to do the Moon's bidding."

Waite stared at him. "They must have gotten *your* blood."

"Ah, well, fortunately, my blood, and the ones who tried to collect it, are nothing but ashes now."

She scooted back on the bed and he winced as the movement sent a lance of pain through him. "That explains all the commotion I heard earlier and the smoke in the sky. Maybe I should have left you in that alleyway."

"And yet, you did not. For which I am eternally grateful. But, at this point…" He coughed. "I never meant to drag you into all this. But it would be in your best interests to make sure I survive, and that I can defeat the Blood Moon. After all, if the Moon finds out you helped me, they'll want revenge on you for doing so."

She looked at him, eyes sharp as a hawk. "And if I don't help, you'll give me up, is that it? Tell the Moon I aided and abetted you?"

"I would never," Sanford said, genuinely shocked. "We're *friends*. Remember I saved your life in Paris, when that auction turned ugly."

Waite looked away. "You saved your own life certainly,

and brought me along, but I was never sure… after London, you know, I thought… but then after it was just the same old sort of letters. In Paris, I'd wondered if we'd have a repeat performance, but then it was all running through corridors full of skulls."

"Ah, Anna." Sanford was suddenly, uncharacteristically uncomfortable. Navigating matters of the heart never came naturally to him. Stabbing people through the heart was so much easier. "I didn't realize London meant anything to you. I thought it was just two friends getting carried away. I'm very sorry, my dear."

She smiled in response and straightened her shoulders. "Ah well, at any rate, we lived on different continents and it wouldn't have worked out. You have your work and I have mine, and that's what we both love most, isn't it?"

"I daresay that's part of why we get along," he said.

She nodded. "All right. Of course I want you to survive, for reasons other than purely selfish ones. I withdraw the uncharitable accusation that you'd sell me out."

"I wouldn't," he grumbled. "But if the Blood Moon uses magic to control my mind, I won't be able to keep any secrets from them, especially that a cult-obsessed bookseller has evaded them for so long." Sanford was beginning to think it might be impossible to stop the Blood Moon from taking his blood. Which meant he needed to make a plan in case that horrid eventuality did come to pass.

The master of the contingency plan.

"I could use a little more help to prevent that eventuality."

Waite groaned. "I've patched you up, Sanford. What else do you need from me? I didn't say I liked you enough to die for you."

"Just three things. First, give me time here to recover. Second, bring me every volume you have that concerns blood magic. I have some notions I'd like to explore. And finally... what's the time?"

She checked her wristwatch, sighing, resigned to his presence. "Just after noon. You were out for some time."

He nodded, not surprised. "I will probably have visitors, perhaps as early as this evening. If a severe woman and a thuggish man arrive looking for me, do send them up, will you? Don't worry, they don't mean me harm. Any immediate harm, anyway. You see–"

She rose. "I don't want to know any details. I must look into my own affairs if this Blood Moon is on your track and now mine. You must focus on healing, but I will see what books I can find for you. Perhaps a finder's fee should be settled on?" She left and closed the door.

Sanford settled back, smiling faintly. He wasn't exactly sure how things were going to work out – there were a great deal of moving parts and several degrees of uncertainty – but he had some good ideas and a temporarily safe place to ponder them.

Honestly, he found this whole experience rather invigorating, stab wound aside.

Altman and the Warden completed their train ride in the company of the *vocera* of the Blood Moon, parting ways at the train station. From there, they took a cab to the center of the city. "Do you think they're following us?" the Warden whispered.

Altman looked out the car window at the sparse traffic around them. Threads of red rose up from the cars behind them and disappeared into the sky where they joined a great hideous knot of convoluted blood magic like a storm cloud. "Oh, definitely."

Back on the train, the *vocera* – or, rather, the Blood Moon within the woman – had filled them in on recent happenings. Sanford had arrived in Madrid early that morning and proceeded to cause great difficulties. "He killed some of my people," the Moon said. "Nearly thirty of them, in fact."

"They must not have listened to reason, then," the Warden said. "Sanford always tries to reason with people first. He hates getting blood on his shoes."

"Reason doesn't enter into it," the Blood Moon says. "I cannot allow such an insult to stand, as I'm sure you understand. But the bulk of my… employees are ordinary people, and those have proven no match for him. I have certain special operatives who I'm sure would fare better, but Sanford has vanished, gone to ground somewhere that I don't have eyes." The *vocera* spread her hands. "The two of you know this man. You might have an idea of how to find him. And if you do – if you lead me to Sanford, or better yet, deliver him to me – I will fulfill your every dream."

"What do you know of our dreams?" Altman scoffed.

"How do you even know who we *are*?" the Warden demanded.

Oh, yes. Altman realized that was a better question.

The *vocera* waved her hand. "I've had Sanford watched since I became aware he was making plans against me. I saw you arrive at the hotel and made inquiries throughout my network. I traced your travel from Lisbon, found your names on the crew manifest of the *Ebon Lion*, reached out to American contacts, learned about the power struggle in the Silver Twilight Lodge…" She shrugged. "I don't claim to know all your secrets, but I know you took part in a coup and tried to kill Sanford and apparently failed. You want to rule his Order, don't you?" The *vocera* showed her teeth. "If there is one thing I have in abundance, it is zealous and devoted humans. Assist me, and I'll send you home with a whole new membership, yours alone to command, and I'll even give the means to subjugate any heretics back home."

"If we refuse?" Altman said.

The *vocera* shrugged. "Then I will find another way to get Sanford. But why shouldn't we make common cause? If we find Sanford, all our problems are solved."

"I am persuaded," the Warden had declared. "We have a partnership."

"Were you really persuaded?" Altman asked her now.

"Of course not. This Blood Moon is a parasitic infection in human form. I don't really care about the squabble between Sanford and this Coterie and some Spanish blood magician. As long as Sanford frees me from the bounds of my oath first, the Blood Moon can tear his head from his shoulders for all I care."

"Agreed," Altman said. "We'll get what we want from Sanford, and *then* hand him over, and take our reward from the Blood Moon, too. Why not?"

This is boring, the partner said. *I want to eat someone. You know how to drive. Let me eat the driver.*

No, be patient, Altman thought back. I'm sure we'll find someone who needs eating soon enough.

Soon, his partner grumbled.

"Estrella, those two in the car up ahead," the Moon said, speaking through the driver. "You are going to follow them. I think they can recognize our family – anyone connected to me by the covenant of blood – but they shouldn't suspect you of working for me, so they won't notice you following."

"But aren't we connected?" Estrella asked, confused. "We're family." She knew the Blood Moon never used her body or spoke through her, but she thought that was because she was special, a protégé, almost a daughter, not because there was something different about their connection.

"We are, my little star, but our connection is special, not like the one with my hu– with the rest of my family. The ties between us can't be perceived by the likes of these foreigners."

What had the Moon almost said? My human family? Something stirred in Estrella's mind, a worm of doubt wriggling. The ghoul-creature she'd sent away had suggested that Estrella wasn't human, that she was something else. But she *was* human, an ordinary person, granted special powers by the Moon who saw potential in her.

Except… the ghoul said *that* was a lie, too. And she knew for a fact that the Moon lied to her sometimes. How could you build trust on a foundation of lies? That was just as impossible as building a just society on a foundation of corpses.

"I understand," she said instead. Now was not the time to confront the Moon about her concerns. She would do that later… perhaps even in person. "So you just want me to follow them? Not, ah… anything else?"

"No need to open your heart to them, little star, no." The Moon sounded amused, and that made Estrella clench her fists. To speak of her most troubling gift in such a flippant way! "If these American fools lead you to Carl Sanford, I want you to take his blood and then hand it off to my *vocera* – she will be nearby."

The *voceras* were the Moon's most dedicated servants.

They lived in comfort, but they lived in waiting, always ready to serve as the Blood Moon's eyes and ears, arms and legs. They did not marry, or have jobs, or maintain any social connections, but the Blood Moon said they were happy to sacrifice their meaningless lives for the greater good. Estrella had met the *vocera* of Madrid a few times – there were others, in Barcelona and Valencia and Lisbon, and elsewhere – but the woman had made little impression on her. She mostly seemed resigned, a shell the Moon inhabited from time to time, like a rich man's summer home in the country.

How could someone who treated people like that be *good*? How could someone like that usher in a perfect world?

What is wrong with me? Estrella thought.

Sanford leafed through the tomes scattered around him on the bed, courtesy of Anna. He already felt better; he was overdue for a rejuvenation ritual, but he'd had so much life- and youth-extending spellwork done over the years that he healed at an unnatural rate. He'd be well enough to move around freely by tomorrow, probably, and he'd be as good as new in a week. Assuming he lived that long, anyway.

He turned a page, and there it was: the passage he half-remembered from research undertaken a decade ago. Sanford knew a bit about blood magic – he'd used it to hide from the Warden and Altman, after all – but he was hardly an expert on the subject. It was just one of many disciplines he'd dabbled in over the years. This book, though, had been written by an expert, a court magician to Elizabeth Báthory.

"The blood is a conduit," Sanford read aloud, translating loosely from the Hungarian. "Blood is life, and any life entangled is a life shared." He sat up straighter, wincing, and shouted, "Waite! I need you to run a few errands for me! To the apothecary, and while you're out, you may as well retrieve my things from my prior lodging! But you'll need to be careful. I'm sure the place is crawling with minions of the Blood Moon."

She stomped in a moment later from her own room, glaring. "Do I look like your servant?"

"Of course not. I will pay you much better for your services than I've ever paid a servant."

Waite rolled her eyes. "What do you want from the apothecary, Carl?"

"Just a few things to… sweeten my blood. You should get a pen and paper. You'll want to make a list."

"Adding even more to my finder's fee," she said. "Will you be able to afford me in the end?"

"Here is close enough," the Warden said. The taxi dropped them off near the royal palace, and she looked at the grand edifice with obvious wistfulness. "Isn't it beautiful? I always thought we should have kings in America."

"They barely have a king in Spain," Altman said. "From what I read in the papers, that palace is a gilded cage. It's the generals who rule here, and once the people with all the guns take over, they don't like to relinquish that control."

"We're all caged, in one way or another." She snapped her fingers, and a hound slithered up out of a drain in the gutter, even though the dog was obviously too large to fit. The hound sniffed around on the ground, and the Warden smiled. "Well, well. It appears our compass is working again. It says Sanford is that way." She nodded. "The direction we were going anyway. He really might be hiding out with that bookseller."

"He's not hiding anymore?" Altman said.

"It appears not. Perhaps his spell of obfuscation faded. Or it could be a trap. But you've got your *partner* to deal with such an eventuality, don't you?"

"I do at that," Altman admitted.

She glanced around. "Do you still think we're being followed by the Blood Moon's people?"

Altman scanned the area. "Strangely… no." He could see a few red threads rising into the sky, but they were all some distance away, too far for him to see who they were attached to. The only people around were the usual array of Spaniards, emerging from their homes, businesses, and bars for their evening perambulations: students, business people, workers. A pretty woman in a dress embroidered with little stars around the neckline standing on the opposite corner caught his eye and then looked away shyly. He felt no stir of desire for her at all. His cursed partner had seen to that.

"Then let's go." The Warden strode forward, crossed the street, and made her way along the crowded sidewalk. People spilled out of the doorways of bars or ate at tables set out in the open air, and they dodged around them, following closely at the heels of the swiftly coursing hound. There were none of the Moon's people in among those crowds. *It's almost like they're avoiding us*, Altman thought.

They continued on their way into narrow side streets until they reached an old brick building with a shop, the hound leading their path. There was a display window full of dusty tomes and a glass door with the words *La Librería de Waite* in gold leaf on frosted glass. Below that, in English and in Spanish, it read "*By Appointment Only.*"

Oh, no, but we don't have an appointment, the partner said.

"This is the place," the Warden said, sounding almost nervous. "Are we ready?"

"We should have the element of surprise," Altman said. "Even if we don't, so what? His power came from the Order, and he's lost all that. He took a few relics and curios with him, yes – I'm not saying he isn't dangerous. But with my partner, what do we have to fear? You saw how easily I tore Akh apart. We can handle one old man, far from home. Once we find him, summon more of your hounds to pin him down and then I'll persuade him to do what we want."

What fun! the partner said.

"Do you really believe it will be that easy, or are you trying to convince yourself?" She sighed. "Either way, this is what we came to do, so we'd best get on with it."

The Warden rapped sharply on the glass until the door was wrenched open by a bespectacled woman with dark hair threaded with gray. "Oh," she said, eyeing them up and down over her dark-rimmed frames. "Thuggish and severe. You're the visitors Carl was expecting. Come in, then."

"*Expecting?*" Altman said. "*Thuggish?*"

"Carl?" The Warden softly laughed. "Oh, Sanford."

"This changes nothing," Altman said sharply. "We proceed as planned–"

"Are you coming in?" the woman asked. "You're letting in a draft."

Duly chastised, they followed her into a quintessential antiquarian bookshop: whether it was a small space or not, it *seemed* small, crammed as it was with floor-to-ceiling shelves full of volumes, with more books piled up in unruly stacks on the floor and numerous rare tomes locked away in glass display cases. Antique maps hung slightly askew on the walls and brass lamps provided haphazard illumination. Whether the shop had begun as one large room or several smaller ones, it was divided into passages and chambers now, with narrow corridors lined by shelves leading to other sections. There was a stairway in the back of the shop, with a dusty velvet rope draped across the bottom. "Sanford is upstairs through the first door on the right. Don't go poking into the other rooms."

"You were expecting us." Altman scowled. "How?"

The woman – Waite, presumably – smirked. "Severe woman, thuggish man. Carl said you'd be along. That's how and that's all there is to it from my end. He's recovering from a rather serious injury so please don't let him overexert himself. I stitched him up once. I don't want to do it again."

The Warden and Altman exchanged a glance and she shrugged. Altman unhooked the velvet rope and made an "after you" gesture to Van Shaw, who preceded him up the stairs.

They opened the door they'd been directed to and found a small bedroom inside, with Carl Sanford on the bed.

He should have looked vulnerable in such a position. Even though he sat up in a bed surrounded by books, with a blanket pulled up to his waist, he seemed like a king on a dais, benevolently considering his latest petitioners. "Oh good, you made it," he said. "I'm so sorry I made you run around Barcelona like that, but I had some matters to attend to before I could meet with you. Your timing is impeccable, though. I'm delighted to see you both. And before you ask, yes, of course, I'd be happy to help you out of your various difficulties."

Altman stared at Sanford, flabbergasted, and couldn't even think of a response. The Warden murmured to him, "Did you still want me to summon my hounds to restrain him, or is he sufficiently bedridden as is?"

"You," Altman blustered. "You. You must…" He trailed off, unsure where to begin. He'd expected anger, hostility, maybe fear, but not this… welcome.

"Indeed I must, and so must you." Sanford smiled at them paternally. "I'm afraid we don't have much time, but we can observe certain niceties before we move on to satisfying your various demands." He put his palm to his chest. "First, let me say, I am terribly sorry that Tillinghast turned on you and left you nothing for your trouble but ruins. I did try to warn you that the man was dangerous and untrustworthy, but I understand why you didn't heed my cautions. You acted in the heat of the moment and mistakes were made on all sides. Let's call it water beneath the bridge."

Altman stepped closer, fists clenched. "Shut up, Sanford. We didn't come all this way to listen to you blather on. We came to make demands–"

"Tut, tut," Sanford interrupted mildly. "I already said I'd grant them. Your brother knew how to take yes for an answer, Altman. Surely, you can learn as well."

"You haven't even *heard* our demands!" he shouted.

The magus waved a hand. "They are not hard to surmise. You wish to be named the anointed head of the Silver Twilight Lodge. Fine. You are so anointed." He made a vague hand gesture. "I will draft any proclamation you like in the presence of any witnesses you specify. I suspect Ms Waite – my bookseller friend I'm sure you met, assuming you didn't break the door down, and if you did you must repair it – even has some nice vellum and ink, so we can draw up a beautiful document. You also want material resources, yes? You need a newLLodge house? Well, Tillinghast absconded with the majority of my wealth, alas, but I can still provide you with a nest egg to get your organization up on its feet. I can also provide you with the blackmail material you'll need to bring your squabbling schismatics to heel, and once they pledge fealty, their sheeplike adherents will come along, too."

Altman felt like he'd tried to climb a set of stairs and missed a step. "You… you'll just let me have the Order?"

Sanford nodded. "Why not? I've moved on to better things. I'm joining the Red Coterie, a far more venerable and powerful organization. But, no, Altman, I apologize if I wasn't clear. I'm not *giving* you anything. What's happening here is we are making a mutually beneficial arrangement. We're making a *deal.*"

You should really let me eat him, the partner said. *This one is dangerous.*

I… we will, soon, but…

Meanwhile, Sanford turned to look at the warden. "Sarah. Dear Sarah. You want to be free of your oaths, yes? Unbound, so your health and power are no longer tethered to the wellbeing of the Order? Even knowing you'd have to give up your powers, which are vast, you barely even use a tenth of them, in exchange for that freedom?"

Van Shaw nodded.

Sanford nodded, benevolent as a saint. "I can do that, too. I oversaw your binding, after all, and I know how to unbind you. But again: I will not do this out of the kindness of my heart. The two of you did betray me, conspire to overthrow me, and try to kill me, after all. I am a merciful man, but even I have my limits. I am willing to wipe our slate clean though, and fulfill your wishes if you'll help me with a little problem first."

"We came here to force you to give us what we want," Altman said. "Not to negotiate."

The man in the bed nodded. "I understand. You can certainly beat me, torture me, and so forth to get what you want. As you can see, I'm in no condition to stop you, but you know me, and you know any agreement I made under duress would be full of traps, pitfalls and poisons. I may go down, but I'll go down fighting. You saw *that* back in Arkham. So why not do this the easy way, instead?"

Altman closed his eyes and pinched the bridge of his nose. This wasn't what he'd expected. But was it… better? A way to get what he wanted without violence?

But I love violence, his partner complained.

"We might as well hear him out," Altman muttered, suddenly wondering why he'd believed he could force the magus to do anything. "What is it you want from us?"

"This and that," Sanford said pleasantly. "I'll also need a favor or two from the entity you invited to reside within you, Altman. Is it listening?"

CHAPTER SEVENTEEN
The Touch of an Outsider

Estrella stood across the street from the bookshop, observing the door and the windows above. Was the assassin Carl Sanford inside, or had the strangers stopped here to pick up something to read? How could she possibly know? Should she try to go inside for a closer look? Or would the people inside try to kill her, if they were the members of some conspiracy? Would she spoil everything by acting or spoil everything by waiting?

She decided to watch for now, until something happened, or until she could no longer bear the suspense. And in the quiet, her mind churned and churned.

Sanford smiled at Van Shaw and Altman, although he hardly felt like smiling. Altman was disloyal gutter trash with pretensions to greatness, but he was inhabited by something that could prove useful in more ways than one. As for the Warden, he'd expected their meeting to make him angry, but in the moment, it just made him sad. Once, she'd been the rock the Order was built upon, someone whose loyalty he found as certain as the sunrise. When she'd turned on him, the foundations of his world had shifted.

No matter. Soon enough, the Warden would help make Sanford a member of the Red Coterie, the first step to founding his *new* Order. They just had to deal with the Blood Moon first.

"You know about my… partner?" Altman said, as usual slower than everyone around him.

"Well, of course," Sanford said, leaning into his pleasant demeanor. "Obviously you needed access to some kind of power to pull the shattered pieces of the Order of the Silver Twilight back together again." He felt no need to mention that Ruby Standish had sent him a letter mentioning Altman's dark bargain. It was always preferable to let one's underlings think you simply knew everything all the time. "Most of the Order's books were lost when the deep basements tore loose from reality and many others burned, but it occurred to me that you might have recovered those volumes that hadn't yet been processed. I happened to look through those, brought in by my Keeper of the Red Stone from his last trip to Morocco, before all the… unpleasantness happened. I knew there was only one volume that could possibly give you power. You really did the ritual, then? You invited *that* thing in?"

"The serpent of the night, yes," Altman said stiffly. "It lives inside me now and grants me power."

Sanford winced. "Tut-tut, Altman. Did you do so little research? The copy of the book you had was horribly defaced, but I've read the full text in unexpurgated form – it was one of the volumes the Order lost forever, thanks to Tillinghast's meddling. First, it's not *the* serpent of the night, it's *a* serpent of the night. They were a whole species. And you aren't possessed by one of those anyway. That book is a true and complete history of the *vanquishers* of the serpents of the night. We don't even have another name for entities like the one living inside you, we just call them 'vanquishers' – they're famed for bringing extinction to a once-great race. It was such a thorough extinction that all we know about the serpents of the night is the information contained in a book written about their conquerors. *That's* what you invited to share your body and mind: a paradimensional predator that thrives on genocide."

"It's always nice to meet an admirer," the vanquisher said from Altman's mouth in a horrible gargle. "What's this favor you need?"

"You like to kill, don't you?" Sanford said.

"Very much so."

"There are people in this city bound by magic to the Blood Moon. Now, it's difficult to tell which people are connected–"

"Oh, I can see them," the vanquisher said. "Red ropes floating out of their heads up into the knot in the sky."

"You can *see* them?" the Warden said. "You might have mentioned that earlier!"

"Like you tell me everything *you* know," Altman grumbled in his own voice.

"Capital," Sanford said. He'd been about to hand over the opera glasses, but now there was no need. "I didn't realize such perception was one of your gifts, vanquisher."

"Even I don't know all the things I can do," that wet horror of a voice replied. "But it's always fun to discover something new."

"Since you can perceive the thralls of the Blood Moon, what I'd like you to do is go out tonight and kill as many of them as possible. Start close to this location and then spiral outward."

Sanford half-expected some protest that those people were innocent victims of the Blood Moon, or at least a perfunctory gasp of horror at the idea of such indiscriminate slaughter, but he didn't get either reaction.

Of course not, he thought. Ruby Standish isn't here.

She'd been the only one of their group with something approaching an ordinary human conscience. Good heavens, Sanford realized *he* was probably the most empathetic and merciful person, or entity, in this room and he was suggesting murder. What a state of affairs.

"Gladly," the vanquisher said. Altman broke in to ask, "Why?"

"Because his minions tried to kill me," Sanford said. "I was stabbed. I'd like to teach the Blood Moon it's better to keep distance between us. They'll show more caution once you cut a swath through their ranks."

"Pah," the Warden said. "I know you, Sanford. You're going on the offensive because you hate being on the back foot. If someone thinks they're hunting you, you must turn around and start hunting *them*."

Sanford shrugged, then winced at the pain that caused in his side. "You know me so well, Sarah. Sowing chaos and uncertainty in your enemy's troops is always a good tactic, though. The Moon's numbers are a strength, but they're a weakness, too. Altman and his roommate won't have to look far to find suitable targets." Sanford waved a hand toward the door. "Well, go on, vanquisher, and vanquish. Come back here around dawn and we'll discuss next steps."

"If I do this killing for you, you'll… do all the things you said?" Altman broke in. "The wealth, the proclamation that I'm your heir, the blackmail material?"

Sanford sighed, impatient. "Yes, yes, we'll work out the details tomorrow. If you act in good faith, so will I."

Altman hesitated, clearly unhappy with that answer, but just as clearly, the thing inside him lusted for murder, and he turned jerkily and darted out of the room.

"Will you really give him control over the Order?" the Warden asked once they were alone.

"The Order is gone," Sanford said. "If I'm not running it, it's not the Order anyway. It might have that name, I suppose, but it will be something different. Something lesser. The Order is my past, and for now, I'm focused on the future."

"That's not really an answer," she said.

"Do you care what happens to Altman, so long as you get what you want? Have the two of you become close since I left?" Sanford stroked his bare chin. It felt so strange. "I suppose you are comrades in arms now, and that does create a certain bond. But then, I thought you and I had a bond, once." He barely kept the bitterness out of his voice.

The Warden looked at him for a long moment, then shook her head. "Do what you will. So long as you free me from my oaths to the Order. What service will you require from me?"

"Breaking such a complex spell will require preparation, but we should be able to do it in the next day or two if I can get my Anna Elizabeth to collect the necessary supplies for me."

The Warden smirked.

"Do you have something to say?" Sanford asked.

"Anna Elizabeth?"

"Forgive me, *Ms Waite*. You and I have other problems to deal with in the meantime. I need you to protect me if the Blood Moon's people try to capture me again. I am not fully recovered and I need my strength before I'm ready to attack the Moon directly. I heal quickly thanks to myriad enchantments over the years, but even I need a moment after a knife wound."

"The Blood Moon asked *us* to capture you, you know," the Warden said.

Sanford frowned. "How rude. Well, don't do that, either. If I'm in the Moon's hands, I won't be much good to you *or* to Altman."

"The Moon made promises," the Warden said. "They can compel you to help us, if we hand you over."

"I understand you don't necessarily trust me," Sanford said. "But need I remind you: *you* betrayed *me*, not the other way around, and I'm willing to bury the proverbial hatchet. Besides, I can't imagine you trust the Blood Moon, either. Why would you believe that a monstrous blood mage who enslaves people on a regular basis will honor any bargain you struck? They would likely take your blood to enslave you and use your powers against you. Why free someone from such amazing magics that they can then directly use? All the Blood Moon really needs to do is keep the vanquisher happy and healthy, which in turn would keep you healthy, if not happy. The Blood Moon would never let you go."

"I have considered it," she said softly.

"At least you know me. You know me better than anyone does, Sarah. Anyway, if you try to take me, I will fight you, and while it would be interesting to see which one of us would win, I'm rather tired. Wouldn't you rather do this the easy way?"

He couldn't tell if the Warden was persuaded or not; she was that impassive. If she was not, this could get ugly.

Then she shrugged. "Fine. I agree. No one will lay a hand on you while I keep watch."

"Oh, they can lay a hand," Sanford said. "If they come for me, I want you to let them take my blood, just don't let them take the rest of me anywhere."

"What are you talking about?" the Warden said. "If the Moon gets your blood, they'll control you, won't they?"

"Ah, but the blood is a conduit, my dear Warden. Do you see that blue jar? I think my concoction has steeped enough. Hand it to me, if you please."

Van Shaw frowned at the bedside table, crowded with bags of herbs and jars of powder, a mortar and pestle, and various small jars of fluids in different colors. There was a blue glass vial with bits of sediment floating near the bottom, and she passed it to him.

Sanford took the bottle, capped the top with his thumb, gave it all a vigorous shake, and then tossed it back, swallowing it in one gulp. He grimaced. "Gah, that's vile. The things I must do..." He handed the vial back, and the Warden put it with the other things on the table.

"What did you drink?" she asked.

"Oh, a great many things in a very particular combination." He held up his fingers, wiggling them at her, and then chuckled as if the movement amused him. "There are some psychoactive compounds, and some sensory enhancers, and... oh, other ingredients, all meant to alter perception and open certain interior doors. All very dangerous, of course." He leaned back, eyes half closed. "I just need to give the concoction a few minutes to properly flood my system."

Sanford let chemical serenity wash over him. He should have been tense with all that awaited him, but the potion he'd taken to loosen his mind also loosened everything else. He decided to simply enjoy it; this might be his last chance to relax for a while, after all.

Estrella watched from the early evening shadows as the thuggish man emerged from the shop and hurried away. She was torn between pursuing him or not. She'd been told to follow the man and the woman, Altman and Van Shaw, but hadn't been given instructions about what to do if they split up.

This was silly. She needed to do something. One reason the Blood Moon valued her was because, unlike the rest of the family, she could take the initiative and act without being given explicit instructions first; she could be given a task and use her own wits to find the best way to accomplish it.

Fine. She would go in and see if Sanford was in the shop, and if he wasn't, then she could pursue Altman – no one could outrun her anyway, not with her gifts. Estrella went to the door and knocked. An older, attractive woman with dark hair answered. "Can I help you?" she asked in Spanish.

Estrella hesitated. "I am looking for someone."

"Another visitor for Carl?" the woman said. "Come in then, he's upstairs. Wipe your feet, please. Altman tracked dirt from the street in here, the pig."

Could it be so simple? Estrella dutifully wiped her feet on the mat. She stepped inside the shop, marveling at the vast array of books – there must be so many stories here, and so many worlds! – and then saw the stairs. She glanced back at the shopkeeper, but the woman was standing at a desk, seemingly repairing an old tome, so Estrella simply ascended. "The door on the right!" the woman below called. "Leave the other ones alone!"

Estrella reached the landing and opened the door, then stepped back with a cry of dismay. There were huge snarling hounds in the doorway, three of them, standing so close together they seemed like a single beast with three heads. There were other dogs in the room behind them, too, perhaps five or six of them, but it was hard to count.

A hard-faced woman in an ankle-length dress stood at the foot of a bed, her fists clenched and her teeth bared, just like the growling dogs. She flickered with an aura of power, bright and silver. So that meant this woman wasn't entirely human. Was she like the irredeemably wicked ones? Like the Blood Moon? Like… Estrella herself?

She didn't want to think about such things. The void in Estrella's chest throbbed, but she hadn't been told to send anyone away. She was here for Sanford; or, more specifically, for Sanford's blood. Having one was the same as having the other.

Estrella could do more than just send people away. She could hurt people. She could shatter their minds and leave them gibbering about shapeless dancers and black stars. She didn't like doing that, but she could, and so she raised her hands.

"Oh, the power in you!" a voice cried out from the bed. "Warden, step aside, let me see her."

The woman at the foot of the bed grimaced and shuffled over, but the snarling dogs didn't move out of the doorway. Now Estrella could see the man sitting up in bed against the headboard. He was clean-shaven and silver-haired, wearing an undershirt, surrounded by books, and holding strange red lenses up to his face. He put the lenses down and then peered at her through – was that a monocle? He dropped both sets of lenses down on the covers and spread his arms wide. "Welcome, friend of the Moon! Aren't you remarkable! *Habla inglés?*"

"I – yes," she said. Estrella had always been good with languages. In fact, she only needed a few lessons in a given tongue to unlock understanding; another gift from the Moon.

"Excellent, my Spanish is very poor," the man in the bed said. "What is your name?"

"Estrella Gullette," she answered automatically, then winced. She probably shouldn't go around telling the Moon's enemies her name. Deception was not her forte.

"Welcome, Miss Gullette. I am Carl Sanford, late of Arkham, Massachusetts, here on extended sojourn in your fair country."

Was the man drunk? He sounded drunk. Or, no, he was bandaged, so perhaps he'd been dosed with something for his pain? Enough laudanum to make him silly, but not enough to send him to sleep?

Sanford went on, his voice mirthful. "I call you a friend of the Moon and not a slave of the Moon because I can see that you are free! There is no tether connecting you to the Moon, no blood magic binding your will to theirs. And that means you serve the Moon willingly. But why? What has he promised you? What could the Moon promise you that you couldn't achieve on your own with all that nuclear chaos bound inside you? Oh, my senses are so vast now, my mind is so open, I can see beyond the boundaries of your body, Estrella Gullette. I can see the door inside your heart. I can see the truth of what you are!"

"I serve the Moon because I believe in the hope for a better world," Estrella said stiffly. "I am the Moon's heir and protégé.

And you are a foul assassin sent by the Moon's enemies in the Coterie."

The man shook his finger at her in mock admonishment. "I would quibble with being called foul, but it's true, I have been sent to slay the Moon. That is a noble goal, Miss Gullette, because the Moon steals blood, forces people to serve them, then kills anyone they can't control, anyone who isn't human, that is. The Blood Moon's compulsive magic only works on humans, as you may have guessed."

"Is that so?" the woman said sharply.

"Sarah, you were made inhuman, not born that way. I'm not sure if the distinction matters, but it certainly could. Would you risk it?"

Sarah scrunched her face in displeasure.

"They – they're wicked," Estrella said, feeling off-balance. This was not going how she anticipated it. "The ones the Moon sends away, they're irredeemable."

"Oh, not necessarily," Sanford said. "The inhuman are just like anyone else. Some are awful, some are lovely. You seem lovely, and you're the least human person in this room."

"Shut up!" Estrella shouted. "I *am* human!" These were lies – they had to be. She pointed to the woman. "She isn't human. I can see her… her *wickedness*, all around her like an aura."

Sanford looked at the woman and lazily nodded. "Ah, yes, the Warden. She used to be a perfectly ordinary human, once upon a time. But she traded away parts of herself for power. Unlike me, she now doesn't just use magic, she *is* magic. That can happen, you know. You can begin as one thing and then become another. Just ask the good people of Innsmouth." Sanford giggled, and Estrella had no idea why. "Why, if you took the Warden's magic away, there wouldn't be enough left of her to stand up, let alone walk and talk and wear a dress! But you, oh, no, Estrella, you were not made. You were born this way."

She stomped her foot and her hands began to glow with a soft purple killing light. "I. Am. A. *Person*."

Sanford held up his hands in mock surrender. "Of course you are! You don't have to be human to be a person. The fact is, somewhere far back in your bloodline, there's a touch of the outsider, that's all. You could come from the line of the Nameless, I would guess, the lineage of great old ones, including some who lived their whole lives as humans, unaware of that twisted thread in their heritage. That touch of the strange originated generations ago, most likely, but sometimes the old bloodlines surge back to the forefront. Occasionally a child in a dark-eyed family comes up blue, or a redhead appears among the blonds, yes? Well, look at *you*!" He clapped his hands, apparently delighted with her. "In you, the lineage of the outsider is so strong. Tell me, child, do you hear the music? The pipes of the Court of Azathoth, that which dwells in the brightly shining dark? I can hear them when I look at you."

No one had ever mentioned the pipes before. Estrella shook her head in vicious denial.

"Your heritage is nothing to hate or fear," Sanford said gently. "It's just… a fact about you. Some people have perfect pitch. Some people never forget a face. And you… well, I don't know *what* you can do, honestly. But these powers you have are your natural gifts. It doesn't matter if you aren't entirely human. Many people aren't. You're still a *person*. And a lucky person, as a resident of Madrid, because the Blood Moon cannot enslave you as they have so many of your countrymen. In fact, your immunity means you could help me."

"No!" Estrella shouted. "I've come for your blood!" She stepped forward, prepared to fight with the dogs, to unleash the violence that tingled in her fingertips but the hounds withdrew, watchful. She hesitated, and then marched into the room. The Warden moved to sit in a chair against the wall, watching her warily.

"Will a little prick of my fingertip do?" Sanford said, extending his hand.

"You'll just let me take your blood?"

"I don't see how I could possibly stop you," he said. "I might not have noticed your nature if I'd seen you earlier, but now I can see so many things, and you ... you are not someone to be trifled with. You could be great, if you let yourself be. But a tree can't grow tall if it's smothered in the shadow of another, eh?"

Estrella shut out his words. She withdrew a needle and pricked his outstretched finger. He didn't even wince. The man's pupils were enormous.

"The Moon is lying to you," Sanford said. "They claim you're their heir, their protégé? No. The Moon is afraid of you, for good reason. I know you don't believe me, Estrella, but I can prove it."

"Shut up!" she shouted, and fled the room with Sanford's blood in hand.

She'd fulfilled her mission. She should have felt triumphant. But she only felt frightened and confused as she hurried out of the bookshop, racing with her inhuman speed past the astonished bookseller, smashing her way through the door and fleeing down the street.

She was "touched by an outsider?" What did that mean? Her powers were the heritage of some ancient association with magic, then, passed down her family line? If that was true, then the Blood Moon hadn't blessed her but merely taken credit for her naturally unnatural gifts. But… why should she believe Carl Sanford, an admitted assassin? Shouldn't she believe the Moon, who'd loved and cared for her?

She reached the alleyway where the *vocera* of Madrid was supposed to be waiting to retrieve the blood, but no one was there. Estrella saw something hidden in what would have been impenetrable shadow to other eyes (to *human* eyes!): a crumpled form on the stones. She swiftly moved in, crouching to examine the shape. It was a person, rolled over, unconscious. No. Dead. When Estrella turned the woman over, she revealed a great gash in the woman's throat.

It was Bernadette, the Moon's *vocera*, killed. How could this be? Estrella lifted her gaze and saw other bodies hidden deeper in the alley. There were none she recognized, but the *vocera* never traveled alone; she was always with her guards. They had most definitely failed to guard her tonight.

Estrella stumbled away from the carnage, supporting herself against a wall, gorge rising. She managed not to vomit on the pavement, but it was hard. She'd been involved in ugly business before, yes, but when she used her powers on people, they just… went away. All this death, this blood, this savagery… her mind spun. She'd had tea in the *vocera*'s house! The Moon's enemies were monstrous.

But according to Sanford, so was the Moon…

Her legs trembled. She clung tightly to her sanity. She had to find another member of the family, pass off the needle, and get the blood to the Moon! Then this Sanford would become part of the family and he'd be forced to stop lying – forced to tell her the truth.

Forced to say whatever the Blood Moon wants him to say, a treacherous part of her mind whispered.

She focused on the future. There were some things she needed to ask the Moon about. Certain inconsistencies and ambiguities. She just needed clarity. Maybe the Moon had kept things from her to spare her feelings, or to keep her from worrying. But how could she serve properly if she didn't understand who she was serving?

You know where the Moon lives, her mind said reasonably. You can see the pillar of power rising above them. It's not even that far from here. Why not just go there and hand over the blood yourself?

Action. She had to take action. That was the only way to wash the horrors she'd seen from her mind. Estrella set out in the direction of the Moon's lair. If she encountered another member of the family, she would talk to the Moon then, of course, instead…

But she didn't. She didn't see anyone in the family at all. She didn't know where all of them had gone.

"That went well," Sanford said as the Warden's hounds crawled under the bed to disappear. "Don't you think?"

The Warden shook her head. "I don't know what any of that was. I saw a woman who isn't yet twenty wearing a dress with stars embroidered around the neckline. What did *you* see?"

"Just what I said," Sanford replied. "It seems a greater perception of the uncanny is an unforeseen side effect of the concoction I drank." He cocked his head and smiled at her dreamily. "You won't believe what I see when I look at you, Sarah."

She shuddered. "I don't want to know."

"A shame," Sanford said. "Since you're the most beautiful thing I've ever seen."

She raised an eyebrow and then looked down at herself, frowning. "You should leave Arkham more often, magus."

He settled back and watched the radiance that coruscated around the Warden like an aurora in silver and waited for the Blood Moon to take control of his mind.

CHAPTER EIGHTEEN
El Matadero

Altman sprawled on a rooftop, clutching at his belly, aching as if he'd just eaten three or four holiday dinners in one sitting. "Why am I so full?" he groaned. "I haven't eaten anything, not really, not food, not even… not even flesh. Right?"

That bodily sensation is your mind's way of interpreting the truth, the vanquisher said. *Which is that we're stuffed to bursting with power right now. We're practically overspilling. Don't worry. I'm going to use up some of that power to make room for more.*

"How many of the Moon's people have we… eaten?"

Oh, it's gauche to keep track, Altman. Taking score reduces the whole enterprise to a game. These people aren't notches on the dinner bell for me, you know. Every one of them is a personal and unique experience, to be savored on its own merits. The vanquisher paused. *That said, probably dozens? We cleared out every thrall of the Blood Moon in a ten block radius. They're starting to run away now. We'll have to roam farther afield for the second course.*

"Could I… could I stay conscious for the next part?" Altman asked.

Hmm. I'm integrated enough that you don't need to sleep so

much anymore. But are you sure you want to? I don't want to
trouble your delicate human sensibilities.

"I don't find your actions troubling," Altman said. "The
death, the killing… it doesn't bother me anymore." The
stomachache troubled him more than his morals. "I don't
know why. I used to kill only by necessity. It was always a
pragmatic act, and while I didn't lose sleep over it, I didn't
especially relish doing it, either. I was never a sadist, that was
more my brother's line. But now I find I *like* the killing."

Of course you do, the vanquisher said. *I've arranged things to
make* you *like it.*

Altman groaned. "What do you mean?"

I've rid you of all your other appetites, the voice said reasonably.
*Eating and sex, smoking and drinking, gambling and dancing,
these are meaningless to you now. I suppress all those urges and
suppress your empathy, too – not that you were burdened with
much of that anyway – and what do you have left? The only outlet
for your appetites that remains is violence. Which just happens to
be* my *only appetite, and so, we become a more perfect union.*

"You've made me into a monster," Altman said, but he
couldn't even be furious or appalled about it for some reason.
Oh. For that reason. Fury, like most other things, apparently,
probably came down to the glands.

A beautiful monster, suited to your purpose, the vanquisher said.
*Even though you know I'm messing with your mind, increasing
your bloodlust, turning you into something very like myself – the
process still works! The knowledge does nothing to change the
effect, just as an opium-eater can know he's an addict without that
understanding lessening his compulsion in the slightest.*

"I might be able to purge myself of you." Altman said this
without much urgency. "I am helping Sanford, and he will

repay me, and I could… I could make him take you out of me. He seems to know a lot about you. About your kind."

Entirely too much, if you ask me. We've been trying to destroy all copies of that stupid book – except for the part including the ritual to call us up, of course. I would have killed Sanford, but you need him to help take over your cult and assisting you in that goal was part of our bargain. I am a creature of bargains, Altman. I can't violate ours, though I confess, it's written very much in my favor. I can cancel our partnership, but you can't. The only way you can get out of our contract is if I release you, and why would I do that, unless I get a better offer?

Altman wanted to weep but didn't. He didn't even really want to, honestly; he just felt that he *should* want to.

What he actually wanted to do was kill.

Cheer up, the vanquisher said. *You asked about flying to the moon earlier. We can't quite do that much, but we can fly above the streets of Madrid. We can fly toward those threads over there. We can swoop down on the Blood Moon's puppets from above like death on the wing. Doesn't that sound fun?*

Nothing, in fact, had ever sounded more fun. So instead of weeping, Altman laughed.

Estrella made it almost all the way to the Blood Moon's lair before a security guard outside the gates of the slaughterhouse and cattle market approached her. The Moon hadn't always lived here. When Estrella was younger, they'd been hidden away underneath a hospital. But a couple of years ago, when El Matadero y Mercado Municipal de Ganados started operating at last after more than a decade of construction, she'd watched the Moon's pillar of power move across the city and settle here.

Estrella wasn't sure why the Moon liked this place, but she suspected it had something to do with all the blood.

The Matadero had been designed by a renowned architect commissioned by the city, and so it wasn't the brutal, functional space one might expect from a slaughterhouse and meat market. Instead, the Matadero was a sprawling array of large pavilions, with an emphasis on simple elegance, but with numerous architectural touches meant to call back to the history of the region, including Moorish designs and decorative tiles. The complex was beautiful, like a temple to appetite, but even so, it was a place full of cows, and it smelled that way.

When she approached the edge of the market, a burly guard rushed forward with a baton in hand, as if ready to attack her, but he stopped short. "Estrella?" he said. "Is that you? What are you… what brings you to this part of the city?"

"Moon!" she cried, delighted despite herself to encounter her oldest friend. "I don't know what happened. I went to find your *vocera*, but someone had killed her and her guards, it was awful–"

"It's the assassin," the Blood Moon said. "Hunting our people, hunting our *family*–"

"But I saw him, Sanford. He's in bed, he's injured. I don't think he's hunting anyone."

"He is a sorcerer." The guard spat in disgust.

Estrella almost laughed. As if the Blood Moon wasn't a sorcerer, too! Her mind was disarrayed, full of fears and doubts, where until recently there'd been only solid certainty.

The Moon continued. "Sanford sent some sort of living shadow to hunt us down. I can't catch more than a glimpse of the phantasmal beast, it kills us before we can even lift a hand to defend ourselves." Then the guard grabbed her hands, the Moon fixing her with a fierce look. "You said you saw him? Sanford?"

She nodded. "I collected a drop of his blood."

"Give it here!" the Moon said greedily, his hands tightening around hers.

"Can't I bring it to you personally?" Estrella asked. "All these years, all this time, you're like my parent, and yet I've never seen you. Never really met you, not in person."

The Moon hesitated, then slowly shook the guard's head. "I'm afraid that is not a good idea, Estrella. It is not safe. If you do not know where I live, then no one can torture you to find out where I live. We have so many enemies. This secrecy, it is for your own protection, do you understand?"

She didn't understand. Anyone who found out she was the Moon's heir would probably assume she knew their whereabouts and torture her anyway; the Moon just didn't want her to be able to tell the truth if that situation arose. Which, fine, was fair enough, but why twist it into a choice the Moon made out of care for her?

Because the Moon lies, her treacherous mind whispered. Because the Moon is using you.

"Just give me the blood!" the Moon said, but Estrella took a step back, her hands slipping from his.

"I have some questions," she said. "There are things I do not understand."

"This is not the time, little star. We are being hunted. We need to gain control of Sanford and make him call off this killer."

Estrella felt a pang for the deaths of her family members, but *she* wasn't the one killing them, and how else could she ever compel the Moon to tell her the truth if not under this kind of duress? "Then you should answer my questions quickly."

The guard went completely still, like a statue. "You forget yourself, little star," the voice said after a moment. "I made you. I gave you all your gifts. I can take them away."

Estrella lifted her hands, letting them glow a faint violet, allowing a touch of her power to show. "Then take them away," she said. "Go ahead. Please. I don't want them anyway."

After a long moment, the guard laughed harshly. "Do not be absurd. They were gifts. Don't be ungrateful. I wouldn't–"

"You can't take them," she said, sorrowful wonder and understanding in her voice. "You didn't give me these powers. I just… have them. The ghoul told me. Sanford told me. I was born like this."

"Lies!" the Blood Moon said. "My enemies are conspiring to turn you against me."

"The ghoul you sent me to remove and Sanford don't know each other," Estrella said in disgust. "It wasn't some story they concocted together. Moon, I love you, I *have* loved you. I believe in our mission, but you have to stop lying to me!"

The guard bowed his head for a moment and then sighed. "Fine. Yes, little star. It's true. I did not make you what you are. I found you, and took you out of that horrible orphanage, and placed you with loving parents–"

"So you could use me as a weapon," Estrella said. "To fight your enemies. Isn't that right?"

"At first, I admit, I only saw your power and how you could be of use to me. But then I got to know you, Estrella, your beautiful heart, your curiosity, your courage, your generosity of spirit, and I grew to love you. That is when I made you my heir."

Estrella wanted to believe that, desperately… but the Moon had pivoted so swiftly, so glibly, and so neatly to this new story. She'd known liars before, people who simply altered their stories when you caught them in an untruth, and told a new lie, one you'd be more likely to believe since you'd pushed them into a "confession." "If you wanted me to be your weapon, why didn't you take control of me like you do all the others?"

"Because I knew, from the very beginning, that you were precious and special."

"It's because I'm not human," Estrella interrupted. "Your powers, your control, it only works on humans. The others, the ones you order me to send away – to *kill*, because nothing from this world can survive in the place I send them, I know that, I think I always knew that – they aren't human, either. That's why they're a threat to you. You kill anyone you can't control. But I can recognize people who aren't human, Moon. You didn't know that, did you? I can see them, a sort of glow, the strangeness in me reaching out to the strangeness in them. I'm not *stupid*. I see the pattern in the people you send me to… to kill. They all glow, because the humans who trouble you simply become part of you, instead. Some of these people you send me after shine brightly, others are dim, depending, I think, on how powerful they are. I used to think that glow was a sign of wickedness, but I knew that couldn't be right. Because *you* glow, too."

"What are you saying?" The Moon's voice was flat. "You have never seen me. You cannot know anything about what I am."

Estrella pointed to the left, where the towering pillar of the Moon's otherworldly power rose up. "I can see your glow from here, Moon. I have always been able to see where you–"

Something struck her on the back of the head. She fell to her knees, stunned and disoriented. "Traitor," the guard said and kicked her in the chest. "Ungrateful, vicious, meddling, stupid–"

The person behind her, who'd crept up and struck her, wrenched her arms back viciously, while the other guard tore her purse away and dumped out the contents. He snatched up her needle case, cracked it open to look inside, and then raced away toward the slaughterhouse. The person holding her arms released her, shoving her down to the ground. Estrella groaned and rolled over in time to see the person draw a knife. She shouted, "No!" and reached up, her hands flaring with purple light like the afterimage of a lightning strike.

The knife clattered to the floor. The attacker was gone. Or... most of him was gone. His legs were still there, from the shins down, faintly smoking. She hadn't sent him away to the place that could be reached through the door inside her heart. Instead, she'd let a little of the power of that place out, channeled through her hands.

Estrella gasped and scrambled back, appalled. She looked at the tower of red smoke that marked the Moon's location. She wasn't sure exactly where the Moon was – probably locked away in some vault below the earth, a bolthole created during the construction of the Matadero by enthralled builders – but Estrella would find her way inside...

Then scores of people began to pour out of the gate, wiry women and massive men, carrying crowbars and hammers and pipes. Some of them were no older than Estrella herself. "What is this?" Estrella cried out.

"These are my family!" The biggest of the men, with biceps as thick as Estrella's thighs, stepped forward, holding a maul. "You can't get to me without coming through them, Estrella! Will you kill them all?"

"You would use their lives to shield your own?" Even knowing what she did now, Estrella was aghast.

The man in front boomed with the Moon's laughter. "They're *blessed* to serve such a divine purpose! They're just people, Estrella. They're ordinary. They aren't like you and me. They don't matter."

"Everyone matters," Estrella said. "Whatever else I might be, I am a person, too. But these people are just bodies to you, aren't they? You really are a ghoul."

"I was born a ghoul," the Blood Moon said through their mouthpiece. "I started out life that way, scrabbling in the colony in the hidden quarter, but I have become so much more. I found my Keys, I transcended my origins, I ascended to new heights, I became a god, self-created! I am nothing that has ever been on the face of the world or the chambers underground before. I am the Blood Moon!"

Estrella took a step back as the man approached her, weapon held high. "But why?" she cried. "You told me you wanted to make the world better, but what do you *really* want?"

"I do want to make the world better. The world better…" The giant took a deep breath and then all of them, the whole massed crowd of thralls, shouted two words in unison: "For me!"

Then they rushed her, weapons raised.

Estrella could have killed them all. She could have sent them all away. Let the void have them. But they weren't here willingly. They were innocents.

And those innocents would tear her head from her body if

she let them catch her. So instead, she turned and she ran with all the speed granted her by the touch of the outsider deep in her bloodline, and while she ran, she wept.

"I have you now."

The voice in Sanford's head was gleeful and rasping and as clearly audible as if the speaker were in bed beside him.

"Mmm, hello, Blood Moon," Sanford said, and the Warden sat up straighter in her chair by the bed, suddenly alert. "So, that's what you really sound like."

"What?" she demanded. "What did you say?"

Sanford waved a hand at her. "Be quiet a moment, would you, Sarah? I'm engaged in a psychic test of wills."

"There is no test," the Moon said. "There is only my will and your submission. I have your blood now, Sanford. My little star brought it to me."

"What a shocking development," Sanford said mildly. "Who could have possibly foreseen such a happening? You'd think I might have anticipated this, since I was here when she took my blood, but no, you have shocked me to my very core. Indeed, I am so shaken, I may never recover."

The Warden could only hear one side of the conversation, but she gave him a thin smile anyway.

Sanford felt incredibly good and relaxed. He'd experimented with various entheogenic and specialized compounds before, of course – inhaled peculiar smoke in remote caverns, sipped the juice of unearthly berries in ceremonies in the jungle, eaten the occasional unlikely mushroom – in his quest for knowledge and understanding of the world's hidden mysteries. But the potion he'd brewed up based on Anna Elizabeth's books on blood magic was something else. The euphoria was a side effect, but a pleasant one. "How do you like my blood, Moon?" he asked. "Ha. Blood, moon? Blood Moon!"

"What do you mean?" The voice flickered with suspicion. "Are you *drunk*?"

"No, not at all. I mean, my blood must be especially delicious, or whatever the psychic equivalent of deliciousness is, as I am a remarkably remarkable individual–"

"Silence, thrall."

Sanford felt a fleeting urge to be quiet, but his psyche was a whirling maelstrom. Nothing imposed from the outside could survive in that environment long before being torn apart in a whirlpool of ideation. Trying to control his mind was like trying to lasso smoke. Once the effects of his potion wore off, Sanford would be vulnerable to the Moon's control, though, so despite his scattered thoughts, he tried to focus. "So let me see if I understand. Now that we're connected, I've got one of those threads extending from the back of my head, up into the cloud above the city? That's the conduit that lets you send your thoughts into my head?"

"Be silent, I said!" Was there a hint of panic in the Moon's voice?

"The thing about conduits, though, is they flow both ways. If you're connected to me, I'm connected to you. Now, you're very strong, or rather, your Keys are. The force of your power usually produces too much pressure for anything to flow the other way, like a water pipe gushing out a hundred gallons per second. Who can swim upstream against a current like that? It would take a nimble fish indeed." He turned his head and smiled at Van Shaw. "I'll be back shortly, Warden. Don't fret if I look slightly dead."

The Blood Moon hissed at him. "Why are you... your

mind is so *slippery*, what have you done? You can't stop me, Sanford, I am the greatest blood magician in the history of the world, it is only a matter of time–"

Sanford ignored the bluster and sent his mind crawling up the tether that attached him to the Blood Moon.

CHAPTER NINETEEN
A Meeting of the Minds

Altman and the vanquisher killed and killed, hunting and murdering the minions of the Moon, cutting off the Blood Moon's tethers in a widening circle, reducing the number of nodes and the Moon's reach, winnowing the Moon's collective might.

Altman and the vanquisher. The vanquisher and Altman. But they were so unified in purpose and delight, now, that the distinction between them was increasingly irrelevant.

Estrella stumbled through the streets of Madrid. She wanted to go home, but the Gullettes, her adoptive parents, were the Moon's thralls. They would kill her, wouldn't they? They would turn on her with the knives used to chop vegetables for dinner, with the scissors used to cut her hair, or with their bare hands, if it came to that.

This city belonged to the Blood Moon, and she was no longer the Moon's heir, but their enemy.

She didn't know what to do. She didn't know where to go. She didn't know who she *was*.

• • •

This process of climbing up his own blood tether was like astral projection, something Sanford had a fair bit of experience with. He simply thought his way up the pulsing filament, moving slowly at first, like climbing a rope hand over hand. Then he grew accustomed to being a bodiless mind and it became more like sledding down a snowy hill, except he was sliding up, toward the ceiling of Anna Elizabeth's spare room.

He even managed to bring his senses along with him, or at least, some of them – vision and hearing, anyway. That was fine. He doubted he'd want to smell or taste or touch the things he was going to encounter soon.

Briefly, he wondered if he'd ever smell or taste or touch anything else ever again. If this worked, he would gain valuable information and knock his opponent off balance in the process. If it failed… well, the worst scenarios were all fairly dreadful. His mind might be obliterated. His soul might be lost forever, his body an empty husk wasting away. He might even be trapped in *another* body. The prospect would have terrified him, if he hadn't left his glands down below. As it was, he assessed his chances of success and found them good enough to go on. There was no great win without great risk.

Sanford's psyche ascended through the ceiling of Anna Elizabeth's building and out into the night air. He kept climbing the blood conduit, ignoring the mewlings and yammerings of the Blood Moon so he could focus.

His vision was panoramic in this psychic form. The city spread out below him, glittering with lights, alive with people and motion. He could see all the blood tethers in the city, now, without the need for the opera glasses, perhaps because he was climbing up one of them, or maybe as another side effect of the potion – the answer might interest occult researchers, but he was more concerned with the practical effect. Sanford slid up the tether, high into the air, pausing to admire the moon – not a blood moon, or a blue moon, or a black moon, or any sort of special moon at all, just a waxing crescent, but it was beautiful, nonetheless.

I should take more time to admire beauty, Sanford thought. All this rush, rush, fight, fight, win, win – what's it all in service of, if not to enjoy the world I seek to master?

The Blood Moon's shrieking redoubled, and climbing the tether suddenly became more difficult. Ah, the old ghoul was trying hard to control him – and the Blood Moon *was* a ghoul, Sanford could tell that now; he'd met enough of them under French Hill and in the Dreamlands, and he could taste the old sorcerer's mind. But something – perhaps long association with the Keys, or just some strange thread in their lineage – made the Blood Moon into something much more than *just* a ghoul, in the way Estrella was more than human. A singular creature, perhaps, unlike any other entity on the Earth or below.

A shame to have to kill such a rare thing. Ah, well. The efficacy of the potion was already waning (just like the moon above) and time was short, so Sanford pushed himself harder.

He ascended his own conduit and entered the great knotted mass of threads above the city. They crossed and recrossed one another like a knot of wriggling worms – oh, the threads were pulsing in time with the heartbeats of the people they were connected to, that made sense! Sanford's pulsed at a stately fifty beats per minute.

He worked his way through the tangle, humming a little, insofar as a disconnected psychic cloud could hum. He climbed over strands, slithered under them, and unpicked the deliberate mess of obfuscation the Blood Moon had created to hide their location.

As Sanford crawled, other threads shriveled and fell away, not a lot of them, but steadily. That was Altman out there, killing the tethered. That was an unfortunate necessity, but the Blood Moon found power in numbers, and so diminishing those numbers would diminish Sanford's enemy. Losing nodes would make the Moon panic – the ghoul had been so secure, so seemingly invincible for so long, that even losing one or two percent of their thralls in Madrid would seem like a terrifying violation. This ongoing massacre would also fuel the vanquisher, and Sanford wanted that dread beast absolutely bursting with power for the inevitable confrontation with the Moon.

Sanford was, in fact, capable of guilt, a fact that would have stunned many of his associates and rivals, but he didn't feel all that guilty about any of this. He hadn't put those humans down there in danger, after all: the Blood Moon had done that. Once the Moon was dead, thousands of people would be freed, himself included. If some had to die in service to that, well, the arithmetic worked out for him.

Ah, and there it was. Sanford reached the end of his tether, but it wasn't the end. It was the place where all the threads joined together in a single knot, hidden in the center of the cloud, like a nerve bundle at the base of the skull. There was a single thread, gossamer thin, reaching back down to the ground, to the source. The Moon had found a way to hide that vast collective blood signature, somehow–

Ah, very clever. There was a slaughterhouse down there, a temple of blood with countless gallons of the stuff spilled every day. The Moon had hidden the etheric signature of their conduit amid all that sanguinary noise. Such an idea wouldn't even have occurred to Sanford. It was neatly done. "I *do* respect you, Moon," Sanford said. "You're very good at this. Please don't take this assault personally. It's only that you're standing between me and what I want."

"I… will… make… you… eat… your… own… fingers!" the Moon shouted, and pushed harder, but Sanford was getting better at surfing the conduit now. He sidestepped the grasping psychic force and plunged down, racing along the final thread, straight into the heart of the Blood Moon's lair. It was like swimming over the edge of a waterfall and being carried along by the doubled forces of gravity and the current. He watched the slaughterhouse rush up, and burst through the roof of a pavilion, down through a confusion of cows and into the earth, into the vault–

Everything went dark as Sanford's psyche overlapped with the Blood Moon's, competing willpowers fighting for control, but then Sanford found a niche where he could safely nestle in the Blood Moon's strange mind and looked out through the creature's eyes.

The vault was dark and filthy, a cavern hollowed out of the rock, the domed ceiling above held up by rough stone pillars. A handful of yellowish alchemical lights attached to columns and on the ceiling illuminated the space, which did not benefit from visibility. There were human and animal skulls everywhere, in piles on the floor and cemented haphazardly to the walls, and long tables heaped with gobbets of raw meat and fragments of bone. Flames flickered in a black metal brazier, sending smoke to stain the ceiling. This was the Moon's command center and dining room, all in one!

Sanford tried to make the Moon turn their head, to look for entrances to the lair, but he couldn't control their body at all; ah, well, that would have been too much to hope for, here in the seat of the Moon's power. But over there, off to the side, visible in Sanford's periphery, there was an immense cabinet – stacked rows of cabinets, like the card catalogs at the Biblioteca Nacional de España.

That must be the Moon's blood library with droplets from all their thralls smeared on slides within, linked psychically to the ghoul itself. In fact… yes, Sanford could feel a tiny speck of himself over there in the cabinet, the drawer still slightly ajar. He was aware of that blood drop's location just as he was aware of the current position of his littlest toe (which, at the moment, was some miles away, but still).

"Hmm, this slaughterhouse only commenced operations recently," Sanford said, his words emerging audibly from the Blood Moon's mouth – ha, he hadn't even meant to do that! "Do you mean to say you've made the place *this* filthy *that* quickly?"

"Get out of my head!" the Moon screamed, thrashing, making the view of the room jerk around. Sanford would have been nauseated if he'd been more attached to his stomach. "How – how is this possible? How are you *in* me?"

"You may be the Blood Moon," Sanford said. "But I am the Blood Magus." That wasn't really true – he dabbled in blood magic at best – but it *sounded* good, didn't it? And he'd need some sort of scarlet sobriquet once he joined the Coterie. Maybe he'd test out a few more, just to be sure.

Sanford felt some small urge to gloat, but he'd acquired the information he needed, and that meant it was time to begin the process of disentanglement. Best to do that now, while the Moon was still panicking at this unprecedented violation.

"Now, let's see," Sanford said. "First, I'm going to take control of your nearest thralls – ah, you've got big strong guards, don't you?" He couldn't actually sense any of the Moon's victims. He'd followed his connection into the Moon, but wasn't strong or savvy enough to flow out of the Moon into any of their minions. Sanford was fairly certain if he even tried, he'd get lost, or maybe even trapped in someone else's body. Repulsive. But it was a safe bet that the Moon had burly tough people guarding their inner sanctum and, well, manipulation was all part of the game.

"No!" the Moon screamed. "No, stop, you can't do this, I won't allow it!"

"I wasn't asking permission," Sanford said. "You're *my* thrall now, don't you see? I'm inside you. All your powers are mine. Oh, you're putting up a token resistance, but I'll knock those walls down in time."

Those walls were impenetrable, invincible. But Sanford didn't need to break through the Blood Moon's shields. Sanford just needed to make the Blood Moon afraid that he could.

The Moon scrabbled across the old bloodstains on the stone floor, toward the blood library. They reached out for a drawer. That was Sanford's first look at any part of the Moon's body: a wiry arm covered in coarse black hair, a clawed hand with gore clotted under the nails. They scrabbled at the drawer, dumped the glass slides inside out onto the floor, and began sorting through them until they found the one containing Sanford's blood, a fresh drop, still wet-looking between the thin sheets of glass.

The Moon took the slide, put it on a table, and then picked

up a scepter made of rose gold – the Moon's Key, or one of its Keys? The Moon used the butt of the scepter to smash the slide, then scooped up the fragments and flung them into a brazier, where they sizzled. "I banish you!" the Moon shrieked.

Sanford had been a little worried about this part. He'd been fairly certain he could frighten and goad the Moon into severing their connection, but what if he ended up stuck in the creature's mind, unable to return to his own body? His research suggested that he should be all right, that minds really preferred to stay in the bodies they belonged to, but it wasn't a certainty.

Luckily, when that drop of Sanford's blood burned, his tether snapped, and Sanford's psyche was ripped from the ghoul, moving slowly at first and then with great speed on through the ceiling, the floor, past the cows, and through the ceiling again, and into the sky, and back down the disintegrating connection on into his own body.

In those first moments, though, rising away slowly, Sanford got a good look at the Blood Moon: a ghoul in ragged robes, adorned with a rose-gold crown covered in sharp spikes and spines like thorns.

Goodbye, Moon, Sanford thought. Until we meet again.

"Sanford!" the Warden cried. "Are you all right?"

"Hmm?" he said. "Oh. Did I seem dead? Apologies." He yawned and blinked heavily. "I need to sleep now, Warden. That took a lot out of me. I don't think anyone will bother us before morning. Altman's vanquisher has made the immediate area rather inhospitable for the Moon's minions, but if anyone does come knocking with ill intent, kill them, would you? This time they won't be satisfied with a chat and a blood sample."

"What is *happening*?" the Warden demanded. "What did you do?"

Sanford snuggled down into the covers. He was sobering up. That was too bad, but it was better to have his wits intact for the next part of his plans. His euphoria was sufficient to carry him into sleep before fading entirely, at least. "Oh, I took care of my little blood problem and found out where the Blood Moon lives. In the morning, when Altman comes back, we'll settle our outstanding business, the three of us – four, if we count Altman's passenger – and then, oh, I suppose I'll have to go and kill the Blood Moon."

"Is *that* all?" the Warden said. "How do you intend–?"

But Sanford was already falling asleep.

Estrella hunched in a doorway, glaring out at the night, and hugged herself, and her fear slowly transmuted into fury. Her mind churned and churned.

Altman stumbled to the bookshop and rattled the door. When it didn't open, the vanquisher did something and the lock clicked free. Altman stumbled inside, bloody and yawning, and shut the door behind him.

Wipe your feet this time, the vanquisher said.

Altman did, mechanically, though that didn't do anything about the blood splashed all over his body. There were only two bedrooms upstairs, Sanford's and the Waite woman's, so Altman limped into the dark back of the shop, found a corner to curl up in, and slept the brief hour before dawn.

• • •

The early morning news reports blamed the scattered mass-acre throughout the center of Madrid on various things: anarchists attempting to sow chaos; republicans trying to undermine the authority of the military government by proving they couldn't protect the people; a secret army of Catalans out to revenge past crimes; criminals killing indiscriminately in a gang war; or a terrible death cult made up of foreigners who hated the Spanish way of life. The exact death toll was unknown, since in addition to the corpses on the streets, others were still turning up in unexpected places: on rooftops, in the branches of trees, and in one case, shoved partway through a mail slot. But even counting the confirmed cases, there were at least a hundred dead bodies and, apparently, no one had seen or heard anything in the night.

If there were any witnesses, they'd been killed, too, or else the things they'd seen had frightened them so much that they would never breathe a word about them to anyone.

"Carl!" Anna Elizabeth shouted and he jolted upright. Oh dear. She looked positively furious. The Warden stood by the head of the bed, as if ready to protect him. It was wonderful how easily she fell back into the habit of obeying his instructions. That boded well for his future plans.

"Oh, Anna, good morning. Might you have such a thing as a soft-boiled egg? I feel a bit peckish."

The bookseller crossed her arms and glared. "Carl, there are a hundred fresh corpses scattered throughout Madrid, and your *thug* is downstairs asleep in my naval history room covered in blood."

"Ah," Sanford said. No wonder she was furious. "Only a hundred? I overestimated the thing's appetite. Well, please, send Altman to wash up and then tell him I need to speak with him urgently."

"I am not your maid. I want you out of my shop, Sanford. Right now!"

Black dogs slithered out from under the bed and began growling. Anna Elizabeth stepped back, alarmed.

"I am very sorry for the inconvenience, Anna," Sanford said, and it was true. He hated the idea of souring their friendship. "I will leave and take my associates and their pets with me later today. There are, unfortunately, some preparations we must undertake first. I will see that you are well compensated for your troubles. I know your finder's fee must be quite large by now."

"And if I insist?" Anna Elizabeth asked. "If I demand that you leave?"

"I would be quite understanding and do my best to comply, despite my injuries," Sanford said. "But that bloody thug downstairs is responsible for the scores of bodies you mentioned. I'm afraid *he* might object quite strenuously if I departed before we concluded our business."

Anna Elizabeth quivered with outrage, then turned and stormed out.

"Please send Altman up!" Sanford called after her, knowing he was pouring salt on the wound. It would take more than a few rare occult items to patch this argument up. She only really called him by his surname when at her wit's end.

Breakfast could wait. He reached over and patted the Warden's hand. "Give Altman and me a little privacy, if you would? We need to discuss his future."

"My future is tied to his!" Van Shaw objected.

"Not for much longer," Sanford said. "After I deal with him, we'll address the issue of the oaths and bindings that tie your fate to the Order. I promise. But you know how Altman is. He gets embarrassed and then he blusters. We'll be able to talk more freely without an audience. Perhaps you could help me smooth this incident over with Anna."

"Unlikely." The Warden scowled and departed, followed by her hounds, who jostled together until they coalesced into a single immense mastiff.

Sanford threw back the covers and got to his feet. He checked his wound and found it adequately improved. He wasn't operating at one hundred percent, but Carl Sanford at eighty percent was more formidable than most at full strength.

As requested when he first arrived, Anna Elizabeth had gone to his shabby rented rooms and recovered his valise and walking stick. She'd offered to settle Sanford's bill and added a sizeable tip in exchange for access, and the clerk had proven open to such bribery. He went to his valise now, resting on the dresser against the wall, and sorted through his belongings. Anna Elizabeth had thrown away his bloodied clothes, apparently – a reasonable action – but he had a spare shirt and trousers purchased at the same shop, and he put them on, wincing in the process. He sat in the chair and was just pulling on his socks when Altman came in, hunched and groaning.

"Suffering from a murder hangover, are we?" he asked cheerfully.

Altman rubbed a hand over his face, leaning in the doorway. "I… think I overindulged."

Sanford leaned back with his hands crossed on his stomach, taking in the sight of the bloodied man. The potion in his blood had ebbed, so he couldn't see any power crackling off the man or the eldritch tendrils no doubt wrapped around

Altman's body like a strangling vine, but he knew they were there.

"*The True History of the Vanquishers of the Serpents of the Night, and the Means by Which to Bind and Command Them,*" Sanford said. "That's the full title of the book you found. It's a shame you couldn't read all the warnings and caveats, but the vanquishers tend to erase everything but the summoning ritual." He paused, then cocked his head. "Tell me, Altman. Have you started to enjoy it yet?"

"Enjoy what?" he growled.

"The killing, of course. People who make imperfect bargains with the vanquishers all go through the same experience. First their former sources of pleasure are twisted or burned away until they can only find joy in violence. I understand that part happens quickly, and after last night… well. If you didn't like it, that must have been a horrible experience for you."

"It was wonderful." The vanquisher's gargling, hissing voice spoke up. "Altman is coming along nicely."

"Let me speak to your host, please," Sanford said wearily. "You and I will talk later."

Altman straightened up and walked into the room, standing before Sanford, probably trying to be threatening. "What is it?" he asked, waspish and cranky.

"I just wondered if you'd hand me my walking stick." Sanford gestured. "With my wound, you see, it's hard for me to get around easily."

"I want to talk about the Order, and how you're going to help me win it back!"

Sanford sighed. "I will, but I'd like to stand up, at least. You're looming over me and you're full of monster."

Altman huffed, stomped to the dresser, and retrieved the walking stick, handing it over.

"Thank you," Sanford said with great dignity. Using the stick in one hand and levering himself up from the armchair with the other, he rose ponderously to his feet. "I want you to know, Altman, that I do understand you. I know what it's like, desiring power and everything power can offer. If I'm entirely honest, I see a little bit of myself in you." A rather less talented version, admittedly. "But."

"But what?" Altman said.

"But I don't forgive you," Sanford said.

He whipped the sword from his walking stick and severed Altman's head from his shoulders in a single scything motion.

CHAPTER TWENTY
Broken Oaths

Estrella looked up and down the mostly deserted early morning street, then darted across to the bookshop. She raised her fist to knock and then paused when a long, shrill scream emerged from within, followed by shouts and other commotion. She considered bursting in but drew back instead. She'd spent too much time rushing into places lately. She needed to learn patience, and to wait, and to listen.

The Warden clutched her chest and collapsed to her knees in the kitchen, her head pounding like someone had cracked her skull with a felling axe. Then, she pitched forward onto her face, jarring her nose badly in the process. She wasn't even aware that she'd made a sound until Waite rushed in, shouting, "What's wrong, what's happened?"

Van Shaw couldn't speak. She weakly rolled over and grabbed onto the neck of her hound, hoping to absorb its power back into herself. The hound diminished, shrinking under her touch, until nothing remained but a few strands of coarse black hair clutched in her fingers. At that point, Waite screamed and ran out of the room. She'd read a lot about magic, it seemed, but apparently hadn't witnessed much, or at least nothing as dramatic as this.

Sanford, the Warden thought in fury. What had he done? She never should have trusted him! He always had plots within plots, and people were nothing but game pieces. She dragged her body along the tiled floor, propelling herself by force of will even as her soul tried to tear itself out of her body and cast itself into oblivion. She might die and disintegrate like her hound before she made it up the stairs, but if she made it to the top, she'd take the magus with her.

Sanford heard the Warden's scream and ignored it. She was a problem for later.

"What have you done?" Altman's severed head cried out in the vanquisher's hideous voice. Said head was on the floor by the dresser, resting on its left ear, mostly facing Sanford. That mouth shouldn't have been able to speak, being disconnected from the body's airways and so forth, but the beast was so fat with power from last night's massacre that it could doubtless make its voice emerge from anywhere.

Sanford wiped some of the blood from his face, then nudged the body with his foot. He kept his sword handy, because it was possible the vanquisher would be able to control the headless corpse, in which case he'd be forced to do a lot of tedious dismemberment. But after a moment it became apparent that separating the brain from the spinal column was sufficient to cut the vanquisher's puppet strings and render it harmless. As long as he didn't get close enough to the still-possessed head to get bitten, anyway.

"I'm terribly sorry about all that," Sanford said, wiping the bloody sword on the bedspread. Anna could add replacing that to his tally. "Dramatic, I know, but necessary."

"You just *had* to get your revenge!" the vanquisher said.

"You just *had* to let your petty stupid human rivalries–"

"Revenge?" Sanford shook his head. "Tut-tut, vanquisher. Altman turned against me, yes, but we were hardly friends. He was only ever an employee. He wanted power and did all he could to attain it. I can't fault him for that. I've schemed my way to the top of many organizations in my time. Of course, I was good enough to actually reach the top and stay there, recent setbacks aside." In fact, Sanford's current plan to scheme his way to the top of the Red Coterie was working out nicely. Although, over these past few days, he'd begun to reconsider some of his goals. He couldn't stop thinking about being high up in the clouds, looking over the magnificence of the city, and wondering what it all added up to in the end. Regardless, he needed to deal with the Blood Moon and soon. He could sort through his ambivalence about other matters later, when the most formidable blood magician in history was no longer trying to destroy him.

Sanford crouched, wincing a little from his wound, and nudged the head with the top of his walking stick, the blade sheathed inside again. "Aren't you impressed? I charmed this blade to kill monsters long ago. It's etched with sigils and anointed with oils, and it cut Altman's head free faster than you could heal him. He always did overestimate his own formidability. His brother was scarier. He's dead, now, too."

"Stop gloating," the vanquisher said. "You cut my host's head off. I don't need to know how you did it. I need to know *why*. Altman was going to help you kill the Blood Moon! His will was weak, his need for approval from his betters pathetic, and you could have kept stringing him along for ages. It wouldn't have mattered to me."

Sanford sat down, cross-legged. "You made the usual

bargain, then? You agreed to help Altman achieve his mortal goals and in exchange, you would receive full and eternal possession of his body after his soul departed?"

The head hissed. "How do you know about our *usual bargains*?"

Sanford clucked his tongue. "Knowing things is my business. Once I realized Altman had made a deal with you, I wracked my brain to remember everything I'd read about your kind. Fortunately, Anna had a monograph on the subject, written by a scholar of the unexpurgated volume describing your conquests. She really is quite wonderful, my Anna. That helped fill in the gaps."

"I prefer to be more mysterious. But yes. That is the deal I made with Altman: my power to achieve his aims in exchange for shared use of his body now and free use after his death."

Sanford nodded. "Altman was too foolish, and too ignorant, to put any other stipulations in place during the negotiations, I take it?"

"Negotiations? Does the lamb negotiate with the butcher?" The vanquisher laughed, a sound like angry snakes in a bag. "I got everything forever, and he got the merest pittance of my power. And now I'm stuck in this useless body unless I can get someone to sew the head back on, and quickly–"

"Oh, no, I'll burn the body," Sanford said. "And the head, too, of course. Then you'll be returned to the place you came from. 'The writhing world,' I believe you call it?"

"Nobody calls it that," the vanquisher complained. "It's poetic license. But it's a terrible place. No fun at all. There's nothing to eat but each other at this point. Why, magus? Why ruin my fun now, when it sets back your own cause? I'm more useful as an ally than a severed head in a fire."

"I did it because you were no good to me inside Altman,"

Sanford said. "I need you to be inside *me*." He tapped his chest. "With that in mind, I've drawn up a contract laying out the terms of our shared habitation of my mortal vessel."

"Ah. Hmm. Go on."

Sanford opened a drawer in the bedside table and withdrew a folder. Anna Elizabeth had been kind enough to bring him pen and paper along with all his other demands when he first arrived. "There are several pages, but I can hold them up for you to read, if you like."

After he'd flipped through most of the document, the vanquisher hissed. "Enough! This is a terrible contract. I am to reside inside you, silently, unless called upon to use the fullest extent of my power for your benefit, in exactly the ways you demand, and I am not permitted to feed on anyone without permission, and I can't meddle with your glands in any way?"

"And when my soul departs my body, after a long life during which you will do everything in your power to keep me alive and healthy, you inherit my body to use as you will." Barring the exercise of the sub-clause on the final page, which you didn't seem to notice, with all the other outrages taking your attention. Sanford kept his satisfied contented smile on the inside.

"Why would I accept such a bargain? It dooms me to years–"

"Decades," Sanford said.

"–decades of boredom!"

Sanford shrugged. "Then say no. You're my first option. I have contingency plans if you prove intractable. This solution to my problems is simply the most elegant." This was also the solution that involved killing Altman. Which, Sanford's grand speeches about pragmatism aside, had been rather satisfying.

"I'll starve," the vanquisher whined.

"Nonsense," Sanford said. "In the writhing world, you all persist without devouring any life essence at all, except one another's. And after last night's massacre, you're filled with power, enough to last you for years upon years. That's why I sent you out there to gobble up everything in sight. One of the reasons, anyway."

"You … are … horrible."

"In my way," Sanford acknowledged. "But listen. Given the sort of life I live, someone is always trying to kill me, capture me, or overthrow me. You will certainly get to eat people again. I promise." He paused. "Said promise not to be considered part of our binding contract as heretofore elucidated. If that's not good enough for you, I'll start that fire I mentioned. Decide quickly. The Warden will doubtless be here soon and she'll be cross with me."

"I hate lawyers," the vanquisher said. "You really enjoy negotiating from a position of strength, don't you?"

"Lamb, meet butcher," Sanford said blithely.

"Fine," the vanquisher said. "Gods, you remind me of my spawnmother, and that is not a compliment."

They didn't shake hands (the vanquisher lacked them), or sign a document, or burn special candles, or draw dread sigils, because all those things were unnecessary: what mattered was the promise, and an entity that was forced by its very nature to abide by all agreements – even those it hadn't read fully. As above, so below. The deal was struck and Sanford shivered as the vanquisher passed from Altman's remnant into his own body. The transition was eased by the dregs of the dissociative potion in Sanford's bloodstream and caused only a brief frisson of discomfort. The head's eyes went glazed and lifeless, just a relic of a wasted life.

Sanford could sense the presence of the vanquisher inside him, like an extra tooth in the back of his mouth, but he'd get used to the feeling. Without the creature meddling with his glands and trying to overpower his mind, he shouldn't suffer the same agonies and fevers that Altman doubtless had. There was no struggle here, only a partnership, unequal in Sanford's favor, just as he preferred.

Something scratched at the door, like a dog begging to be let in. She'd made it up faster than he'd expected. Sarah really was a remarkable woman. Sanford opened the door and looked down at the Warden on the floor, who'd dragged herself up the stairs and onto the landing, despite her visible disintegration after the death of Altman and the Order. Her hair came out in clumps, and her face was drawn and haggard, like a skeleton under a thin sheet of cloth.

"Hello, Sarah," Sanford said. "My oldest friend."

"Are the candles really necessary?" the Warden rasped from the bed where Sanford had placed her. He was still recovering from his wound, but she weighed barely as much as a sack of feathers now, so it had been no great struggle. "You want to watch me die in more flattering light?"

"Do try to have a sense of occasion, my dear." He'd found a few candles in the dresser and arrayed them around the room. He thought back to that night so long ago, when the Warden lay atop the obsidian stone of sacrifice in the woods of another world, surrounded by Seekers holding blazing torches. This setting hardly compared, but Sanford would make do. Once the last candle was lit, he turned off the lamp by the bed, so only candlelight illuminated the room.

"Don't 'my dear' me," Van Shaw snapped, some of her own

thorniness emerging even in her extremity. "By killing Altman you've killed me!"

"Now, now, Sarah, you did bring this on yourself. You were quite healthy when I was the one in charge of the Order of the Silver Twilight." He sat on the bed beside her, taking one of her gnarled hands in his. If she'd tried to shake him off, he would have obliged her and let go, but she didn't. *Do we all want comfort, at the end?* he wondered. He'd find out in time, he supposed. "But you decided Altman was a better choice to lead."

"It wasn't that," she rasped. "I was a prisoner, a fixture of the Order. You never treated me that way in the beginning and then time went by, and I became nothing but a tool to you."

I'm not your maid, Anna Elizabeth had said. The accusation echoed in his mind, making him uncomfortable.

"And I just knew Tillinghast was going to beat you," Sarah continued. "I knew, because he convinced me to turn on you, and if he could convince *me*, there was no hope for anyone else. You got complacent, Sanford. You assumed you were at the top of the wheel of fortune forever, and it would never turn and put you facedown in the mud again."

Sanford chuckled. "An astute observation, albeit one I would have argued with vociferously if you'd made it back then. I understand why you did what you did, Sarah. But, alas, you are bound to the Order, and the Order is dead, now, its leader headless on the floor."

"You can lead us again." She clutched at him weakly. "Just… just declare that the Order is yours again, let the membership know you're alive. Your claim is better than anyone else's."

"No thank you," he said politely. "I will rebuild what I lost in time, but such a declaration wouldn't be useful to me at the moment."

"Then please… free me… you promised… from my oath." Her eyes were wide and pleading, and one pupil was much smaller than the other.

"Ah, but you see, if I released you from your oath, you would still die," Sanford said. "I suppose I should have mentioned that. I wasn't lying earlier, when I said you're not really human anymore." Neither was Sanford, since taking the vanquisher into himself, not entirely. "You are composed more of magic than you are of flesh. The truth is, the oath can't be broken without breaking you in the process. That binding is intrinsic to you now: your very nature is to be a protector with your strength tied to something else. Like the tales of the Fisher King, who prospered when his nation prospered and sickened when his nation did."

Van Shaw groaned, a sound of inhuman anguish.

He patted her hand. "All is not lost. Hear me out. The reason I bound you in service to the Order of the Silver Twilight, and not to me personally, is because I hoped the Order would outlive me. I wanted you to watch over my creation forever. But, alas, I have outlived the Order, instead." Sanford listened to her labored breathing and decided to stop drawing things out. The Warden had betrayed him, yes, but he had all the power now, and there was no reason to see her suffer any longer. Gloating was like salt; a little seasoning improved things, but too much spoiled the dish. "I cannot release you from your oath, WWarden, but, if you're willing, I could facilitate a transfer."

"What… do… you mean?" She struggled to speak each word.

"Your life must be bound to *something*. So, I could bind your life to mine."

She was silent for a while, gathering strength. "I was your employee before, but now I would be… your thrall. Forced to protect you and serve you, as I once served the Order, to put your needs above all else, even my own life."

"That's what I'm offering, yes. You would retain your considerable powers, and while you'd be bound to remain in my company, you'd get to travel far more than you did when you were bound to the–"

"You're no better than the Blood Moon," the Warden said. Her voice was a hoarse whisper, but no less contemptuous for that.

"I have noted the resemblance in this particular instance," Sanford said, "and I can't say it pleases me. I would keep you on a long leash, but it's still a leash. The alternative is I let you die, which, believe it or not, would grieve me mightily. Let me know what you choose."

"I thought I would choose death, if I had the choice again," the Warden said. "But now… in the moment… I find I fear the darkness. More… after all the things I've done… I fear finding something *other* than darkness. I will serve you." She tried to spit but couldn't manage it.

"Then let us speak the words of binding, my dear Warden."

Once the rite was done, Sanford trembled again. He could feel the Warden, too, and it was much more than an extra tooth or a splinter in the mind. It was more like a whole extra set of limbs, a whole body that he could move as easily as his own.

But he wouldn't use Van Shaw that way, at least not unless he had no choice. He didn't need to use her like a puppet. She was sworn to defend him, *personally*, and to further his interests, and help him every way she could. There was a positive feedback loop there, too, because the stronger Sanford got, the stronger *she* became, and the better she felt.

Everything was working out just as he'd planned. Transferring the Warden's bindings from the Order to himself had been his endgame all along. He needed a Key to prove himself worthy to join the Red Coterie, and artifact of immense paradimensional power... and that Key was the Warden. She'd been transformed long ago, remade in a ritual under alien skies, connected to ancient powers, and even she didn't realize the full extent of her abilities. She wasn't a person, anymore, not really. She was a living artifact, a nexus of power. Now, she was Sanford's to wield.

He just had to take care of the Moon, and show the Coterie his Key, and take his place among them. And then, take his place at the *head* of them, in time.

He would have thought that having victory in his grasp would have felt more... stirring.

The Warden sat up with a gasp. She looked at her hands, smooth and strong again, and touched her hair, long and lustrous. "Sanford, I... I feel so good. It was never like this before. How are you so powerful?"

"I always was," he said blandly. The real answer was, "Because I contain a vanquisher, flush with the life essence of hundreds of victims," but it pleased him to let her be impressed. "Come, Warden. We have a Moon to kill. He's hidden under some slaughterhouse."

The door flew open and Estrella stood there, wreathed in purple light. She'd looked that way before, too, but last time, Sanford had been under the influence of a potion that revealed the hidden world. Now that aura blazed visible for anyone to perceive. "What wickedness are you doing?" she demanded.

The vanquisher coiled and uncoiled inside him, eager to be called upon, to unleash devastation. The Warden leaped up and over half a dozen hounds came snarling out from under the bed. The last one to emerge wasn't even a hound, but some sort of black lion. The Warden's powers really were expanding. How wonderful! Especially since they were effectively an extension of his own.

"Peace, peace," Sanford murmured, lifting a hand before violence could erupt. He gestured toward the armchair in the corner. "Have a seat, Estrella. Tell me what's on your mind."

She unclenched her fists, stared at him, looked at the headless body on the floor, and then moved slowly to the chair. "You are covered in blood."

"Indeed. Neck wounds can be messy. You haven't ever noticed?"

"I have never cut off someone's head." Her voice was small and a little lost.

"In truth, it is not an experience I can recommend." He cocked his head. "Have you come to kill me, Estrella?"

She shook her head slowly and Sanford relaxed. Even with the Warden… and the vanquisher… and his rings and amulets… and the myriad advantages of old age and treachery… he wasn't at all confident he could best this girl in a fight. The touch of the outside was strong in her.

"You're different now," she said.

"I am much recovered from my wounds, yes, thank you."

"No, I mean you… you're not human anymore. How? How can you go from one thing to another?"

He smiled. "Ah, you can perceive that? The touch of the otherworldly upon me? That is a useful ability. Yes, I have taken on a little extra help. I must face the Blood Moon, you see, and I am told they have an artifact that allows them to compel the obedience of any human in their presence. It was necessary for me, then, to become something other than entirely human."

He felt the vanquisher seethe inside him, but it didn't speak or complain.

"Oh." Estrella reached out and absently stroked the head of one of the black dogs, who consented to the touch without complaint. Estrella sat silently for a long moment and then looked up at Sanford. "Can I come with you?" she asked. "To stop the Moon?"

CHAPTER TWENTY-ONE
The Lair of the Blood Moon

Sanford pressed a small bag into Anna Elizabeth's hands before leaving the shop. The Warden and Estrella waited in the street. "For your trouble. It should cover, ah… everything."

"Where's the thug?" Anna said, frowning at the bag. She opened it, looked inside, and gasped.

"Altman? He… had to leave."

"I didn't see him leave," Anna said.

"Ah, well, he has magical powers, you know. He can do all sorts of things." In fact, Sanford had been concerned about disposing of the body, and his best plan had been to leave it on the street and let the locals think Altman was a late victim of last night's massacre. The Warden suggested that her hounds – and her ebon lion – could eat the body, though it would make her feel ill, since they were, in a way, extensions of *her*. Since that also made them extensions of *him*, Sanford didn't love the idea, either.

Then Estrella had offered to "send the body away," and Sanford had been very curious about what that entailed.

The girl asked them to stand behind her, and once they did, a coruscating black and purple light filled the room for a moment. When it stopped, Altman's remains were gone.

"I've gotten better at doing that," Estrella said. "The first few times, I accidentally sent away nearby furniture, and sometimes bits of the floor and walls. But I have become much more precise."

"Where do they go?" Sanford asked.

She shook her head. "I do not know. A ghoul I met once said I had a portal hidden inside me."

Oh, that was *very* interesting, and terrifying, because like conduits, portals opened both ways, and if she could send things to some… other place… then denizens of that other place might be able to travel here through her. But Sanford didn't have time to investigate those possibilities right now. Perhaps he could track down the Scholar, later, and ask her about the phenomenon – she'd escaped the Lodge, and she knew all sorts of interesting things. Who knew where she had ended up now?

It was pointless to muse about the future when the present still needed to be secure. Now, he patted Anna on the shoulder. "I really am terribly sorry for all the fuss and inconvenience. And, even more so, for the unkind things I said to you."

"Carl." She scattered the gems on her palm. "Are these diamonds?"

"Mostly," he said. "I know money cannot make up for everything–"

"Of course it can." She gave him a savage grin. "With this, I can get that first folio that's coming up for auction. And the misprinted Gutenberg Bible that reads 'Thou *shalt* suffer a witch to live.' And…" Her eyes positively gleamed with bookish acquisitiveness.

"Capital," Sanford said, relieved. "I look forward to hearing about all your triumphs in your next letter. I'll let you know once I have an address again. Don't forget to write me back, my dear."

She ignored him entirely, going to her desk to leaf through an auction catalogue. With a small smile, Sanford eased out onto the street, shutting the door behind him. He didn't have very many friends, and even fewer who'd never betrayed him, not even once. He was glad to hold on to one of them for a little longer.

Sanford faced his troops. A stern woman in a long dark dress, with large black dogs (and one small lion) jostling around her feet, and a young Spanish woman with dark eyes and a dress patterned with stars.

He smiled. No conqueror had ever led a deadlier army. "Let's go and have a word with the Moon, shall we?"

They paused a few blocks from the slaughterhouse. "He's still there," Estrella said. "I can see his pillar of power, stretching into the sky. I thought he'd move when I located him."

"Ghouls tend to hide more than they tend to run," Sanford said. If he'd realized Estrella could have led him right to the Moon's lair all along, he might have foregone all that business with letting her take his blood, and drinking the potion, and following the conduit into the lair. But not even the Blood Magus could know *everything*. "The Moon will be surrounded with fighters, and I'm sure they have minions out on the streets now, pricking people with needles, trying to replace the ones Altman killed."

"I don't want any more killing," Estrella said. "Those people, the Moon's prisoners, his slaves, they didn't mean anyone harm. They had no choice."

"Ah, well," Sanford said. "Altman was a savage killer,

consumed by bloodlust. We aren't like that." The vanquisher writhed and Sanford thought, Settle. "But, Estrella, well, the Moon…"

"I know the Moon must die," she said. "I don't mean that. I mean the others. The people the Moon has surrounding their lair, used as living shields. The ones he uses for bodyguards. I don't want to kill them. I won't let *you* kill them. You have to find another way. I don't know how, I know they're everywhere, there are hundreds of them between us and the Moon, but…"

Sanford spread his hands. "Estrella, darling. The minions of the Moon are only humans. Tell me, Warden. Do humans see you, if you don't want them to?"

"Of course not," she grunted. "I can't abide being stared at."

"And with my newfound power, I, too, can hide from human eyes. And we can hide you, too, Estrella. We can just stroll right in and pass all those tedious mortals by."

Estrella nodded seriously. "Then let us go."

"Stroll right in" was a bit optimistic, as it turned out. The cattle market was closed today, the gates shuttered, and every entryway lined with the Moon's people. Sanford and his band slowly circled the grounds until they found an untended stretch of wall, and then they all scrambled up to the top. Sanford didn't even need to use his gloves this time, thanks to the strength his new junior partner gave him. Access to the vanquisher's power could easily become intoxicating; Sanford would have to watch himself. The monster inside him was a seducer, even with all he'd done to contractually defang the beast.

They dropped down on the other side of the wall, into

one of the cattle yards, and picked their way through the churned mud and stoic animals. The cows couldn't see them, exactly, but animals could sense the otherworldly, especially the predatory variety, and the cattle jostled and shied away without ever fully stampeding. The skittishness of the herd made it easier for them to reach a metal gate and climb over that.

Sanford surveyed the array of pavilions. The air here reeked of cow flatulence, meat, and blood. What a terrible place to make your lair! Unless you were a ghoul, who savored the stench of open graves, Sanford supposed, and a blood magician who benefited from the confusion of overlapping etheric signatures. "Do you have any idea where we might find the entrance, Estrella?"

"The center of the pillar of power is there." She pointed to one of the largest pavilions. "Over the killing floor."

"Of course it is," Sanford said.

They walked along, rounded a corner, and found a human wall, innumerable persons wide and five or six people deep. The crowd was armed, wielding everything from chains to fencing foils to heavy stones. The living wall entirely surrounded one of the buildings, and there were more people lining the edges of the roof.

"There's no sneaking through that," Sanford said. "We may be essentially invisible, but they'll notice us shoving our way through." He considered. "You said no killing, Estrella, and I quite agree, but would you object to a little, shall we say... roughhousing?"

"Do not do any permanent harm to them, please," she said.

"I think I can arrange that. Warden? Do you think you could...?"

"I know." Her voice was miserable. "I know what you want, and what you need. The same way I used to know if the pipes in the Lodge were clogged, or there were termites in the walls, or broken windows. I can *feel* your need." She clucked her tongue, gestured, and sent six hounds – the size of black bears, with teeth like bear *traps* – and the lion racing across the courtyard.

Judging by the reaction of the Moon's guards, the creatures were visible now, because scores of the thralls screamed and rushed forward, weapons raised, attacking the animals. But the Warden's hounds moved so swiftly and fluidly that none of the blows landed. The lion grew in size and knocked over a giant of a man. Estrella cheered quietly, making Sanford wonder if she had some personal connection to the brute. If so, it wasn't a fond one. The dogs grew, too, nearly to the size of ponies, and nipped at people, driving them back.

The phalanx that surrounded the slaughterhouse didn't disappear, but it sprouted numerous gaps as the hounds sowed chaos. Sanford moved quietly forward, padding with inhuman stealth, followed by the Warden and Estrella. They found the thinnest part of the barrier and slipped between a six-foot-five bodybuilder with muttonchops and a woman in a nun's habit, and then they were inside, beyond the wall of flesh.

The interior of the slaughterhouse was dark, full of tiles, metal, and echoes, but empty of cows. There was no slaughtering happening here today. Not yet, Sanford thought. The Moon must have control over all the employees and supervisors in this place. Sanford was surprised to find the facility so bloodless, having expected deep red stains, and then he noticed the hoses on the walls. They must wash the walls and floors down every day. The Matadero hadn't been operating for too long, and it was still possible for them to make all the blood vanish.

"We are walking into the pillar of the Moon's power now, we're so close," Estrella said. "It is like walking into a tornado, but without motion. The Moon is directly below us. There must be a way down, a hidden door…"

The vanquisher roiled, and Sanford allowed it to speak. *I am good at finding openings to slither through. There's a hatch on the floor, over there, hidden behind that pillar. I can taste the lock. It's a good one.*

Sanford beckoned, and the three of them gathered around a wheel set into the center of a metal bulge in the floor. Sanford laid hands on it, and the vanquisher manipulated the locks, and then the wheel spun freely in his hands. He had a terrible vision of a shaft crammed with people, humans clinging to a ladder, shoved in shoulder to shoulder, packed too tightly to pass through without killing them.

He lifted the hatch and looked down into the hole.

The Moon apparently didn't have a mind as devious as Sanford's, because the shaft was not jammed with bodies. Then again, the Blood Moon had no reason to think Sanford's approach would be a stealthy one. After last night's grotesque excess, they'd clearly prepared for a brawl instead.

Sanford descended first, sliding down the ladder into darkness. The Moon's basements weren't as pleasant as the ones Sanford had ordered to be excavated beneath the old Lodge house. The walls here were rough stone, the floor uneven, and there were bones strewn everywhere underfoot. It was like a ghoul's lair, which, to be fair, is exactly what it was, however rarefied the ghoul's nature. Sanford led Estrella and the Warden. The alchemical lights provided a sickly glow.

Why have any illumination down here at all? Ghouls didn't need such things.

They passed a chamber full of cots, each with a steamer trunk at the foot, like in a barracks. This was where the Moon's onsite security lived, no doubt. Then they passed another chamber, this one a shower room, with hoses like the ones up above dangling from the walls. A third room was a jumble of scrap cloth and white bone fragments, no doubt the Moon's garbage heap. Sanford nudged Estrella along before she could look too closely. The young woman had seen enough horrors of late. No need to let her dwell on the eating habits of her former patron.

The lion growled, a low rumble, and the hounds joined in, looking into the midden just as half a dozen figures burst up from the filth on the floor, holding lengths of twisted metal and sharpened bone. The Moon hadn't sent *all* his guards above, it seemed. These people were filthy, bare-chested, all matted beards and wiry muscle, and Sanford wondered briefly what their role was down here – butchers, trash collectors, something more foul?

The lion and hounds pressed into the doorway, snarling. "Don't kill them!" Estrella shouted. The vanquisher turned over angrily in Sanford's mind.

"You rather limit our options, child," the Warden complained. The savage fighters inside swung their weapons at the beasts, but the beasts did not retaliate.

Sanford had a thought. "What is it they call it in American football when several people leap upon the one carrying the ball, and form a great ugly mound of bodies?"

The Warden rolled her eyes. "I believe it's called a dogpile. Very well. I can spare them. You've given me new reserves of energy."

The hounds in the midden room multiplied, dividing like amoebas under a microscope, pushing the fighters toward the back wall. The hounds weren't biting or scratching them, but simply *pressing*, furry bodies milling about, knocking the thralls over at the knees and then climbing on top of them before they could rise, pinning them to the ground in a heap of flesh. Soon the interior of the room was a moving carpet of black fur, and the occasional groan or cry.

"The hounds will keep them pinned," the Warden said. "But that's pretty much all the beasts I can conjure." The lion, clearly too dignified to participate in such an activity, waited at her side. "The Moon knows we're here now, though. The people upstairs will come for us soon."

"Then we'd best hurry on." Sanford resumed walking quickly.

Behind him, Estrella fell into step beside the Warden and said, "Thank you. For sparing them."

"I don't relish killing," Van Shaw said. "I don't mind it, but I don't enjoy it."

The tunnels curved and twisted, descending in a spiral, with innumerable branching corridors at each landing, but Estrella used that pillar of power for dead reckoning: the signature of the Blood Moon was impossible to hide from her otherworldly eyes, and she simply led them again and again toward its center.

They finally reached a metal door, as solid as a bank vault. Sanford chuckled as he felt the vanquisher reach out eagerly to manipulate the mechanisms inside. The pins and teeth disengaged with a *thunk*, and the Warden hauled the door open. Her hounds had returned or else she'd conjured fresh ones. The lion twined around the Warden's legs.

The chamber beyond the door was familiar to Sanford. This was the sanctum of the arch-ghoul, the lair of the Blood Moon. The place was bloody and befouled, a pile of old blankets in one corner for a bed, rotten meat strewn around, the whole altogether hideous.

The Moon themself stood in the center of the vaulted space, their back turned to the library of blood, facing the intruders, the white dinner plate of a skull moon-mask beneath a crown of thorns and fangs. They were clearly a ghoul, body like a cross between a man and a dog standing upright, limbs thin and wiry with muscle, ribs prominent and belly concave despite all the human flesh in their larder, a physical display of their eternal hunger.

Sanford and his friends were invisible to humans, but the Moon could see them well enough. "No!" they screeched, lifting their hands, one clutching that short scepter like a mace.

"Or, rather, yes," Sanford said. "Shut the door, would you, Warden? We don't want the Moon's people interrupting us. Vanquisher, please make sure the door doesn't open until we're done here."

A trivial use of my power, the vanquisher complained.

Sanford sighed. The contract said, "Do not speak unless spoken to," when he should have made it, "Do not speak unless asked to do so," but it was too late to amend things now. He'd just have to live with the irritation.

Sanford strolled toward the Moon, jauntily twirling his walking stick. "You're smaller than I thought," Sanford said, walking in a slow circle around the creature. "I've met ghouls before, of course, but, well, the way people talk about you! The great and terrible Blood Moon. I was expecting something more impressive."

Sanford stopped, leaned on his stick, and arched one eyebrow, but the Moon just stared at him. Ghouls were formidable fighters, but the Blood Moon had used other bodies to do their fighting for so long it seemed they couldn't remember how to use their own. "I will take your blood again," the Moon said. "You and the woman. You are only human." The Moon reached up to touch the crown, as if afraid they might have lost it.

"There are no humans down here, I'm afraid," Sanford said. "Just us monsters, eh? Do you have anything to say before I strike off your head? Some parting words for Estrella, perhaps?"

She walked closer, hands clutched before her, face anguished, but at least she wasn't glowing purple.

The Moon stared at her, then tore off the flat mask and flung it aside. The face beneath was snouted, mangy, snarling, ancient. "You. Stupid little star. I gave you everything. And you betray me!"

"You fed me lies and told me it was honey," Estrella said. Were her eyes glowing purple? Just a little? Oh dear.

"I know how you feel, Moon," Sanford said. "But as someone who has also felt the sting of betrayal, allow me to share a hard truth I have only recently come to accept. We must acknowledge that we are somewhat responsible for those betrayals. If we were better people, our allies might not turn on us the first chance they got." He glanced at Estrella. "Oh, I'm terribly sorry. Did you want to do the honors?" He drew the sword, letting the stick-sheath clatter to the stones. "I don't mean to presume."

Before Estrella could answer, the Moon shrieked. "Stop! You can't kill me!" They pointed their scepter at the blood library, scores of wooden cabinets stacked beside and atop one another, stretching into the darkness. "If you kill me, they all die! Everyone connected to me! That means the people upstairs. Your parents. Everyone whose blood flows to me, through me, they are tied to me. I bound our fates together. The conduit flows both ways!"

Sanford hadn't anticipated such a dead man's switch. Dead monster's switch? He really did have to give the Blood Moon some credit for vile ingenuity.

"What are you saying?" Estrella asked. Sanford suppressed a sigh. Well, she was young yet. She hadn't learned to expect and accept the worst.

"The Moon's life is entangled with that of their thralls," Sanford said. "If the Blood Moon dies, his death will travel out along every blood tether, and all those people will die, too."

"That sounds familiar," the Warden muttered from her place by the door. Sanford could hear her clearly, despite the distance and her quiet. That was a side effect of their connection, and not one that he loved. He could also hear the hammering of fists and feet and weapons on the far side of the vault door. Those people wouldn't make it through soon, but they would eventually. The Blood Moon didn't care if they wore their fists down to stubs in the process, after all.

"This madman might let all those people die," the Blood Moon said, almost cooing to Estrella, pointing their scepter at Sanford. "But *you* wouldn't doom all those innocents. I know you wouldn't. You're good. I raised you to be good–"

"Because someone good was less likely to threaten you," Sanford interrupted. "And as for this madman." He touched his chest. "I'm not inclined to let tens of thousands of people die today either." Not that he cared about them, particularly, but Estrella did, and anyway, letting them all die would be inelegant. "We've reached a stalemate. Fine. We'll engage in some negotiations. We can take death off the table. Relinquish your Keys and we'll permit you to go into exile–"

"Die screaming in my teeth!" the Blood Moon shouted. "That is my counteroffer!"

Sanford spread his hands. "You see? We're already negotiating."

"Sanford," Estrella said, speaking softly in his ear. "You told me how you followed the blood into the Moon's mind and drove him to destroy your blood sample…"

"Yes?" Sanford said.

"That cut off your connection to him, didn't it? With no harm to you?"

"Yes, that's right. If there is no blood, there is no sympathetic connection." He gestured to the library. "I considered that. I know some spells to make fire, but that's a lot of wood and glass and blood to burn up. Causing an inferno in an underground chamber like this… well, even with our myriad talents I'm not sure we would survive."

"But I can just… do this," she said. "Avert your eyes?"

Sanford realized what she meant and smartly turned away.

"Little star, no, what are you doing!" the Moon cried, and then the room filled with purple light and there was a whooshing *crack* of displaced air. That hadn't happened when she sent the corpse of Altman away, but she was moving a lot more matter this time.

The Moon screamed and fell to the floor, crawling across the bare stones to the place where their vast library of blood had been, scratching at the bare ground with their talons as if they might find the cabinets buried underneath. "Where did you send it? Where did it all go?"

"Into the unlighted chambers beyond time and space," Estrella murmured, swaying slightly. "Into the nethermost blight that churns at the heart of infinity. I could feel it, that's where I sent *everyone*, into that nuclear chaos, that gulf beyond the world of angles and shapes." Sanford caught her when she tumbled. "Sorry," she said into his chest. "I never… never sent so much before. I thought opening so wide would crack me in two."

"Rest, now, Estrella. Warden?" He turned to ask for her help, but she was instantaneously there, responding to his will. She supported Estrella and led her across the chamber to help her sit down against the wall.

The pounding on the door had stopped. There would be a lot of confused people in that tunnel. The ones who'd lived here, subject to the direct influence of the Blood Moon's crown, might not have tasted anything like real freedom for years.

Sanford looked at Estrella, who was still just a girl in many ways, a girl with a passageway to the realm of a blasphemous god inside her. She leaned her head on the Warden's distinctly un-matronly shoulder, yawned, and went to sleep.

Good. There was no reason for her to see this.

Sanford advanced on the Blood Moon, who sat slumped on the cavern floor, all grandeur and grandstanding gone. Sanford plucked the crown from the Moon's head and flung it clattering into the corner. Best not to give in to the temptation of wearing it. That kind of power would corrupt Sanford far more than he was willing to be corrupted. He tore the scepter from the ghoul's unresisting claw and tossed that aside, too.

The Blood Moon gazed up at him with a look of sly hope. "So," they said. "About that offer of life in exile."

Sanford lifted his sword. The vanquisher turned over in his mind, eager, imploring without words. Sanford sighed and lowered the sword. "Oh, fine. Go ahead."

He let the beast inside him feed, and oh, the Blood Moon was sweet.

Sanford sat at a small round table outside a cozy wine bar in a cobblestoned square in Madrid next to a statue of some old poet rendered in bronze. Someone had put a red flower in the statue's hands earlier, and just moments ago, a young man had stomped over and torn the flower away, throwing it onto the stones in disgust. Were these symbolic acts, something to do with local politics? He decided he didn't particularly need to know, or care. He just enjoyed the sunshine and took another drink of full-bodied red wine. These Spanish varietals were growing on him, or else overexposure had ruined his palate.

Estrella sat across from him, sipping a glass of cava. The Warden was in another chair, not drinking anything, a small black housecat winding its way around and around her. Madrid was known as the "city of cats," and the locals even called themselves "gatos" and "gatas." Back in the eleventh century some soldier had scaled a wall like a cat, leading his people to victory, and subsequently changed his name to Gato, and by something akin to contagious magic, the people of Madrid considered themselves part of that illustrious and courageous line. The Warden had heard the story and liked it, apparently, for she'd allowed her black lion to shrink into something more manageable and it traveled with her constantly, like a familiar. Sanford didn't begrudge her anything that made her happy. So few things did.

The days since the Blood Moon's death had been eventful. The local papers were calling it an "epidemic of amnesia," since the broken blood connection had left gaping holes in people's minds.

Poor Estrella was an orphan now, too. Her adoptive parents had frowned at her in confusion, remembering her vaguely as a lodger, but not as their daughter. It seemed she'd seldom interacted with them when the Blood Moon wasn't controlling their bodies and their recollections were accordingly scattered.

Estrella had cried about that, but less than Sanford would have expected. He'd rented her a room adjoining his in the hotel for now. People assumed she was his daughter and the Warden looked about thirty years old, now, so those same people assumed she was Sanford's wife – a little scandalous, yes, but not too disastrous for Sanford's reputation – and Estrella's stepmother. Being bound to Sanford's life and bursting with his power was good for Van Shaw's health.

Sanford raised his glass in greeting when he saw Thorne approach and was pleased to see the dapper figure of the Claret Knight strolling with him. The two of them sat at the directly adjoining table, the Claret Knight signaling for a waiter while Thorne stared at Sanford. "Well," they said at length. "You actually did it."

"I never doubted myself for a moment," Sanford said. He nudged a wooden box under the table with his foot, sliding it across the stones to Thorne. "The crown and scepter are in there."

Thorne raised an elegant eyebrow. "You weren't tempted to keep them for yourself?"

Sanford shook his head. "They are powerful, but the sort of power they offer… it isn't to my taste."

"I thought you liked being a leader of men." Thorne paused to order a glass of wine from the waiter, then returned their unwavering gaze to Sanford.

"I do," Sanford admitted. "But to do so using the crown? There's no challenge there at all, and thus no satisfaction." He'd spent years developing his skills at manipulation, coercion, and influence. Using the Blood Moon's Keys would be cheating.

"How admirable." Thorne's voice was so flat it was impossible to confirm or rule out any irony.

Sanford reached into his pocket and withdrew the opera glasses, sliding them across to the Claret Knight. "Thank you for the loan."

"You are most welcome," the Knight said, plucking up the case and putting it away. "We come with glad tidings, Mr Sanford. With Thorne's sponsorship and my support, and that of our allies, we are pleased to offer you a position in the Red Coterie." He coughed. "That is, if you possess a Key. If you don't wish to keep the crown and scepter, you must have something else in mind."

"You are joining the Coterie?" Estrella asked, frowning.

"Well," Sanford began, but the Warden, rather astonishingly, interrupted him.

"*I* am Sanford's Key," she said, voice dripping with bitterness like poison from a serpent's fangs. "I figured it out, Sanford. That's why you bound me to you. To *wield* me. To make me a tool for your ambitions."

"Interesting," Thorne murmured.

"You don't mean…" the Knight said, and then squinted at her. "But… ah. Hmm. I see. He's turned you into a sort of… living relic, hasn't he? Oh, my. Most irregular. But Sanford did vanquish the Blood Moon as agreed, so…"

"Perhaps *I* can speak?" Sanford said.

"Of course, kitten."

Sanford hadn't entirely made up his mind about what to do until just that moment, but he'd been stewing, gnawing, and thinking for days. The hardest thing had been to figure out what he actually wanted, instead of what he assumed he wanted, or thought he must want. "Do you know why I wanted to join the Coterie in the first place?" he asked Thorne.

Thorne shrugged. "Power. Influence. Access to our networks."

"Yes, but for what purpose?"

"To become strong enough to seek revenge on Randall Tillinghast," Thorne said. "The one who orchestrated your downfall."

"That's right, but you skipped a step," Sanford said. "The truth is, I wanted to *rule* the Coterie. I planned to manipulate you all, and turn you against one another, and trade favors until you all feared me, or wanted to please me, or owed me. I know you don't really have a leader, but I intended to do everything in my power to become first among equals, at the very least. And once I was ascendant, *then* I was going to track down Tillinghast and crush him."

"Ha," the Claret Knight said. "Good luck herding *these* cats." The old man shook his head. "No one can fault your ambition, Mr Sanford, but I don't think your plan is likely to work. You aren't the first to have such notions. Trying to make everyone in the Coterie pull in one direction is like trying to make a swarm of bees line up single file."

"This confession is very troubling," Thorne said, stern and cold.

Sanford shook his head. "Tut-tut, you know better than that. I wouldn't have told you my plan if it was *still* my plan. The truth is, I've spent most of my life engaged in, essentially, politics. I manipulate, I bribe, I blackmail, I threaten... and I am good at those things." He swirled the wine in his glass, thoughtful. "But recently, since the Order was taken from me, since I was driven from my home, I've had to do things differently. I sojourned for a time in the Dreamlands and discovered new capabilities in myself there. Then I came to Europe, friendless, destitute – by my standards – and hunted. I fled from murderers, climbed across rooftops, outsmarted monsters, jumped from a moving train – it was moving slowly, but still. I matched wits with, let me remind you, the greatest blood magician of all time. And I *liked it*. I liked it more than sitting in my office, pulling strings, orchestrating events from the shadows. Even when I was tangling with Tillinghast, despite the fact that I lost the battle, let me stress, not the war, I still felt alive, more alive than I'd been in ages. I didn't realize how stagnant I'd become." He glanced at the Warden. "As a good friend told me recently, I got complacent."

"So?" the Warden said bluntly. "What does all this self-discovery mean in practical terms?"

"It means, I was so focused on getting back what I'd lost that I never stopped to ask myself if I even wanted it anymore. And the truth is... I don't. I want revenge on Tillinghast, yes. That ember hasn't stopped burning. But the Order, frankly, looking back, it was a burden to me, and it bound and limited me as much as it empowered me. Moreover, I fought Tillinghast once as the head of an Order, and it didn't work. My position gave Tillinghast more people to turn against me and more levers to pull to bring about my downfall. No, if I want to defeat Tillinghast, I shouldn't use a method that's already failed. I should try something new."

"So you no longer wish to join the Coterie?" Thorne said.

"No, not really," Sanford said. "I'm as surprised as you are, believe me. Besides, what would I even call myself? Should I be the Garnet Magus? I'd have to wear a garnet stickpin all the time. Too limiting. The Carmine Conqueror? Bah. I already *have* a friend named Ruby, so I can't use that as part of my sobriquet. She'd find it too hilarious. The Blood Magus? I tested it out once or twice, but I've had my fill of blood magic." He shook his head. "No, the Coterie doesn't have to make me a member to reward me for defeating the Blood Moon." He smiled at Thorne, showing all his teeth. "Your lot can simply owe me a favor."

The Claret Knight chortled and raised his glass. "Just so!"

Thorne shook their head. "Sanford, Sanford, Sanford. I'm sure we can work something out to our mutual satisfaction." They bent to pick up the wooden box. "In the meantime, I suppose we're done here."

"I did have one small suggestion to make." Sanford raised a finger. "This imposing individual is the Warden, once a woman named Sarah Van Shaw, and now so much more. She would, yes, have been my Key if I'd joined your group. But if she is amenable, and you are as well, I propose that you let her join the Coterie instead. You only need to hear her talk about this place to realize she is fascinated by Spain and loves the country. I daresay she'd be a better steward of this land than I would have been."

Thorne sat back up. "But the Warden is in thrall to you."

"We would change that, of course. If you want to, Sarah." Sanford gestured around him. "The Warden must be bound to *something*, that is the nature of her magic, to entwine her life force with something else, to protect and defend it. She was once bound to protect the Order of the Silver Twilight, and for these past few days, bound to me. But what if we bound you to the city of Madrid, instead, Sarah? We could loosen the strictures a bit, I think, to give you more leeway, and let you roam all over, say, continental Europe at least? You'd weaken the farther you got from Madrid, but with the power of the whole capital feeding you, I doubt you'd even notice."

"Are you serious?" The Warden's cat crawled up onto her lap and stared at Sanford.

"You always wanted to travel and live abroad." He nudged the box on the ground. "I was thinking, if the Coterie likes this plan, that the Warden could hold on to the crown and scepter, too. Because–"

"She would never misuse them," Estrella broke in, smiling wide. "Because she knows what it is to be bound to the will of another and would not use that power for her own purposes."

"I certainly wouldn't." The Warden looked stunned, but, for once, in a good way.

"We'll have to discuss this with our other members," Thorne said.

"But I think it's a ripping good idea," the Claret Knight put in. "Having a trustworthy soul to oversee the crown and scepter would be wonderful. And if your wellbeing is bound to the welfare of this city, Warden – or, dare we say, *Red* Warden? – then you'll be an excellent caretaker for this territory."

The Warden stared at Sanford, and the cat in her lap shifted in color from pure black to ginger. Sanford didn't think she even noticed, but it made him smile.

"Sanford," Van Shaw murmured. "I don't know what to say. I thought this trip would end with you or I or both of us dead."

"To be fair, it easily could have." Sanford reached out, and took her hand, and gave it a squeeze.

Letting go of power like her, and membership in the Coterie, didn't feel at all natural. But it did feel right.

Sanford was packing up his valise and seriously considering hiding some sort of pocket dimension in the bag so he could acquire a proper wardrobe again now that he was no longer bound to matching with red when someone knocked at the door.

He opened it without worry. The vanquisher wouldn't let any harm come to him. It had instructions to defend him from attack without needing to be formally asked. But there was no one who meant him harm in the hall. Only Estrella, wearing a new blue dress she'd bought with the funds Sanford had gifted her to get back on her feet. Between helping her and the restitution he'd paid to Anna Elizabeth, his coffers were dangerously low. However, Sanford was a man of myriad talents and there were always ways to get money.

He ushered her in. She sat primly on a chair while he continued packing his bag. "Are you well?" he asked.

"I think so," she said. "I am still figuring things out. And I have a lot of things to figure out. About myself, and the world, and… and everything."

"Such is the work of a life, my dear."

"Where will you go?" she asked.

"In search of my nemesis." With the vanquisher inside him, Sanford might yet prove a match for the vicious sorcerer/ shopkeeper who'd ruined his life, but he didn't intend to walk around any longer with that parasite inside of him. "Tillinghast put together some sort of expedition, a group of relic hunters, and if I can track some of them down and question them, I might find a thread I can follow back to Tillinghast himself. I'm headed to Greece, first, though. I have some business to attend to." There was a stipulation in the contract allowing the transfer of the vanquisher to another host, as long as that host was "materially superior." "A gentleman on the isle of Serifos owes me a sizable favor, and he is probably immortal, which unquestionably makes him superior… though not as well suited to the vanquisher's purposes."

The thing inside him writhed, outraged, but it could not speak unless he spoke to it, and Sanford never intended to speak to it again.

"I've never even left Madrid," Estrella said.

Sanford nodded. "Now you can travel anywhere you like."

"Can I go with you?" Estrella blurted. "Please? I wouldn't be any trouble."

"Estrella," Sanford said gently. "I know the Blood Moon was special to you, despite everything. But I'm not, ah, a suitable, er, parental figure."

"You are a *magus*," Estrella said. "You know all the things I wish to know. You took one look at me and understood the source of my powers. I don't want to be your daughter. I want to be your apprentice."

He blinked at her. "I've had acolytes, but an apprentice? No. No, not really one of those. I am not sure I'd be any good as a teacher. But I suppose… I could show you a few things and, more importantly, show you how to teach yourself. Hmm." He made a snap decision. It wasn't like him, but he was trying to embrace change. "If you like, you may accompany me to Greece. We can see how we like one another's company with no promises made on either side. Would that be acceptable?"

"Perfectly." Estrella bounced up from the chair and clapped her hands. "I must go let Sarah know. She'll be so happy. She told me you're absolutely miserable when you don't have someone to be witty and world-weary and urbane around."

Estrella bounded out of the room, and once she was out of earshot, Sanford allowed himself the indulgence of a laugh.

His plans had taken quite the change since he left Arkham, but he foresaw that they might be pleasant changes, indeed.

"Capital," he murmured. "Capital."

ACKNOWLEDGMENTS

My thanks as always to the good people at Aconyte, especially Charlotte Llewelyn-Wells and Gwendolyn Nix for their editorial skills, and to the Arkham Horror developers for allowing me to play in their world. My agents, Ginger Clark and Nicole Eisenbraun, handle the business end of things so I can focus on making stuff up.

I'm grateful to my spouse Heather and our teenager River for making our house such a welcoming creative environment. Thanks to Katrina, Emily, and Aislinn for putting up with me even when I'm distracted and talking to myself, and to writer Molly Tanzer for always being up for Mythos talk (and any other kind).

We had to get Carl Sanford out of Arkham for this book, but the reason he's in Spain, specifically, is because I spent a couple of weeks there in November 2023, participating in literary festivals in Barcelona, Valencia, and Madrid, and falling in love with the country. Countless people made that trip great, more than I could mention in even twenty pages of thanks, and I'm grateful to all the organizers and participants and readers I met, but I do want to mention a few specifically: my traveling companion and occasional collaborator Sarah Day, who kept me company on the back half of the trip; my Spanish editor and publisher Cristian Arenós Rebolledo, who arranged the sojourn (after I had to cancel twice due to the pandemic!); writer Ada Hoffman, who was my "exploring Barcelona" buddy; editor and author Cristina Jurado, for making me feel welcome from day one; Marjorie Eljach, who runs the amazing Sui Generis Madrid festival; Daniel Perez Castrillón, for showing me around and being a fount of knowledge and enthusiasm; the editor Maria Pilar san Román, who first brought my work to the attention of Spanish audiences, and whom I was so pleased to finally meet in person (this book is dedicated to her); and to writers Paul Tremblay and Stephen Graham Jones and their partners Lisa and Nancy, who were part of my favorite night of the whole trip, drinking and eating and laughing late into the night in Madrid.

And thank you, dear readers, for watching Sanford fall and rise and, dare I say, grow?

¡Salud!

Tim Pratt, Berkeley California, January 2025

ABOUT THE AUTHOR

TIM PRATT is a Hugo Award-winning SF and fantasy author, and finalist for the World Fantasy, Sturgeon, Stoker, Mythopoeic, and Nebula Awards, among others. He is the author of over twenty novels, and scores of short stories. Since 2001 he has worked for *Locus*, the magazine of the science fiction and fantasy field, where he currently serves as senior editor.

timpratt.org // bsky.app/profile/timpratt.org

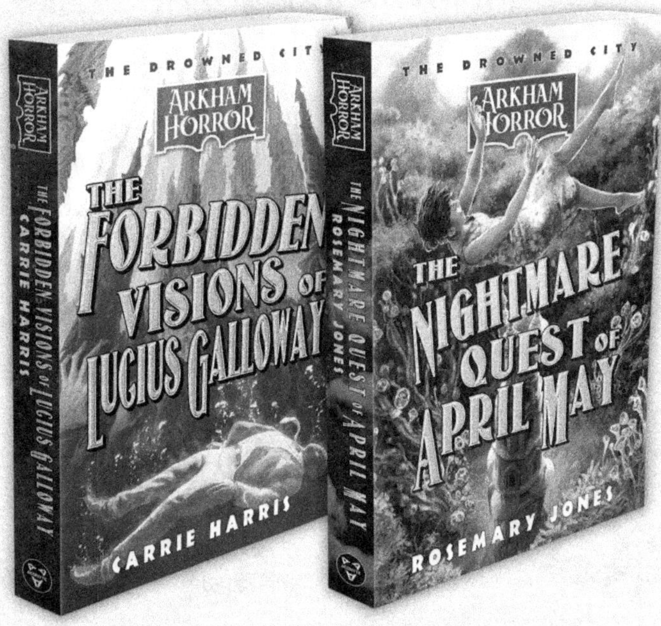

ARKHAM HORROR

Prepare yourself for the terror
of the Drowned City!

THE DROWNED CITY
ARKHAM HORROR
THE FORBIDDEN VISIONS of LUCIUS GALLOWAY
CARRIE HARRIS

THE DROWNED CITY
ARKHAM HORROR
THE NIGHTMARE QUEST of APRIL MAY
ROSEMARY JONES

Read the brand new prequel novels to the
Arkham Horror: The Card Game
The Drowned City expansion!

ACONYTEBOOKS.COM
ARKHAMHORROR.COM

Choose your Investigator.
Choose your Path.
Decide your Fate.

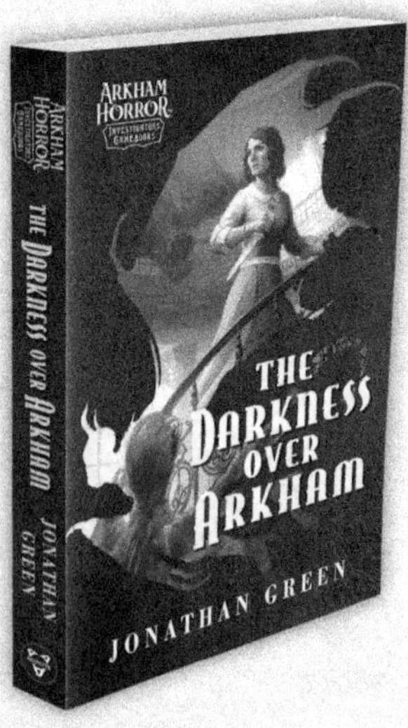

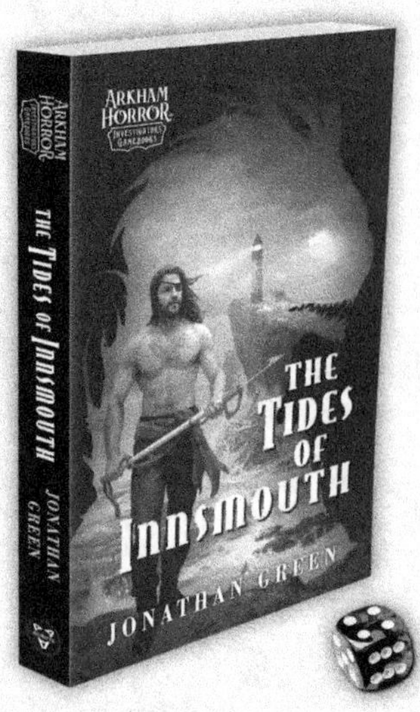

Take on the mantle of Investigator and explore the world of Arkham Horror in a whole new way as your choices change the story.

ACONYTEBOOKS.COM
ARKHAMHORROR.COM